THE WRONG GENTLEMAN

LOUISE BAY

Published by Louise Bay 2019

ISBN – 978-1-910747-59-9

BOOKS BY LOUISE BAY

International Player

The Wrong Gentleman

The Earl of London

The Ruthless Gentleman

The British Knight

Hollywood Scandal

Duke of Manhattan

Park Avenue Prince

King of Wall Street

Love Unexpected

Indigo Nights

Promised Nights

Parisian Nights

The Empire State Series

Hopeful

Faithful

Sign up to the Louise Bay mailing list

www.louisebay.com/newsletter

Read more at www.louisebay.com

ONE

London

London's buildings were lit up by the afternoon sun, the Regency moldings standing out, proudly on display. I couldn't remember the last time I was out on the street and I'd looked up just to enjoy the view rather than to check for anything out of the ordinary. It was almost as if I were in a different city, even though I'd worked two streets away for the last seven years. I was always so focused on work or people. Reading situations and atmospheres.

I spotted the bookshop I'd been looking for and headed down some stone steps to the entrance. When was the last time I'd been in a bookshop? Even now I wasn't sure what I was looking for—inspiration and ideas, I guessed. Places to visit, hobbies to master in the next few months. The last time I'd had free time I'd been in school with no money to do anything.

As of yesterday, my life was very different.

The travel section caught my eye and I headed right. I

wasn't sure what I wanted to do. I'd never done a beach holiday before, and I couldn't imagine I'd be much good at lying on a sun lounger and drinking cocktails. It wasn't really my style. Perhaps trekking. I'd never been to Costa Rica before, and I'd heard that it was beautiful. I started to pull out travel guides and flick through them.

"Landon Wolf, is that you?" a familiar male voice called from behind me.

I turned to see an old army buddy, Harry Reynolds, bounding toward me. I might not notice architecture, but I knew people, and I doubted Harry had ever been into a bookshop before. Our meeting was no coincidence.

"Reynolds," I replied, setting the book I'd picked up back on the shelf and holding out my hand.

"Fuck, so great to see you, mate," he said as he took my hand, shook it, and pulled me into a hug.

"It's been a while," I replied. "But you look good."

"I'll take that as a compliment from the best-looking bastard on the planet. What are you doing here?" He glanced around.

"What are *you* doing here is more of the question. Didn't realize you could read."

He chuckled. "Oh you know, just browsing. But now I've seen you, I might have an interesting proposition for you."

I knew us running into each other was no accident. "Browsing?"

"Okay, I tracked you down. You've changed your number," he said. "And I have something I want to talk to you about. Let's get out of here. We can talk on the street."

My stomach dipped. If he didn't want to be overheard, I wasn't sure I wanted to know what this proposition of his was. I knew Reynolds had started up his own private-security business shortly after I'd started mine, but we'd never crossed professional paths. I didn't want to start now.

"So, I hear you sold up," he said as we got to the top of the stone stairs and out onto the pavement. The papers were only signed yesterday, so he must have his ear very close to the ground.

I nodded. "Yeah, got an offer too good to refuse." Once I'd started to get higher end work and consistent government jobs, I started to get offers from buyers. I wasn't interested at first—I liked the job too much but holding out just made the offers go up, so when I was offered a consultancy position at MI6 the same week as I got another multimillion-pound offer for my business, I'd decided the time was right.

"I heard that. Good for you. So, does this mean you're at a loose end?"

I frowned and shoved my hands in my pockets as we began to walk toward Fleet Street. "I don't know where you heard that."

"Harvey told me that you had a couple of months to yourself."

That made sense. Since leaving the SAS, our mutual friend, Harvey, had worked freelance doing all sorts of shit. I'd put a call in to him, asking him if he wanted to join me on a trip, but he'd been busy.

"He said you two were working together," I said.

"For a few years now. I've got him in the Med at the moment, security for a VIP."

I didn't respond. I couldn't think of anything more boring than standing around in the heat, pretending I was guarding the safety of someone, when in fact, I was just there to make them feel important.

"He mentioned you had some time off before . . ." He

frowned. "Whatever it is you're doing next."

"Yeah. I'm looking forward to doing nothing for a few months."

Reynolds chuckled. "Yeah we both know that's bullshit."

It wasn't exactly bullshit, but it wasn't exactly the truth either. I *couldn't* do nothing for any period of time. It wasn't who I was. But I was looking forward to doing something new. Fresh. Exciting.

"I have a proposal for you," he continued. "I'm short-handed and have just been given a terrific job. I just need the right person for it."

I shook my head. "I'm not your man, Reynolds. I don't do field work." I'd had plenty of men who used to work for me. My time was better spent strategizing and building my business. I had nothing left to prove in the field.

"This is hardly field work. Think of it as more of a paid holiday."

"I don't need the money, trust me."

"Yeah, I heard you did well. But seriously, this job—it's dead simple—just keeping a log of a guy's movements and who he associates with. Better than simple, you get to spend your time on a superyacht in the South of France."

I chuckled. "You think he wouldn't notice if I was on the same yacht as him?"

"Ahh, but you'd be a member of the crew. I've arranged to have one of my men work as a junior deckhand. The idea would be you'd just keep tabs on the guy. See if anyone else comes on board."

"I'm not interested." I wanted to spend the summer doing what I wanted to do. Not following some rich guy around. "Get someone else."

"It's not like you have anything else planned. You said it yourself."

I shook my head. "I'm sure you can find someone else. There are plenty of good operatives out there."

He stayed silent for a few seconds. "This is important. I don't want to give this job to just anyone."

"But it seems straightforward. What's important about it?"

"The target is . . . a challenge. He has dangerous connections. He may be doing business with some people we both worked hard to eliminate when we were serving. I need someone who can handle themselves if the need arises."

"So what about Jones or Greenley or—"

"There are about five guys out there who I trust with something like this. Two the client has passed on. Jones is busy on another job, Greenley is known by an intermediary of the target, and then there's you. I need you, mate."

I groaned. I was really looking forward to getting some time off, but Reynolds was asking for my help and I'd fought side by side with him. There wasn't much I wouldn't do for a man who'd placed his life in my hands, and I'd placed mine in his. "What kind of dangerous?"

"The target has started dabbling in illegal arms trading. His legitimate business isn't doing so well, and he likes to live the high life, so he decided to supplement his income. He started off selling to governments in South America but he's getting more ambitious. Greedy."

"Meaning?"

"He cares less and less who might be the victims of the weapons he's selling and who he's selling to. My client has intelligence that the target has made contact with a splinter group of Islamic State and a meeting is imminent."

I gritted my teeth. "Your client is the CIA?"

"You know I can't tell you that."

I also knew that if it wasn't the CIA, he'd say so. Was I prepared to turn down a chance to protect civilian life?

"And your client doesn't want to get its hands dirty?"

"Oh, they are plenty dirty. But this is a resource intensive job, so they are using internal and external people."

I stuffed my hands into my pockets.

"So, as well as getting a holiday on a superyacht, you'll be helping to bring down one of the bad guys," he said. "And you know how we all like to do that."

He'd pressed on my Achilles' heel. Like most ex-Special Forces, one of the things I enjoyed most about serving in the SAS was the ability to impose justice where other military or political interventions hadn't worked—we were often a final solution. And most of the time we did what we set out to. Now with an opportunity to stop arms getting into the hands of Islamic State, how would I go trekking in Costa Rica knowing someone less capable was handling this job? Someone who might miss something important?

"And all I'm doing is checking this guy's movements? On and off the yacht?"

"Yeah, you call it in when he leaves or comes back. And you tell us when people come aboard."

"Am I planting surveillance devices or searching his—"

"Absolutely not. We want to keep it light. He doesn't think he's on anyone's radar. And we don't want him to think that's changed. We can't risk you being caught."

So much for Costa Rica. I wasn't going to say no to Reynolds. I couldn't. Partly because of our history, but mostly because of the opportunity to do something for the greater good. It was how I was wired. "You're going to owe me for this," I replied.

Reynolds' shit-eating grin said it all. He knew he'd got me.

TWO

Skylar

"This summer I'm going to make it my mission to find you a man," my best friend, August, announced to the restroom mirror where she was trying to fix one of her false eyelashes that seemed to have set a little wonky.

"You'll never find anyone rich enough," I replied, before I popped my lipstick-covered lips and slid the tube of color back in my purse.

"Are you serious? We're in the South of France. This is the playground of billionaires. You're bound to find someone even without my help. But just to make sure, you *will* have my assistance. I won't even charge you."

I rolled my eyes. "You're going to be my introduction to the world of billionaires?" August might be my ride-or-die BFF, but even she didn't know that my supposed requirement of a wealthy, single man who was going to keep me in the manner to which I was happy to become accustomed was just a front. A red herring. A smokescreen. Fact was, I didn't want a husband. Or a boyfriend. Or any man. But that was harder to explain.

"Don't sound so incredulous. As a wingman it's easier to have the courage to go up to strangers and introduce myself, to talk my way into the best parties."

"I'm not sure courage is something you lack even when you're not playing wingman. Anyway, you should focus on you and Harvey. He's a great guy."

August grinned, one eye with eyelashes of a super-model, the other looking like she'd just woken up after a night on the gin. "He really is. I think he might be the one."

I shouldn't have laughed, but whoever August was dating was *the one*. Her dating history was a complete roller coaster, and I was happy to sit and watch on the sidelines rather than be in a car of my own. Not dating had some huge advantages.

I didn't have to watch sports—either on TV or worse, live.

I was focused on my job, which meant I was one of the best stewardesses around. Even if I did say so myself.

And I didn't have to put up with the inevitable heartache that came with dating. Heartache from having your expectations dashed. Heartache from someone not loving you back. Heartache from being constantly disap-pointed in someone.

A couple of times when I'd first met August, I'd suggested to her that maybe she take a break and tried to point out the upsides, in being single but she wasn't inter-ested and told me I was being depressing and cynical. It was shortly after that that I came up with my story about only being interested in billionaire-husband-material men. It seemed easier to be labelled picky than cynical.

"You know we're meeting up with a friend of Harvey's tonight. He pointed him out in one of his army photos. He's h-o-t," she said, spelling out the word.

I groaned. The last thing I wanted was a setup. "So, if he's an old army buddy, already he's not rich enough."

"But he's British. Doesn't that count for anything?" she asked.

"The only thing that counts is the number of zeros in his bank account."

"You're so unromantic. You might fall in love with him and then you won't care if he's rich or not."

I laughed. "I'm practical. Why fall in love with someone poor when you can marry someone rich?" There would be no falling in love in my future. All I was interested in this summer was making as much money as possible. Just like last season and the one before that and every single one since I'd started in yachting. My savings grew every year, and I was on track to creating my future and ensuring I'd never have to depend on anyone for anything ever again.

"Well, even if you don't end up falling in love with him, you might enjoy a little flirtation. Maybe a roll in the hay before the season gets going."

I leaned against the counter, watching as August sighed and ripped off the false eyelashes from both eyes. I nodded encouragingly at her lack of lashes. "Better," I said. "And you know I don't do one-night stands."

"I can kinda follow your logic that you don't want to distract yourself during the season." She paused and scrunched up her nose. "Well, not really, but anyway, I get that it's a rule of yours during the season, but technically the season doesn't start until we step on board tomorrow morning. That means tonight is—"

"I'm not having a one-night stand. Especially with some random army guy. Not my type."

"You don't have to marry him. But seriously, the body on Harvey . . . He left the army years ago but these ex-military guys love to work out."

"Well, that's another reason to say no to him. I don't want any guy who has an ass smaller than mine seeing me naked."

August painted on her best shocked face. "So you're going to spend your entire life a virgin?"

I turned and wiggled my ass at August. "Looks like it."

"You have an ass Jennifer Lopez would be jealous of. But whatever. I just want you to be happy, my friend." August pulled out some mascara and added another coat to her natural lashes.

"I am happy. I'll be even happier when those tips start rolling in."

"But I want you to find the love of your life."

"Benjamin Franklin is the love of my life."

"I'm serious, Skylar."

"So am I."

"I know you want to be comfortable. Financially. And that's totally understandable. Coming from—well, you know, given what you've been through. But having someone who loves you is important too."

Love was bullshit. Something people made up to sell greeting cards and wedding venues. I wasn't interested. I liked certainty, and I could provide that for myself.

"This is going to be the summer of love. I promise you," August said.

"If you say so." There was no point in arguing with August when she had her mind set on something. "Now, are you done with your eyelashes? Can we get out of this restroom and go and get a drink?" After a conversation like that, I could see a tequila in my future. I didn't need a man. Alcohol could keep me warm at night and had the added bonus that it didn't leave the toilet seat up.

THREE

I always enjoyed my reinventions. Reveled in the change. From student to soldier. From SAS commando to business owner. Tonight, I was somewhere between a multimillionaire playboy and junior deckhand. Tomorrow morning, the three-day-old scruff on my chin would have to go, as well as the expensive watch and Italian shoes.

I closed the door to my hotel suite in the grand, five-star hotel in the center of Saint Tropez and dragged wet fingers through my hair as I headed to the lifts. I had few concessions to vanity. Aftershave, hair products, and moisturizer were for a different kind of man. I'd known times when soap had been a luxury, so it was all I'd ever need.

As I walked into the darkened bar, the buzz in my veins, the sense that what was about to happen was both an ending and a beginning, reminded me of the night before a deployment. I hoped tonight would be familiar in other ways, too—a few beers and some banter with Harvey, who I had a bone to pick with because he had told Reynolds I might be up for a field assignment. I'd forgive him, we'd drink some beer, and somewhere during the evening, I'd find a pretty blonde.

Some soldiers liked to have the certainty of someone at home waiting for them. They enjoyed the messages and letters on longer deployments, the home life they returned to in between assignments. That wasn't me. I hated the idea of a part-time girlfriend or wife. I didn't do things by halves. And anyway, I'd never yearned for stability or repetition. I thrived on change—it was one of the reasons I'd sold my business. That and the millions of pounds that now sat in my bank account. Military men rarely got rich, but then I'd always been an exception.

I scanned the noisy bar for Harvey, reading the room as I did.

In the far-left corner, an argument was turning heated between two guys in their thirties who'd had too much to drink. In the booth next to them, a group of girls on a hen night were enjoying a tray of shots. To my right was a mixed group of women and men, but their body language didn't read friendly, more like business associates. Maybe a new superyacht crew getting to know each other.

Standing on tiptoes and leaning over the bar was a pretty blonde. Almost-white hair fell down her back in gentle waves that hit her waist, emphasizing her firm arse. More casually clothed than the women with the hen party, she wasn't part of their group. The way she held herself suggested she was local, but as I stopped behind her, she ordered tequila with an American accent. Wearing black strappy heels, she looked like she'd be about five-five in bare feet. Golden skin.

Yep, my radar had been set off—she was definitely in

the running for tonight's blonde. I just hoped she stuck around long enough for me to order her next drink.

Spotting Harvey on the other side of the bar, I made my way through the crowd. As I neared, his arm dropped from the girl he was with and he greeted me in a big bear hug.

"I can't believe you're here, mate."

I slapped him on the back. "Me neither. It's good to see you. It's been a while."

"Seven years."

"How's the leg?" I asked.

"All good," Harvey said, straining a smile. Harvey had lost his nerve after being shot at.

"Good. So when you apologize, I'll know it's not because you're scared of what I might do to you because of an underlying injury." I grinned.

Harvey chuckled. "Scared of you? I know you're way too worried about messing up that pretty face to come toe-to-toe with me."

I hadn't lost my nerve as a commando. And it certainly wasn't vanity that had seen me leave. I'd lost my hunger to be the best on every day, and I knew well enough that led to mistakes. I had to be all in, and if I wasn't, it meant I needed a fresh challenge.

"Reynolds tracked me down because you told him I was free."

Harvey shrugged and glanced at the girl next to him. "This is my girlfriend, August."

This conversation would have to wait until we were alone. "Very nice to meet you," I said, shaking her hand. "Are you yacht crew as well?"

"Yeah. Interior. Season starts for me tomorrow. Harvey says this is your first season?"

"That's right. But I'm not doing security like this guy." I

nodded toward my old friend. "I'm just a deckhand. Any tips?"

"A ton. Whatever your bosun says, nod. Be nice to the interior team." She pulled her mouth into a wide grin. "And don't shit on your own doorstep. Relationships on board can get messy."

Harvey nearly choked on his drink. "Yeah, no danger of that. Landon here doesn't do messy or relationships."

August rolled her eyes. "I'm glad we're on different boats this season. It's easier, even if we won't see each other as much."

"Well I'm looking forward to it," I replied. "It's been a while since I had my meals cooked for me and my washing done."

"The money doesn't stink either," Harvey said. "That's why we're all here."

"Although I'm going to find Skylar a rich husband this summer. It's my mission," August said as she glanced over my shoulder.

I turned to see the blonde from the bar coming toward us with a tray of drinks. She was even more beautiful now I could see her properly. Her hair fell around her face, ice-blue eyes and a button nose—she had that pretty look that Scandinavian girls had. And she had a body that only a gay priest could ignore. Large, luscious breasts, completely covered by the black top she wore, that small waist I'd noticed earlier, and hips that flared out into the perfect hour glass.

Jesus. She was white hot.

"Tequila," she announced, glancing at me and placing the tray of shots on a table.

"And that's why you're my best friend," August said.

"I need to get another glass," she said.

"I'm more than happy to share yours," I said, wondering what her tequila-covered lips would taste like and giving her my best *I-want-to-see-you-naked* smile.

She shook her head. "I don't think so. I'll get you another glass."

Ouch. There weren't many women who didn't respond at all to some of my not-so-subtle flirting.

Skylar came back from the bar with another glass.

"I'm Landon," I said as she handed me a full glass, alcohol slipping over the sides.

"Skylar," she replied and threw back her shot. She meant business.

Hopefully there wouldn't be too many shots done tonight. I didn't want her to get too drunk—I needed her sober for what I had planned.

"Skylar's single," August announced.

That was good to know.

"Single implies I'm available. Which isn't true," Skylar said.

"You're available to the right guy, though. Right?" August asked.

"Yes, but it's a high bar," she said.

August groaned. "What else is on your list?"

"No liars. No married men. No gay men—no matter how rich. No priests. No—"

"What's going on here?" I asked Harvey.

Harvey rolled his eyes. "Some shopping list that Skylar has for a boyfriend."

"There's nothing wrong with having high standards," Skylar interrupted. "Most people settle way too easily."

I laughed. "Interesting. So you get guys to fill out a pre-qualifying questionnaire?"

"If that's how you see it, you don't have to apply," she said.

I wasn't in the market for a wife. I was an all-or-nothing kind of guy—be it work or relationships. Work I was all in, and it didn't leave time for anything else. But I wouldn't say no to a *night* with Skylar.

"Someone so beautiful can have all the criteria they like, I guess," I said. I wasn't sure if Skylar was incredibly wise, totally jaded, or a little bit wounded, but I knew I wanted to find out a little more. "So, where can I get my hands on your questionnaire? I might want to fill it in," I asked, leaning forward to make sure she heard me over the music. And to get a little closer. I caught a strain of honeysuckle—such a pure and innocent scent for someone so . . . cynical? Or was she just focused on her end goal?

She shrugged. "Applications are closed. I'm sorry."

"I know this season you're going to find your perfect guy," August said. "I can just feel it."

"You're more concerned about it than me," Skylar said. "I'd rather be alone than miserable."

Did she just assume she'd be miserable if she wasn't alone? I wanted to be the man who changed her mind. Just for the night. "Maybe you've just not met the right guy yet," I suggested, genuinely curious about her reaction.

"Yeah, that must be it," she replied.

I couldn't help but grin at her sarcasm, and she smiled in return and tilted up her chin, allowing me to imagine biting the underside of her neck.

Maybe she caught the dirty thoughts running through my head, imagining what her skin tasted of, because her smile faded and her chin dropped. "It's not like I *need* a man," she said. "I'm perfectly able to look after myself."

"I'm sure," I replied. I couldn't help but cast my gaze down her phenomenal body.

I caught August nudging Harvey.

"Well for tonight, Landon will look after you," August said, taking a sip of her drink and wincing.

"I don't need *anyone* to look after me," Skylar said.

I believed she meant it, but I suspected that someone to look after her was just what she needed. I was prepared to take the job tonight.

"Is Landon not rich enough for you, Skylar?" Harvey asked.

If only he knew.

"Something like that," Skylar replied. "Although he has nice shoes. And his watch is decent."

Decent? My watch was the most expensive thing I owned. I'd only closed the sale on my business two weeks ago, and my watch was the only evidence of the multiple zeros sitting in my bank account. "I'm just a lowly deckhand. I'm sure I wouldn't meet any of Skylar's criteria," I said. "And I'm not wife shopping, that's for sure."

Skylar's eyes lit up. "There you go. He's a committed commitment-phobe. We're not going to ride off into the sunset together, August. Sorry to burst your bubble."

I chuckled. "The sun went down some time ago. Far more interesting things happen after dark."

Skylar rolled her eyes at me. "And lots of scary things come out. Coyotes. Vampires. Grave robbers."

If there was anything that I liked more than a beautiful blonde, it was a beautiful blonde who challenged me. "Well, I promise I'm not a coyote or a grave robber. Not sure I can be definitive about not being a vampire. I do sometimes like to bite."

She tried to hold back a smile, but I saw it tugging at the

edges of that delicious mouth. "You're smooth, British Boy, and everything I don't need."

I was pretty sure I could offer her what she needed tonight. "Is that right?" I grinned at her.

She looked right at me as if she were trying to reach in and grab whatever I was thinking and then just shrugged and scanned the bar as if looking for someone more interesting to talk to. Was she faking it or was she really not interested?

"So tell me more about your list of criteria. Does it leave room for . . . attraction? Passion?" I asked as my gaze trailed down her body. When I first saw her, I'd thought of her as pretty, but I could think of a thousand words more appropriate. She was way beyond pretty.

She rolled her eyes. "Love. Passion. Attraction. At best they are temporary feelings and at worst they lead to bad decision-making and horrible consequences."

I couldn't think of a response. I was hardly a proponent of emotion and feeling. It wasn't me at all. But I wanted to dig deeper, understand a little more about why Skylar had come to such a conclusion—I was pretty sure she didn't have SAS training as an excuse. So, what was it?

"And don't think you're going to convince me to change my mind—even with that accent and jawline."

I was clear that Skylar hadn't meant to admit that she was attracted to me. But it was all the encouragement I needed. "I don't need to convince any woman to spend a night in my bed," I replied, catching her small intake of breath as I spoke.

"Is that right?" she asked, her tone a little less confident than before.

"Believe it or not, women sleep with me even though

I'm not a billionaire and don't offer them a ring as soon as we meet."

"Well, I guess that's their lookout."

"Maybe. Or perhaps they just think I look like a man who knows how to make a woman feel good."

Beneath the polished beauty that Skylar wore so effortlessly, I could tell there were things she was hiding, scars that she covered with her story about having a checklist for a man. It might be true. But I had a feeling it was just a front, and I wanted to take her back to my hotel, undress her, and have her tell me all her secrets.

"You seem to be pretty sure of yourself," she said, as she shifted her weight from foot to foot, pushing out her hip toward me, and I had to resist the urge to smooth my palm down her curves.

"I might be the lowest ranking member of the crew," I said into her ear. "But believe me, I don't fuck like a deckhand."

FOUR

Skylar

Landon was everything to avoid—tall, super good looking, charming, and *British*.

I'd have to initiate my best defense.

"So how long have you known August?" he asked as we both glanced across the table as my best friend and her boyfriend tried and failed to keep their hands to themselves. Harvey was a decent enough guy. A summer fling. But then August didn't know the consequences of succumbing to love and passion. She didn't know what I knew.

"About two years. We met yachting. But what about you? You know all about my criteria, but I don't know anything about you other than you were in the army with Harvey."

"Yeah. I've not seen him in a while, but he doesn't seem to have changed. He said yachting was fun, so I thought I'd give it a try."

I laughed. Maybe my defenses wouldn't have to be so strong. Landon was *so* not my type. I was attracted to serious, focused men rather than drifters. Not that I dated—but theoretically. "You thought you'd give it a try? Just like that? So since you left the army, you've been just going from job to job, giving stuff a try?"

Landon generously grinned at me. I was being a little provocative, but I wanted him to take the hint and find some other girl who would fall for those husky-like eyes and hard body. A strong jaw and wide, wide shoulders wasn't enough to hold my interest. "I've been doing private security since leaving the army."

"Like being a security guard and stuff?"

He shrugged. "That kind of thing."

That would explain his body. He'd have to stay in shape for a job so physical. And it would probably mean he wouldn't be a complete waste of time as a junior deckhand. He would likely have some common sense too.

"So your first season starts tomorrow?"

He nodded. "Yeah. I'm looking forward to a change of pace. Five months floating on a luxury yacht. How hard can it be?"

"There's a little more to do than stand around and look pretty," I replied. Yacht work was hard, and this guy was clearly as green as they came.

Instead of getting irritated with me, Landon just chuckled. "Well, it's good to know you think I'm pretty."

"That's not what I—" What was the point in denying it? The guy was gorgeous, and he clearly knew it. I took another sip of my second drink, then put it back on the tray. I didn't want to get drunk. Not with temptation like Landon around.

"I have to pee," August shouted across to me. "Come with me."

I was happy to have a break from being close to Landon.

It was nice a man so handsome was interested, but I needed to stay focused on my goal, and it was beginning to feel like I was on a double date.

August led the way to the restrooms and spun to face me as soon as we were inside. "So, what do you think?"

I opened my purse and pulled out my lipstick. "About what?"

"Landon, of course? Jesus, he's hot. You two look great together."

I popped off the top of my Maybelline SuperStay lipstick, the brand all good yacht stewardesses used, and began to needlessly reapply. "You know he's not my type. He's ex-army, thirty-something years old, and still hasn't found a career?"

August hiked herself up onto the counter. "You're so judgy. Harvey's ex-army. I swear that guy is so good in bed, I might actually marry him."

I smacked my lips together. "I'm not judgy. I'm practical. What's the point in being interested in a man like Landon when he could never make me happy?"

"We could double date all season. We'd both have a reason to ditch the *Sapphire*'s yacht crew and get away from the boat for a little bit."

I smiled. Having a reason not to socialize with your colleagues was good, but not worth me abandoning my strict no-man policy.

"Is Landon on Harvey's boat?"

August shrugged. "I guess. But I'm sure we could coordinate days off."

I rolled my eyes. "Not going to happen. I need to stay focused. Chief stew of the *Sapphire* is a big deal. And you never know, if we do a good job, we might land a long-term contract after this season." For career yachties, a two- or three-year contract was always the job to get.

"What are you so focused on a two- or three-year contract for? There's always work."

"There's always been work *so far*. If I got a two- or three-year deal . . ." Guaranteed income. The money was good in yachting, but it was never certain. I might have savings and I might not have ever spent a season jobless, but a three-year contract would give me some additional security.

"Can't you forget about that for tonight? Surely you deserve one night of fun."

Landon was definitely the kind of guy who could over deliver on a single night of fun, if that was what I wanted. "You know I'm not capable of picking fun over sensible, and you're friends with me anyway. You have to put up with me."

August groaned and slid off the counter. "Just enjoy your last day of freedom. A kiss with Landon might take the edge off the thought of all that hard work that the season has in store for us."

August had struck my Achilles' heel. I loved a good kiss, and with my no-man rule firmly in place I couldn't remember the last kiss I'd had. Landon's full lips and defined cupid's bow probably meant he would be one of the best kissers I'd ever met.

Another reason not to go near him.

"You clearly don't want to pee. Let's go," I said.

August shrugged and followed me out, circling her arms around Harvey's neck when we arrived back at our table. "Have you missed me?" she asked as we both sat.

"No." Harvey laughed. "Drink your drink."

"Anyone want to go for some food?" Landon asked as

August began to kiss Harvey's neck and paw at his clothes. "August seems hungry."

"Not for food," August said, turning to Harvey. "Take me to bed or lose me forever, you big stud."

"If she's going to quote *Top Gun*, she could at least get it right." I shook my head.

Landon's eyes lit up. "Right?"

I smiled and patted him on the leg, instantly regretting it as I caught his scent as soon as I touched him—clean and masculine—and his thigh? It was like I was hitting the trunk of a tree. I wondered if the rest of his body was that hard.

I glanced up at him and found him staring at my mouth.

"You wanna grab some dinner?" he asked. "I'm hungry and don't like eating alone. I'll pay if it tips the balance."

I rolled my eyes. "I don't need a man to pay for dinner."

"Let's get out of here and you can explain what you do need a man for."

Was I really going to agree to breaking bread with a perfect stranger? It wasn't as if I had anything else to do. It was the last night before what would be a back-breaking season, and I was in no rush to go back to my hotel room.

"Sure. Why not."

I leaned over to August. "We're going to go."

August's eyes lit up. "That was a fast change of heart, but I'm happy."

"We're just getting something to eat." As I said it, I wondered if it was the truth. Landon was good looking and attracted to me. I was playing with fire.

We said our goodbyes and headed out into cool, May air. In just a few hours, August and I would be in uniforms, cleaning, serving, and blending into the background. At least this year we were on a private yacht so although the client would no doubt invite their friends aboard, there would be less variation, which would make it easier to learn likes and dislikes and give the client what they wanted.

Occasionally I let myself fantasize about what life would be like to have my every whim anticipated. I couldn't imagine what it would be like to be able to spend an entire summer aboard a yacht as a guest, worrying about nothing but tan lines and whether my pedicure had chipped.

I wasn't sure it would suit me.

"So you must know Saint Tropez pretty well," Landon said as we walked along the waterfront.

"I guess. I've been yachting for . . . eight years now, so yes, that's seven summers that have started here." I glanced up at him, his strong profile highlighted by the streetlights, the scruff of his beard darker and more masculine outside the bar. "You've never been here before? I would have thought clients who can afford security would have Saint Tropez on their itinerary."

He caught me staring up at him and held my gaze. "If I'd known what I'd discover here, maybe I'd have made it part of my itinerary a little sooner." He grinned.

I couldn't decide whether I should roll my eyes at him or just relax and enjoy the compliment. I'd always vowed to avoid spending any time with men who were attractive because I didn't *want* to be attracted to them.

"But then I guess I still wouldn't be meeting your criteria," he said, nudging me with his elbow.

"Exactly right," I said, pulling my gaze away from him and concentrating on the cobbled street.

"So what's with this criteria? Do you have it written down?"

Despite myself, I laughed. It sounded ridiculous when he said it like that. "Memorized."

"So you're not trying to find love?" he asked.

"Are you? The come-to-bed eyes, the compliments, the attention—the god-damn accent. You want to confess something to me, Landon?" Mockingly, I furrowed my brow, trying to be as serious as possible. "Are you falling in love with me?"

He chuckled. "I guess not. And by the way, the accent and the eyes? I can't help it."

I sighed at his innocent act. "I'm not sure we're so different," I replied. "You have your criteria. I have mine. Our end goals are just different. You want an uncomplicated fuck with a woman you don't have to make breakfast for in the morning. Why are my criteria any worse than yours?"

"Touché," he said.

"You agree?"

"That everyone has criteria, and you seem to think you have mine figured out easily enough. I guess I've never thought about it in terms of having a list before. It feels unnatural." He paused and we kept walking.

"So, why isn't love on *your* list?" I asked after a few minutes.

He shoved his hands into his pockets. "I guess it just hasn't happened yet. I'm an all-or-nothing kind of guy, and being in the army, I'm not sure it's possible to be *all in* as far as relationships are concerned."

"How long have you been out?"

"Same time as Harvey—seven years."

"And you still feel the same, even in private security?"

Landon slid his arm around my waist and pulled us both to the other side of the road. Before I could push him away or ask him what the hell was going on, he nodded toward a group of drunk men coming toward us and leering at women in their path. Looked like they were on a bachelor party trip, but I wouldn't have noticed them. "I've been totally focused on building a life outside the army, I guess. I'm happy enough," he said, releasing me and continuing our conversation as if he hadn't touched me.

But he had. And his touch had felt comforting and protective.

Strong.

Safe.

I'd never felt that way from a man's touch before.

And I wanted to know if every time he touched me it would feel that way.

One night of uncomplicated sex was becoming more appealing. Even if Landon was Harvey's friend, it wouldn't be hard to dodge him for the rest of the summer. And it wasn't as if he was going to cast a magic spell and make me fall in love with him. I could put my no-men rule away for one night and just enjoy myself with a man I was physically attracted to.

"You look like you're deep in thought," he said.

"I'm trying to decide how bad an idea kissing you would be."

He chuckled. "You're full of compliments." He stopped and turned to me and I stepped back and faced him. "Either way, you know it's going to happen."

"You're very sure of yourself."

"Like I said, I'm all or nothing and when I saw you, I just knew that you'd be a great kiss."

I tried to bite back a grin. I'd been thinking exactly the same about him. Those eyes. That accent. That gorgeous mouth.

He was right. I knew it was going to happen.

FIVE

Landon

A hotel room said a lot about a person. About their wealth and how they liked to spend their money. About their tastes and habits. I'd say Skylar was careful with her money but still enjoyed her comforts. Other than that, signs of Skylar in the room were fleeting and that made her intriguing to me. Everything was neat and ordered. Clothes put away, her book—a romance—and a clock the only things by the double bed. The toiletries in the bathroom lined up. Nothing was out of place. From what she said, she'd arrived a couple of days ago—plenty of time for a person to settle in and get messy if that was who she was.

If I didn't know better, I'd say she'd done a stint in the armed forces.

"You didn't say where you were staying," she said, kicking off her shoes.

"Just on the other side of the port." I didn't mention that it was the hotel where we'd had drinks. That would give too much away.

I took off my suit jacket and placed it on the back of the chair before taking a seat on the bed where I could watch her relax before she came closer.

She glanced at me from the corner of her eye and took off her earrings. I didn't get to witness them much, but I liked women's routines. They were so different from a man's. The way they removed jewelry, undressed. The stuff they put on their face and then took off.

"You want a drink? Water?" she asked, reattaching the clasp on the necklace she'd just taken off.

I shook my head. "I like to watch you. Undress for me."

Heat colored her cheeks. Skylar was so confident on first impression that she didn't seem to be the kind of woman who blushed. Perhaps that was why her reaction felt so much like a victory.

Every time I thought I had her pegged, had figured out what type of girl Skylar was, she showed me something contradictory. I'd only known her a few hours, but she was like some beguiling puzzle, that the more I examined, the more determined I was to solve.

She turned away and reached for the side of her black dress. The grating of the zip drove the blood right to my cock, and I had to hold in a groan. Keeping her back to me, she let her dress drop and stepped out of the fabric.

Jesus, even in the dim, half-light, the sight of her curves in just a few scraps of lace was more than I could have imagined. Her waist provided a delicious, narrow center of the hourglass, her hips and breasts generously providing the counterbalance.

She glanced at me from over her shoulder. Was she still shy?

"Come here," I said.

She turned and took her time. The way she seemed to

think about and consider every move was entirely arousing. Was she a tease or was she genuinely weighing up the options and deciding for herself what she most wanted to do?

I didn't rush her, and she finally walked toward me, her hips gently swaying as she put one foot in front of the other. She stood as close to me as she could without touching me. From this angle, every part of her I wanted was on display.

I ran my knuckles up her inner thigh to the edge of her underwear, then nestled deeper. She was going to need to hold on to something, keep herself steady as I broke through her barriers and claimed her body. Any distance she put between us would tumble away as I made her come.

I dipped two fingers under the lace and found her hot and wet. She tipped her head to the side and blinked lazily.

I let my fingers explore, and as I did, it was as if her heat spread from her body to mine and my blood began to simmer in my veins. I grabbed her arse with my free hand to hold her in place. She gasped, her eyes widening, as my fingers dug into her flesh.

I nodded, my fingers working faster, deeper, more rhythmically.

"God," she choked.

Her pulse tripped against my fingers and she became increasingly unsteady, but despite her protests, I kept working my hand and her hips began to tilt in time.

"Oh God," she said again, her knees buckling.

I held her steady and kept going—I knew what would make her feel good. She might think I was just some deck-hand. Some guy she just met who would never come close to satisfying her.

She was wrong.

"Hold on," I said. I might not know this woman, might

not have her figured out quite yet, but I could tell she was close. My hand was covered in wetness. Her body screamed its desperation to let go despite her reticence.

"Hold on," I growled, louder this time, pushing two fingers into her.

She screamed and fell forward, bracing herself against my shoulders.

Her silence finally shattered, I basked in every moan every *yes* every *oh God* as my erection pressed against the fabric of my trousers, desperate to replace my hand. Fuck, she looked beautiful like this—finally out of control, her criteria ripped to shreds, coming on my hand.

Her fingers grasped the cotton of my shirt, her entire body tightening and then loosening as she floated down from her climax. Reluctantly, I withdrew my hand as her legs gave way and I pulled her limp body onto my lap.

My satisfaction was all about her tonight, which was unusual. I usually liked to start a sexual encounter with a blow job. It wasn't that I didn't like turning women on— more that there was something about Skylar that meant I wanted to try a bit harder. She deserved me to work at it. For her.

I gazed at her, enjoying her softness, her warmth, as she pressed her body against mine. Her orgasm-induced haze lifted, and she stiffened as if she'd given away state secrets and had just realized what she'd done, but I held her tight, determined that the mask she wore stayed off.

"You're beautiful," I said, cupping her neck. I hadn't even kissed her yet, but I knew it would be one of the most memorable of my life.

As if she didn't know whether to encourage or discourage me, she circled her fingers around my wrist.

My heart drummed in my chest as if in warning, of what?

My gaze dipped down to her full lips then back up to those ice-blue eyes and I pressed my lips against hers. She tasted of silk and candy floss—sweet and sexy. I groaned and pressed my tongue against hers. Her fingers dropped from my arm and her body relaxed again. She was trying to hold back but it was futile when she was with me. Guys she dated probably didn't give a shit about her pleasure, didn't understand that the biggest turn-on was to make a woman so weak with desire that she'd do anything for you.

Her fingers found my shirt buttons and began to pull at them. "Jesus, you're hot," she said, gasping as she pulled back.

I grinned. "Back at you."

"And this is a good shirt," she said, frowning as she felt the cotton between her fingers.

I wasn't about to admit that the shirt had cost me a couple hundred pounds. She didn't need to know that I had far more money in my bank account than the average junior deckhand, or even the average captain. Just because I could afford to be a guest didn't mean I'd want to be. I liked to be active. To be purposeful. It didn't matter how much money I had, I'd still never be the kind of man Skylar was looking for. And I wasn't looking for anyone.

I stripped off my shirt, wanting it out of the way, and Skylar stood and unclasped her bra.

I swallowed. I'd never seen more perfect breasts—high and round with nipples jutting out for attention. Fuck, I'd known at the bar she was my type. I couldn't have been more right.

She reached for my shoulder, placing her index finger against the scar of an old bullet wound. Her eyebrows pulled together, and she stepped toward me and placed a kiss over the mark.

I froze.

I'd never had a woman notice it before. Nobody had touched me there since the doctor who treated me.

It was so unexpected. So unfamiliar. So uncomfortably intimate.

She glanced down at me but didn't say anything. There were no awkward questions for me to deflect. No pity in her eyes for me to discourage.

She had no desire to expose my vulnerability, and I couldn't help wondering if that was because she had her own secrets, her own scars.

Fuck, I barely knew this woman and already I wanted to understand her better—know her. Body *and* mind.

Women never intrigued me in the way Skylar did. I needed to shake it off.

Remember why we were here.

I stood and took off my trousers and boxers, and when I looked up, I found Skylar staring at my cock the same way I'd stared at her breasts. I gripped the base, pulled my fist, and couldn't help but groan when Skylar, her eyes still pinned on my dick, licked her lips.

Shit.

There was nothing like the feel of that desire from someone else. It didn't matter that I'd only known her for a few hours, I got the feeling she didn't look at most men the way she'd just looked at me.

"I like you, too," I said as my dick twitched under her inspection.

She nodded and stepped forward. "You have a really nice penis."

I chuckled and she looked up at me, a small smile on her

face. "You have a really nice everything," I replied, scooping her up and placing her on the bed. "And I want to see *everything* from *every* angle."

She rolled to her front, and I trailed my fingers up the back of her thigh and over her full arse cheeks, then I gave her a short, sharp slap. "All fours, please."

"So polite with your 'please'," she said, doing as I asked.

"I'm British. We're polite. But don't let that fool you." I reached between her legs, plunging my fingers into her, coating my hand and then smoothing her wetness over my cock. "It doesn't mean I'm well behaved."

I took a step to the other end of the bed so my crotch was opposite her face. "Taste yourself on me," I said.

She moved to sit on the edge of the bed.

"No. From exactly where you are. Don't move."

She placed her hands back on the mattress and shifted slightly.

My insides tightened as she opened her mouth and tried to capture the tip of me.

"Just a taste," I warned.

As much as I liked to think otherwise, I knew I couldn't handle this woman's mouth around me for too long. Not when she encouraged so many thoughts and questions in me.

Slowly, she took me in her mouth, my crown hitting the back of her throat. I let out a deep exhale and stepped back, needing that perfect bliss to be over. I spotted my wallet and pulled out a condom. It was time for the main act to start. The urge to fuck was heavy in my veins.

I rolled on the latex, watching her, watching me.

"I hope it feels as good as it looks," she said.

I chuckled. There was the funny, demanding woman from back in the bar. "It will, don't you worry about that."

I'd never had any complaints, and Skylar wasn't going to be the first.

I gripped my cock at its base and pulled her to the edge of the bed.

"Ready?" I asked, pushing the hard tip up to her clit and then pausing at her entrance.

"Landon," she moaned as I thrust into her.

She was tight and needy and the way she arched her back, curled her toes, combined with the look of shock on her face made me believe I wasn't typical for her in any way. In so many ways she was exactly my type—blonde, beautiful, and up for some fun—but below the surface, like white noise, there was something telling me this girl was not like the others.

"Relax," I whispered, smoothing my palm up her back, then gripping her shoulder as I pistoned my hips. The relief at being inside her relaxed my muscles and I did what came naturally to me—I fucked her like it was my job, through her second orgasm, not breaking rhythm as her climax clenched my dick like a vice. This was what I knew. Skylar might have knocked me a little off balance, but fucking was my comfort zone. Sweat gathered at my hairline, down my back, at the tips of my fingers, but I couldn't stop.

She collapsed, and reluctantly I stopped what I was doing, turned her to her back and pulled her legs either side of me. She squeezed my hips with her thighs, which interrupted the steady beat of the pulse in my neck. She smiled up at me, her body boneless and weak, and for a split second I questioned myself—and I wanted to question her. Was I giving her what she needed? I was a reader of people, but Skylar? I couldn't figure her out.

"Okay?" I asked. Because I *wanted* it to be okay. I mean I knew it was good but I needed to hear it from her.

I leaned over her, and she slid her palm against my cheek. "More than okay."

I released a breath, dropped a kiss on her lips and twisted my hips as I drove into her, her back arching in response. Her breasts swayed, and I tried to block out all the questions I had for her that were circulating in my brain and focus on the physical. I wanted to come, wanted *her* to come again. But I wanted more than that. I wanted to know every part of her. Who was she?

"Landon." She clawed at my chest, her mouth dropping into a perfect "O" then her tongue darting out as if begging for more. That tongue. That mouth. Her beautiful eyes.

"Fuck," I spat out as she tightened her muscles. I snapped my head up and found her lip caught between her teeth. Was I fucking her, or was she fucking me?

I wasn't going to last much longer.

But neither was she. The slight tremor of her legs, her hands curled into balls at my chest—she was close. My orgasm growled at the base of my spine like an engine being switched on. There was no stopping it now. My jaw tightened, and I knew if I closed my eyes the imprint Skylar had made on my brain would only get brighter in my imagination. She was tough, skeptical and suspicious on the outside and like warm honey and spun sugar on the inside. I wasn't sure which was the biggest turn-on.

"I'm close," I warned her and, as if my confession triggered something in her, she dissolved beneath me, her fists relaxing and her palms finding my back, pulling me closer as if urging my climax on.

I let myself go, my orgasm flooding every sense. Usually my orgasms were all about me and what I felt—the chemicals rushing through my veins. But in that moment, all I could see, taste, feel, hear, smell was Skylar. She was the only thing I could think about.

I groaned, my mouth on her shoulder as my body folded against hers, wordless while our breathing evened out.

Holy shit. What had just happened?

Skylar sighed. "You're welcome to use the shower before you go." She pressed her palm against my arm and pushed before she slid out from under me.

I watched the expression on her face—she was serious. She was expecting me to leave. Fuck, my ears were still ringing, and my muscles were wrung out, and I wasn't entirely sure I wouldn't want to go again in ten minutes.

"It's been a slice of heaven," she said with a yawn.

I couldn't ever remember being asked to leave before. I was the one who was usually counting down the minutes until it seemed acceptable for me to pull on my clothes and skip out. "You worried that if I make you come again, your criteria will start to crumble?" I asked.

"If that's what you need to believe." She pulled out a t-shirt from under the pillow, covered her delicious body, and rolled away from me, feigning sleep. At least, I think she was pretending.

I guess that was me dismissed. If she hadn't been so damn beautiful, so completely alluring, I might have been a little irritated. But she was so confounding that nothing was a surprise.

I scanned her body as she brought the sheet up.

For the first time in a long time, I wanted to stay the night. Ideas of how I'd engineer another meeting with her ran through my head. I couldn't ask her. She'd say no. I wouldn't even get her number successfully at the moment.

I shifted off the bed, dressed, then bent over and placed a kiss on her shoulder. "Sleep tight, beautiful," I whispered and headed out. This girl might be the only woman I ever wanted to sleep with more than once. And ironically, she clearly wasn't interested in anything but tonight.

Hopefully a night's sleep would sweep her from my mind.

SIX

Skylar

I didn't do headaches, unkempt hair, or bleary eyes, even when I was hung over. Which I wasn't. I wish I could have blamed last night on the alcohol. As I pulled my wheelie case behind me up the dock, I had to dampen down a smile. No, I wouldn't have wanted to be drunk last night. Every second was etched on my memory just like it should be. I was pretty sure I'd remember Landon for the entire summer.

Jesus, that man knew what he was doing in the sack. I'd had three orgasms. *Three.* I didn't know that was possible. It had certainly never happened to me before. Landon undressed me and poof, I was orgasming left and right. But it wasn't just the physical pleasure he'd provided. He'd taken control of my body and for some reason I'd let him— even though I knew better. When he looked at me, it felt safe to surrender to him. And although that was liberating, it was also terrifying. I'd never felt such desire for a man. I'd deliberately avoided any guy who might have any kind of power over me.

"Hey, Skylar," a familiar voice called from behind me.

I stopped, erased my grin, and turned around as August half walked, half ran up the dock. "You're early," I said.

"Yeah, I wanted to catch up with you after last night. How was it?" she asked. "He looks like he knows his way around a woman's body."

Of course Landon was experienced. I dreaded to think how many women he'd been with, not that it mattered. I just didn't want to imagine that last night was normal for him. Because it hadn't been normal for me. Anything but. "I guess," I replied as I pointed at the 162-foot superyacht in front of us, the word Sapphire painted on its side in swirly blue writing. "This is us."

"The name is so cheesy," August said.

"His pet Chihuahua, apparently. The interior's lovely. Did you see the photographs?" I asked, hoping the pictures weren't from a hundred years ago or from another boat or something.

"No, there weren't any online."

Yachts owned by private owners didn't often share images online. If you were rich enough to own a superyacht, you didn't need to shout about it. "I requested them." There was no way I was accepting a job without understanding what I was walking into. Yachting was only glamorous as a guest. Staff quarters were never great, but some were better than others, and I always wanted to know what the place I'd call home for the summer was going to look like.

"Of course you did."

We hopped out of our shoes and lugged our bags onto the bow of the boat. "I'm meeting the captain at twelve. Let's go figure out rooms." I checked my watch. We had an hour. The rest of the crew wouldn't arrive until after my meeting, and I would have allocated crew cabins by then. We had two days until the owner arrived—plenty of time to get things shipshape.

"You haven't told me about your night with Landon. How was it?" August asked.

At just the mention of his name, my heart began to thud against my chest. I needed to forget about last night. Focus on today, but I couldn't stop my grin creeping back onto my face. "He's a charming guy and he knows it."

"I knew you'd like him."

"I didn't say I liked him." I led the way into the main saloon of the boat. It was exactly how the pictures had depicted it. It was all simple glamour—dark woods, low lighting, modern. It looked like a New York townhouse.

"This is beautiful," August said, taking in the room as she spun a full 360 degrees. "Is this real gold leaf?" She peered closer at the bottom of the bar at the far end of the room, which had been covered in luminescent squares.

"I can't imagine if you have the money this guy has that you fake your gold leaf," I said.

"He's a Texan, right? This has more of an East Coast vibe," August said.

"That's what I was thinking. Maybe his wife is from some old Boston family or something."

August shot me a look.

"What?"

"I thought you'd know. Walt Williams is divorced. He's forty-three and not bad looking from the pictures I've seen, and he's definitely not married."

"I had no idea." I'd worked with the captain before and, wanting the potential of a longer-term gig, I'd decided to try a private boat. The interior looked nice and it paid well, but

I hadn't looked into the owner's background other than to check he wasn't Russian, because those kinda boats had all sorts of stuff going on that I wanted no part of.

"I thought you might have your eye on him."

"You thought we were here husband shopping?" The divide between guests and crew on charter yachts was clearly drawn. Messing around with a guest could cost you your yachting career. It had worked out for a friend of mine who was currently married to a gorgeous English guy, but mostly, stewardesses got fired for looking at a guest the wrong way. But things were different on a private yacht. Whatever the owner wanted, the owner got, so August could be forgiven for thinking that maybe that's why we were here.

"I thought you were husband shopping, yes."

"I had no clue." If I'd been serious about landing a man with money, I would have looked Walt up.

"His grandfather made a shit ton of money in oil apparently, and he's now doing some alternative fuel stuff. He's been in *Forbes*." August peered into the cupboards behind the bar, presumably checking out storage options.

It wasn't often that August was more prepared than I was, and it caught me off guard. I should have done my homework—supposed husband material or not. I should have looked up Walt's preferences and checked into his history to see if I could figure out how I could make his stay more special. I'd talk to the captain. He might have some ideas. "We're going to have to impress him." I trailed a fingertip along the windowsill, trying to figure out how much cleaning there was to do.

"You mean *you'll* have to."

"I mean *we*. The other interior member is green. First time on a yacht. We'll have to hide her until we've trained her up." Plans started ticking through my head. I wanted to make sure we maximized the tip.

"You can arrange rotas so you have maximum face time with him," August said.

I nodded, less enthusiastic than I should be. "I guess." I hoped August didn't get too fixated on Walt being potential husband material for me. "It's not really professional to flirt with the guests, even if he is the owner. The tip should be our priority."

Pity stretched across August's face that she combined into a smile, then pulled me into a hug. "Great things are going to happen for you this summer. I just know it."

August meant well, but it was her, not me, who needed a man to have a good summer.

"I mean, look how it started off. A night with Landon. Are you going to tell me how many orgasms you had last night, or am I going to have to wait ten days until I can get you drunk?"

"Three, not that I was counting."

"Wow. That's impressive."

"Yes, he was." He was so confident and assured. Not at all like the drifter he described himself as. "I've never . . ." I wasn't sure I wanted to say the words out loud, but August and I shared most things. "I've never experienced anything like it."

I glanced up at August, who was grinning at me. "You two looked really good together. Harvey says he's a great guy."

"Yeah, well it's a good thing I'm never going to see him again. That man is one hundred percent pure temptation." The memory of the way he looked at me as if I were to be cherished set off goosebumps across my skin. And the confidence with which he claimed my body? Just the thought of it made me shudder.

"He and Harvey are bound to have drinks again. We could see if we could arrange to meet up with—"

"August, no. You know Landon's not what I want."

She rolled her eyes and sighed. "Because he's so incredibly hot and great in the sack."

I was looking for ways to explain to August or just myself that it wasn't just him being good in bed that had made last night so memorable. Maybe it was the way he'd put me first. Or had seemed to lift some kind of weight off my shoulders when he took charge.

I shook my head. "Men like Landon aren't where my future lies, and I have to stay focused." Landon talked about passion and love, but I'd lived in a house full of so-called passion and love. I'd seen the misery it brought.

"I just can't help it. I want you to be happy."

"I am happy."

"A man like Landon could add to your happiness with orgasms though."

I'd been clear what would make me happy since the first night in the group home. And it wasn't a man. It was cold, hard cash. Money of my own meant I never had to rely on a man who wasn't worthy—a man who turned out to be a monster, not the father or the husband he pretended to be. "Landon doesn't even know my last name. Probably doesn't know the last name of the last ten women he took to bed. And that's fine with me." I was relieved that yachting made it so easy to move on—physical separation would cure me of the memories of last night. He hadn't taken my number and I'd not taken his. Thank God. I might have been tempted to use it if I had and that would spell disaster.

"Maybe, but you could just have a summer affair until your perfect husband came along. You deserve a little fun."

"You're so sweet, worrying about my fun. But I'm fine. Last night was more than enough. My fun bucket is full." August might argue that a casual fling would be good for me, but a man like Landon was dangerous. A man who still had me thinking about him? Who looked at me like he had? He was way too much of a risk. "Can we drop it?"

August shrugged. "I guess."

"Thanks." I needed to stop thinking about Landon and focus on the job. I drew in a deep breath and led the way down the narrow corridor. We needed to find the rooms pronto, so I could allocate them without any arguments breaking out.

"We're rooming together, right?" August asked.

"Of course. We both know we drive each other crazy. Better the devil you know, right?" I shot her a grin over my shoulder.

"Great. That means I can borrow your fake tan without you noticing."

I laughed and spotted a hand rail. "Stairs," I announced and headed down.

The staff bedrooms were right at the bottom of the boat. Other than the captain, crew never had windows. Or more than a bed's worth of personal space. Most people went into yachting for the money and the opportunity to travel. I was all about the money, but the tight space had started to get to me.

There were seven doors leading off a bright, cramped hallway.

"This light is horrendous," August said.

"Will you check those are all bedrooms? I'll check starboard." I nodded at the doors on the port side of the deck. "One." I let the door slam behind us. "Two, three, four."

"Yes," August said. "All three exactly the same cramped, slightly smelly crew rooms."

"Perfect. Can't wait to get unpacked. At least they're all the same and no one will get their panties in a bunch because they don't have the best room. Having said that, let's take the one port aft so we're away from the stairs."

We dropped our hand luggage on the beds, and I pulled out a pad of sticky notes and a Sharpie and began to assign rooms from the crew sheet I'd been given. I kept the engineers together and the first mate with the third engineer. The bosun and the chef were the only ones who had names against the positions. The most junior deckhands together and the most junior member of my team with the senior deckhand.

"Do you know why the owner's got a whole new crew?" August asked.

"Captain said it was a condition of him coming aboard. He wanted to pick his team."

"I guess it means we all start from the same point," August said.

"Yes, it's better from my perspective. Fresh slate and everything." I'd only worked a couple of seasons with an already-established team and it had been pretty miserable.

"The start of a beautiful summer."

I'd usually be full of enthusiasm at the beginning of a season, but last night had tipped things upside down, and a little off-kilter. Maybe it was the way my legs were still weak.

"I hope so," I said. "Let's find the galley."

"It's bound to be. I mean, look how it started off. Me with Harvey. You had a night with Landon."

I shot August a look. "We're not talking about that. Remember?"

"Killjoy," she muttered behind me.

"Of course I'm a killjoy. I'm chief stew. It's my job." I grinned.

As we got to the top of the stairs, a door marked "Galley" caught my attention. "Perfect," I said and pushed my way through the two-way door.

"Captain!" I said, seeing the avuncular Desmond Brookes at the table, reading *USA Today*.

"Skylar. You're a sight for sore eyes." I swore if he swapped out his captain's uniform for a red and white suit, he'd look exactly like Santa.

He greeted me with a hug.

"How is Mrs. Brookes?"

"Perfection, as always."

I grinned. Captain and Mrs. Brookes were the ultimate love match, and I hung on every word when he talked about his wife. "It's good to know the perfect couple does exist."

August cleared her throat behind me. I'd almost forgotten she was there. "This is my good friend, August. Second stew. August, this is the best captain ever."

"Well," he said, extending his hand to August, "until you piss me off, that is."

I slid into the banquette seating, opposite the captain. "So tell me everything. What's the owner like? A party animal or bookworm? How are the crew? Do you know them all?"

August had disappeared around the side and it sounded like she was wrestling with the coffee machine before a crash outside the galley and the squeak of the door suggested crew were arriving early.

"Erm, Skylar," August called.

"Black Americano for me, please," I replied. "Double espresso for Captain Brookes."

"Sure. But before I do that . . ." She appeared in front of us both and glanced behind her. "You know that thing you were saying about that thing we're not talking about?"

Why was she bringing up Landon in front of the captain? It was so unlike August—she was always so protective of me. "We can talk about that later. I just have a few things to talk to the captain about."

August jumped from foot to foot. "I understand. I just thought you'd want to know the crew has started to arrive."

My stomach began to roil. What was the matter with her?

"Captain Brookes?" a husky, male, British voice asked.

I took a couple of seconds to focus on the figure walking around August, who looked as if she was trying to block his path.

Captain Brookes stood and held out his hand just as Landon came into view.

My breathing stopped and my heart clattered against my ribcage as I stared at that familiar face.

"Landon James, I'm your new junior deckhand," he said as he clasped Captain Brookes' hand.

This couldn't be happening. My detour, my one-night stand, the man who'd given me three orgasms last night and stared into my soul couldn't be working on this boat. It just wasn't possible.

SEVEN

Skylar

Landon James.

Landon freaking James.

How had I not figured out we were on the same boat last night?

One hundred percent pure temptation, the man who'd acted like he knew me or at least wanted to, who seemed to be able to make me feel desired and protected in just a few hours of knowing him, had followed me onto the yacht. Hopefully he wouldn't be looking for a replay of last night any more than I would be.

I would just have to ignore him.

Pretend he didn't exist.

I sat at the internal dining table, hunched over my laptop, trying to concentrate. I was trying to do the provisioning—making sure our chef had everything he needed and the interior crew had everything the guests might want. I had to do my job and concentrate on getting this boat ready for Walt Williams. Focus on my future and not some silly decision I'd made when two tequilas in.

"Skylar?"

I snapped my head up to find August in the doorway.

"Did you know he was going to be on board?" I asked. The question had been bugging me since I'd finished my meeting with the captain.

"No! I swear, I had no idea. I thought he was on Harvey's yacht. I can't believe you didn't know."

I blew out a breath. "Nope. What are the odds?"

"How did you leave things with him?"

"It was just a hookup. We didn't exchange promise rings." Landon being on board was no big deal. I had to keep telling myself that.

August slumped into one of the chairs across from me. "Okay, well, you're both adults. Things should be fine."

August was right. Things *should* be fine, but that same feeling that allowed me to surrender to him was telling me that Landon was trouble. For years I'd stayed clear of men. I didn't want to waste time. I didn't want to be distracted. It was easy to fall for a hard body and a pretty smile. But I knew how much misery such a decision could bring. And it *was* a decision.

So I was deciding that Landon James was no longer attractive to me.

"Right," I agreed. "He's a junior deckhand. I won't have much to do with him."

August's silence told a different story. With just twelve crew members on a 162-foot yacht, it was impossible to completely avoid anyone. I'd just have to do my best.

"Like you said, on days off, you'll be doing other things. Except . . ." August trailed off.

"What?" I asked.

"I don't know. I mean, maybe there's a reason why he's here." She concentrated on drawing circles on the glossy surface of the table rather than looking at me.

"A reason?"

She shrugged. "Yes, you ended up meeting Landon. And now he's on board. That's a pretty big coincidence."

"An unfortunate one." God, I hoped it didn't get around that we'd slept together. I could trust August not to say anything, but I had little idea of who the hell Landon was. What if he told the whole crew? I had rank over most of the crew on board. I didn't want to be disrespected because I'd slept with a junior deckhand.

"But maybe it's fate."

"Don't be ridiculous. We all make our own fate. I just hope he doesn't tell anyone. I don't want Captain thinking I'm unprofessional." Last night I'd been blown off course, but I wouldn't let it happen again.

"He doesn't strike me as a sharer. He didn't even say which yacht he was on."

"Yeah, but I didn't tell him we were on the *Sapphire*, either."

"True, but he's older. More mature. You didn't fuck a nineteen-year-old who can't believe he just got laid. Landon doesn't strike me as a man who needs to shout about who he's slept with or show off about anything."

I'd met Landon less than twenty-four hours ago, but August was right. He was cool, calm, and confident. He wasn't just another junior deckhand. Perhaps I'd pull him aside and warn him how quickly gossip spread on a yacht, just to ensure he didn't make a silly mistake.

"I'm sure he'll continue to be discreet. My relationship with Harvey and his history with Landon during their time in the army provides the perfect cover if you two are a little familiar. No one would know that anything is going on with the two of you."

"August, seriously. How many times do I have to tell you? It was a one-off thing. Whatever I'm looking for, Landon James isn't it."

"I know," she said, slumping back on the chair. "I'd dropped it, but I just think it's weird that he ended up on the same yacht as us."

"It's a coincidence. And that's it." This was a warning that even one-night stands were a bad idea. I needed to be stricter about my no-man rule. "Someone like Landon . . ." I'd only known him a night but underneath that hard body was a sea of complicated. "It's never going to happen."

Last night had just been a one-off. No more than that. There was no fate. Just coincidence. Just a one-night stand.

EIGHT

Landon

I hadn't lingered in the crew mess, making my excuses and asking for directions to my bunk, and then I deliberately went the wrong way. I wasn't interested in exploring the staff quarters. I wanted to know the guest areas inside out. I came across a staircase off the main saloon. The plush, plum-colored carpet told me it led to guest quarters, and I followed it down. Being early onto the yacht today should allow me to explore without anyone noticing. At the bottom of the staircase were six polished mahogany doors. I tried the brass handles and found them all locked. Crouching, I eyed up the mechanism. They would take under ten seconds to unlock. Dropping my bag on the floor beside me, I pulled out a kit from my back pocket. The black leather case looked like a wallet but was far from it. It contained everything I needed to pick a lock. With these locks, I wouldn't need much.

Within ten seconds, I was in, and I quickly checked the back of the door to see if there were any other locks and then did a sweep of the room, checking for the safe, cameras, other security measures along with places to hide things—always easier to identify those when not under time pressure. There was nothing unexpected. I headed out and repeated the process for all six rooms.

As I closed and locked the last door, Skylar called out to August at the top of the stairs and I froze. If anyone caught me down here, I could just say I was lost, but there was no point drawing attention to myself. The voices passed and I made my way back upstairs without making a sound.

The last person I'd been expecting to see on the *Sapphire* was Skylar. It had been a shock, but I hoped I hadn't worn it on my face as obviously as she had. I'd never experienced a woman so entirely uncomfortable in my presence. Maybe it was because she'd given up her criteria last night and she didn't like being reminded of her weakness. Her being on board just brought complications. I was here to do a job. I wasn't arrogant enough to think that Skylar wanted a round two—especially given she'd basically asked me to leave in the early hours of this morning—but I knew well enough that it meant that she'd probably notice more than usual. And I didn't want anyone paying me unnecessary attention. I'd have to be even more cautious now.

I found my cabin, my position written in neat black handwriting on a Post-it on the door, and dumped my bag. The room was more comfortable than I'd been expecting—only as wide as the built-in bunk beds and the walkway to the bathroom. It would be difficult for two people to be changing in here at one time. Training barracks were worse. There might have been a little more space in the army, but there was a hell of a lot less privacy. Sharing with just one person was a complete luxury. Hopefully my roommate wouldn't end up being Skylar. That could be a real problem.

I glanced around and decided to take the bottom bunk— that way I could come and go more easily without my room- mate noticing, if they were in bed. My next job was to stow the weapon Reynolds had provided. The room was small, but I was sure I could find a place. But I wasn't expecting trouble. Not if I did my job properly and no one noticed what I was doing. After searching underneath the mattress and in the few built-in cupboards, I decided to tape the gun to the ceiling of the air conditioning duct. The vent cover came out without any trouble, and I put the miniature screwdriver under the mattress after I'd screwed it back on. Hopefully I wouldn't need to use any kind of self-defense while I was on board.

I checked my watch. Twenty minutes still until I'd been told to arrive, and I was almost done. The next job was to sketch a map of the yacht, so I could make sure I knew all the places Williams could have a private conversation. Reynolds might not be looking for me to do anything other than observe, but I wasn't going to waste an opportunity to listen in to some conversations if I got the chance.

Outside my door, someone cleared their throat. Was it Skylar? She seemed to be everywhere I was at the moment. Would she knock before she came in? I closed the notebook I'd been making notes and drawings in and stashed it under my pillow. This morning I'd been wondering if I'd been an idiot for not getting Skylar's number and even thinking such a thing had irritated me. It wasn't in my character to give any woman I was with a second thought. What was it about Skylar that had gotten under my skin? Last night had been confounding and inexplicable in a number of ways that my mind was still trying to work through. I was good at reading people, but Skylar wasn't remotely easy to read. Confident and self-assured one minute yet demure and almost shy the next. Usually, I could see past a mask but with Skylar it wasn't so much a mask as a layer of riddles she wore. I'd considered calling Harvey to get her number. It had been a long time since I'd even thought about a woman after a night together. Perhaps now that I'd sold my business, it would be possible for me to consider a relationship. Maybe I'd have time to focus. But not yet. If something was worth doing, it was worth doing well, and I was focused on the job for Reynolds this summer. Despite Skylar being beautiful with a fantastic body and exactly my type, there was no way I'd have followed through last night if I'd known I'd see her again, let alone be working with her for the summer while I was on an operation.

My case unpacked, I pulled out my laptop and opened up the encrypted folder of material that Reynolds had given me on the target. I'd studied the information, but it never hurt to remind myself of the details. So many things that seemed like they were superfluous in a file could turn out to be vital in the field.

This might not be a job that required anything more than information gathering and reporting, but the stakes were high. Lives depended on me staying focused and no one figuring out I was there to be anything but a junior deckhand.

I scrolled down the first document. The yacht owner was forty-three-year-old Walt Williams—the target. He was three generations rich but now the family business was more than just oil. International arms trading and money laundering were now at the heart of the Williams' family fortune, with Walt at the head.

The more I studied the file, the more obvious it was that

what I was doing here could have a real impact. I was helping to bring one of the bad guys down—save innocent lives. And even though I'd willingly sold my business, being part of an operation like that, however small a part, warmed my veins and drove me on. It was why I'd accepted the consultancy job at MI6 and not just retired a rich man.

A knock at my door had me flipping down the screen on my laptop.

"Come in," I said, and Skylar poked her head around the door, first seeing me and then scanning the rest of the room. My eyes followed hers, wondering what she was looking for, and then I realized she was just anxious.

I refocused on Skylar, who smiled but it wasn't a familiar grin. More like a nervous reaction. "Urm. Captain wants an all-crew meeting in an hour," she said.

No doubt the captain would simply put a call out on the radio and wouldn't expect Skylar to round people up. She'd wanted to speak to me, and I was going to help her out. "Come in. My roommate hasn't arrived yet."

Skylar smiled nervously. "I'm not sure—"

Her pretty features bore no evidence of our late night. In uniform, with barely any makeup, she no longer looked like a woman who'd be right at home as a guest on one of these yachts, but she was still self-assured, elegant, and beautiful.

"Or you could show me where I can do some ironing?" I grabbed a shirt from where it hung in my half of the wardrobe and held it up.

"Yes, good idea," she said and spun around and headed out.

"Laundry room is by the kitchen, but the interior staff will do your ironing regardless of whether it's your uniform."

I followed her up the spiral staircase, getting another view of her tight legs and generous arse. Fuck, she'd been fantastic last night. Even if she'd cut things short and thrown me out before I'd managed to catch my breath.

"I know, but with some things I'm particular." It was true. I hadn't had anyone do my ironing since I'd left home. I'd even cancelled the laundry service that my building used because they weren't good enough.

"Well, don't burn anything or leave the iron on or anything. Do you want me to show you how to use the steamer?" she asked as we entered a small room, two washing machines and two dryers on one side, the ironing set up on the other.

"No, I'm good. I know how to work an iron." Was she going to spit out whatever it was she'd come by my cabin to talk to me about? "Good to see you again, by the way. Though I didn't think it would be so soon."

She folded her arms in front of her and backed away from me as much as the tiny room would allow.

"Yes, about that—you didn't mention this was the boat you were going to be working on."

"Neither did you."

Her shoulders slumped slightly. "I just wouldn't have—you know—if I'd known."

I leaned back on the dryer and crossed one leg in front of the other, rather enjoying Skylar's awkward side. I'd only seen confident, surprised, and . . . vulnerable. "Well, then I'm rather pleased you didn't know. I had a great time last night."

She glanced at my shoulder. "Working together, it's important to be . . . professional. I think it's better if we can just forget all about last night. Pretend it never happened."

She was deliciously cute when awkward, but of course I

couldn't tell her so. Her presence on the boat was just as difficult for me as mine was for her. I didn't want someone paying unnecessary attention to anything I was doing. "I'm not sure I'll be able to totally forget any time soon, but we can agree to no repeat performances."

She blinked rapidly. "Oh. Yes. Well, exactly."

Had she thought it would be more difficult to convince me to keep things platonic between us? "So we're on the same page," I said.

She nodded. "Good."

I raised my eyebrows at her too-wide smile.

"Good luck," she said. "I guess I'll see you in the all-crew briefing."

"See you then, Skylar."

It was a good job I had motivation to keep things platonic or I could imagine feeling her hot, naked body next to mine tonight. Maybe once the season was over and Walt Williams was in handcuffs.

NINE

Skylar

There was a distinct chill in the air as we all lined up on the dock, waiting for Mr. Williams to board the *Sapphire*. As usual, I'd kept my makeup natural and fresh, touched up the chips on my manicure, then dabbed some of my Hermès perfume behind my ears. Even if I was cleaning up after guests rather than a guest myself, it didn't mean that I shouldn't look the part.

I linked my hands in front of me and pulled my shoulders back. I stood between the captain and August, who held a tray of champagne. There were only two people missing from the lineup. The bosun and Landon. I didn't have to turn around to know Landon was coming up behind me. In just two days, I'd figured out his footsteps sounded like the captain's, but they tended to be spread out more, as if his strides were longer. Not that I was noticing anything about Landon. I was just keeping track of him so I could avoid him.

The deck crew seemed professional. Because August

and I had worked together for a few seasons now, she could show the other members of the crew the way I liked things done, which took some of the pressure off. I wasn't starting from scratch. If Landon hadn't been on board, I'd say it was the start of a great season. But there was something about the man that threw me off balance. I didn't do one-night stands but somehow he'd overrode my sense and been an exception. And the sex had been . . . unexpectedly phenomenal. Usually I found it easy to stick to my no-men rule, but there was something about Landon that was immediately compelling. I didn't buy into the idea that men were protectors, but with him if I hadn't known better, I might believe that he could stand between me and anything that might hurt me. And it hadn't just been the way he'd moved me out of the way of the drunks the night we met. It was just his entire way of being. It was as if he was there to look out for danger and head it off before it came too close.

I'd never felt anything like that, and it was both completely unfamiliar and entirely alluring.

And it was another reason why him being here was so inconvenient. I didn't want to be anywhere near the first man I'd ever felt was *alluring*. Landon might *seem* like a natural protector, but human nature was far more complicated.

So far Landon had acted like we were just familiar strangers. I hadn't come across him other than passing him on deck or in the mess at mealtimes. He was polite, professional, and clearly relaxed in his new position. I'd just have to be the same.

August nudged my elbow and I scanned the dock to find a group of five people coming toward us. Two women in caftans and three men, cocktails in hand, following them. I recognized Walt straightaway. He was at the front of the pack, his tan a little deeper than I'd seen in his photographs. He was better looking in person, and he was handsome in the shots I'd seen. He had a dazzling smile. Unlike so many yacht guests, Walt seemed to be able to carry off casual dressing, and avoided the bad habit so many rich men fell into of thinking jewelry other than a watch was acceptable.

My gaze fell on the four people following Walt—two men and two women. Were they two couples or was one of them Walt's significant other? One of the men slid his arm around one of the women and pecked her cheek. Okay, so it looked like they were a couple.

"Captain," Walt said. "Happy to have you on the team." Walt's gaze darted to me and I smiled my warmest, most professional smile. "Thank you for agreeing to take the helm of the *Sapphire*."

"It's my honor," the captain said. "We have a great team for you."

Before the captain could turn to introduce me, Walt had fixed his smile on me. "I see you have found some very beautiful people to work with you, Captain."

"This is Skylar, the best stewardess I've ever worked with."

"And you know how I like to be surrounded by the best." Walt finally broke our gaze and nodded at the captain.

"Anything you need, just ask," I said, keeping my smile wide and professional.

"I'll remember that," he replied.

He made his way down the lineup, shaking hands with the crew.

"Skylar," he called from where he stood by Landon and Marge. "Please show me aboard."

I glanced at Captain Brookes, who gave me the nod, and I stepped out of line to join Walt.

"May I take your briefcase?" I asked, deliberately avoiding Landon's gaze.

"You may not, but please arrange for our luggage to be collected from the end of the dock."

"It's already done, sir," I said, leading the way onto the main sundeck.

"Oh yes, 'sir.' I do like that. What else am I going to like about you, Skylar?"

The sliding doors into the main saloon opened and we stepped through. "Everything, I hope, sir. I want your stay to be the best you've ever had."

"Well, you're setting the bar mighty high," he replied.

Before I had the chance to respond, Walt pulled in a deep breath. "Good, the decorator has freshened things up in here," Walt said. "How's the rest of it looking?"

"It's a beautiful yacht, Mr. Williams."

"Please. I prefer Walt. Or sir. But yes, she is beautiful, isn't she? The best you've worked on?"

"Absolutely," I lied. It certainly wasn't the worst, but some of the charter yachts I'd worked on were bigger and more glamorous.

"Good. Have you worked in yachting long?" He handed me his now-empty cocktail glass and sipped on the champagne he'd taken from August.

"About eight years, sir."

"And before that?"

"I was back home in Ohio."

"I took you for more of a California girl," he said. I wasn't sure what he meant by that, but I decided to take it as a compliment.

"Thank you. And you're a Texas man from what I understand?"

"Born and bred."

"You get back often?" I asked. Life in Texas must be very different to life on board a luxury superyacht.

"Not as much as I'd like. But it's where my heart is." He rested his palm on his shirt.

I smiled, warmed by how down-to-earth he seemed and continued our tour.

We stopped by the kitchen, spoke to the chef, and Walt made a point of speaking in French, which seemed to genuinely impress Chef. And me.

"Okay, I'm going to freshen up, and then I'd like some lunch," Walt said as we exited the kitchen.

"Of course. As you saw, Chef has all your favorite dishes on the menu."

"Thank you, Skylar."

"Thank you. Let me know if there's anything you need." My smile was genuine. Walt seemed like a great guy. Respectful of the crew, down-to-earth, and friendly. My day —my summer—was looking up.

TEN

Landon

Portside of the top deck, I bit down on an apple and watched as sailing boats passed us heading out of the marina. My shift didn't start for twenty minutes, and I was taking the opportunity to listen in on a conversation Walt was having in the hot tub with one of his male guests, Bob. Spying wasn't part of my brief—all I had to do was report everyone's comings and goings—but it was in my nature to over deliver. And anything I could do to stop the bad guys from killing people. It wasn't as if I didn't know how to cover my tracks and not get caught.

I'd not heard anything interesting so far. The two of them were talking about Walt's oil business.

"Have you heard from the new client?" Walt asked just as the wind changed direction and the voices became muffled.

I stepped closer to the bow so I could hear better.

"Thursday, I think. And then I think we'll need a trip.

It's not like these guys can enjoy life in the Med without going detected."

Shit. Which Thursday?

"Will they come onto the yacht?" Walt asked. "It's very private. We can bring them out by tender."

"We don't get to call the shots on this one. Going on what my contact has told me, they will want to do a social dinner. So it doesn't look like a meeting. You know, with wives and girlfriends. It's all about building trust. These guys don't make friends easily."

This had to be about more than an oil deal.

I missed their next exchange. The next voice I heard clearly was Walt's. "But Vivian is on a job at the moment. Won't be around the next couple of weeks."

"You just need to find yourself a date. But that's not going to be a problem. Not for a man with a yacht like this," Bob said as he and Walt chuckled.

"Jesus, she's beautiful," Bob said as Skylar appeared at the top of the spiral staircase with a tray of drinks.

Bloody hell. We were just getting to the good bit and now Skylar was interrupting. Bob and Walt were bound to clam up before I got to hear which Thursday they were talking about or who they were going to meet. I checked my watch. My shift was about to start, and I didn't want to be late.

"Fucking right," Walt agreed.

I took a few steps to my left so I could see better.

"Gentleman, I brought you some champagne," Skylar announced as she approached the hot tub. "And some nuts." She set the tray down beside the bubbling water and handed out the glasses. Walt checked out her arse as she handed Bob his drink. Fucking idiot.

"Would you like to join us?" Walt asked. "The water's beautiful."

"I'm afraid I have to make sure your lunch is on track and order some more of your favorite Cognac. I want to make sure everything's perfect for you."

Walt grinned.

"Can I get you anything else?" she asked.

A horn from one of the nearby boats sounded and she glanced in my direction, catching me watching. She didn't react, just turned back to Walt.

"I don't think so, darlin'. Not unless you're ready to hop in with us," Walt said.

"You're out of fresh towels. I'll send some up," Skylar said without missing a beat. She was keeping it professional —good for her.

I tossed my apple core overboard and headed to where the fresh towels were stowed for the hot tub toward the aft deck. It wasn't my job, and I wasn't on shift, but it meant one less job for Skylar. From what I'd seen since we started, Skylar was incredibly diligent and hard working.

After distributing the towels, I headed down to the galley to begin my shift, which normally started with me emptying the bins in the kitchen. The fact that I hadn't emptied a bin in years made me grin to myself. Reynolds had been right—a summer with nothing to do wouldn't have suited me. And I'd never minded physical work. Being a deckhand was actually fun. There was a lot to do, and I was learning new stuff, but nothing was particularly difficult.

Skylar was at the sink when I pulled out the rubbish.

"Why were you up on the top deck? You shouldn't be listening to guests' conversations," she said.

"I wasn't listening to anything. I was enjoying the view and eating an apple," I said, feigning ignorance.

She fixed me with a stare that told me she wasn't buying it.

"And I already took them their towels, so no need to ask anyone else to do it."

"Thanks. But you could get fired if you're a nosey parker."

Was she looking out for me or just making sure that guest privacy was respected? "Thanks for the warning, but those guys don't have anything to say that I want to hear." I tied off the first bag and started on the recycling.

Skylar was perceptive. I just hoped I'd planted enough doubt in her head that she didn't give my being on top deck a second thought again. I needed to fly under the radar and get this job done.

ELEVEN

Skylar

"Anything you need from shore?" Peter, the bosun, asked as he stuck his head around the crew mess door.

"You're going ashore?" I checked my watch. "Tell me they're not going out to dinner." It was just after six and Chef had already done all the preparation. Why would he be taking guests to shore now?

"No, I'm picking someone up."

I stood. "No one told me. Are they staying over? Do I need to refresh a room? Who is it?"

Peter shrugged. "Friend of the owner, apparently. Captain asked me to get them, but I'm not sure of the arrangements. Can I collect anything for you?"

"Not for me. You should ask Chef, though. And you should tell him that he has another mouth to feed as well. Actually, no. I'll tell him. I have to go up and find the captain anyway. He didn't say anything about a preference sheet when he spoke to you, did he?"

"Nothing. I got the impression that he'd only just found out himself."

I straightened my skirt and headed upstairs.

"Chef, do you know anything about this new guest?" I asked as I entered the kitchen and August came in with an empty tray of champagne glasses.

"You're not on for another thirty minutes," August replied.

"Change of plans. We have a new guest coming on board and I have no idea who it is," I replied. "I'm going to speak to the captain and then we need to check over the empty cabins." I hated to be caught off guard. I should have checked those cabins since charter started.

"Are they coming to dinner? And will they stay?" Chef Anton asked.

"I have no idea. Radio Peter if you want anything from shore. I'm going to the bridge to find the captain and as soon as I catch a clue, I'll be back."

I turned and almost ran into Landon, who was coming in. "Hey, where's the fire?" he asked.

"Up my ass. Excuse me. We have a new guest coming aboard."

"We do? Who?"

I shifted around him. "No idea. Trying to find out." I pushed through the swinging kitchen doors as Landon started asking Anton questions about the new guest. Why did he care? It wouldn't change how much work *he* had to do. I took the stairs two at a time to the bridge just before my radio began to ring out.

"Skylar, Skylar, this is the captain—"

I knocked on the door to the bridge and went in when he answered.

"You heard about the last-minute addition to the party?" he asked.

"It's why I'm here." I was used to dealing with chaos and last-minute plans. The problem was guests didn't see the effort that went in behind the scenes and had no idea the work we'd have to put in for an additional guest.

"A business associate of Walt's is coming aboard," the captain explained. "They'll be joining the owner for dinner and will be staying over."

"Just one additional guest?"

"Yes. Do you have a room ready?"

Relief and frustration mixed in my lungs. "Yes, but I want to check them all over." I made a mental note to check them each morning so we weren't so unprepared next time that happened.

"Do we have a preference sheet for them? Do we know what nationality they are or even if it's a man or a woman?"

The captain shook his head. "Don't sweat it. From what Williams said to me, as long as he's happy, that's what counts. He's used to being the boss."

"I guess that's what's made him successful."

Captain Brookes shrugged. "I guess."

"Well no complaints from me on that score. Makes things easier when we're just trying to please one person."

The captain smirked. "That's for sure. Tell the rest of the crew. Perhaps you can find out a bit more when you show whoever turns up to their room."

"I'll let the team know. And I'll just make sure Walt doesn't have any expectations we don't know about. Thank you, Captain."

Men like Walt liked to impress business associates. I had to make sure everything was perfect. If I made him look good, hopefully it would be reflected in our tip.

TWELVE

Skylar

Finally everyone had gone to bed. I just wished *I* could. I checked the time over the stove—two thirty. Then I surveyed the damage. There were unwashed plates and glasses piled everywhere. And that was just the kitchen. The main saloon was a mess. It was going to take me hours to clear up. August would be on shift from six thirty, and I wasn't sure I'd be done by then.

I pulled open the door of the dishwasher and began to unload the clean dishes so I could reload it. There might only be six guests aboard, but they had kept me plenty busy tonight.

"Hey," a male voice said from behind me.

I snapped my head around, already knowing it was Landon—he was the only other crew member on duty.

"You all finished?" I asked.

"I think so. It's my first late shift, but I got the hot tub area all cleaned up and towels restocked and stuff." He glanced around. "It looks like a bomb went off in the lounge. And in here."

"Yup. When the guests are wanting every cocktail under the sun, one after another, it doesn't leave much time to clean up after them."

Landon reached into the dishwasher and pulled out two glasses and put them away.

"You don't need to help me. I've got it."

"I know," he said. "But we're a team, right?"

Exterior crew rarely offered to help out the interior crew. Perhaps Landon didn't realize. "Yeah but interior is my job. No one expects you to start washing dishes."

"Are you telling me I *can't* help?" he said, pulling out the basket of silverware from the bottom of the machine.

"I'm saying that you don't have to."

He nodded and began to sort through the utensils.

"Seriously, Landon," I said.

"I heard you. But I'm not going to bed and leaving you with this mess." He said it with such authority that goose-bumps pebbled across my skin.

"That's the deal between interior and exterior crew," I explained.

He rolled his eyes. "You don't like accepting help, do you?"

I turned away and began to wipe down the juicing machine that had been put to use tonight when Walt had decided he wanted to wash down each cocktail with freshly squeezed OJ.

"Have you always been the same?" Landon asked as I rinsed out my cloth.

"I accept plenty of help. August—"

"She's paid to help you. It doesn't count."

What was it with Landon? It always felt as if he was

challenging me and trying to uncover parts of me that no one else had seen. "I accept plenty of help." I couldn't think of any more examples to give but I'm sure there were a ton. "I just don't expect help. There's a difference."

"That's interesting," he said as he began to stack the now empty dishwasher with dirty glasses, his muscles dancing beneath his shirt as he moved. "Why don't you *expect* help?"

"Why would I? Why should anyone *expect* help?"

He frowned like I'd just said something shocking. "Well some people *like* to help."

I dropped a new filter into the coffee machine. "That's fine, but it's the *expectation* that's the issue. If you don't expect anything, you can't be disappointed." I would have thought that was obvious. The easiest way to be disappointed was to have unrealistic expectations of people.

"I've always thought that people live up, or down, to your expectations. So if you don't expect anything, you definitely won't get anything."

I grinned and then stopped myself. Landon was always surprising me. "How very . . . hipster-y of you," I replied. I didn't know him very well, but he hadn't come across as the kind of man who thought about things like that.

He chuckled. "I'm pretty sure I don't qualify as a hipster. In any way. It's just my own personal philosophy." He stacked the dishwasher like a pro. I guessed that was a skill people developed in the army.

"Not a hipster but a philosopher, hey?"

"We all have our own rules and theories we live by, Skylar."

"And a psychologist too. And I thought you were just a pretty face." And a nice ass, I didn't say.

"Someone's defensive."

I shrugged. "Not at all. I guess I just had such low expectations of you."

He laughed and the smile reached his eyes, his face, his entire body and I stopped what I was doing and took it in. Landon didn't strike me as a man who laughed very much, which was a shame because it suited him.

I bit back my own smile, conscious that I shouldn't be enjoying our interaction. I'd found him attractive before I knew almost anything about him. I didn't want to find out he was a great guy who was fun to be around and a little more thoughtful than I expected on top of that. "You should go," I said. "I'm almost done here."

Landon scowled at me. "What's next?"

"Seriously, you go on to bed. I'll finish up here. It's a one-man job." Him being so close was making me uncomfortable. The more he talked, the more I wanted to listen. The closer he was, the more I was drawn to him. I wanted to hear about all the other philosophies he lived his life by. I wanted to remind myself how his skin felt under my fingers. And I knew that was dangerous.

"Bullshit. What's next on your list?"

I shrugged. "I'm not sure." I needed space. What was his deal? Why didn't he just go to bed? At least that way one of us would get some sleep.

"Again, bullshit. You know exactly what's next. This interior runs like a train. Tell me and I'll do it."

He'd noticed how I ran the interior? I tried not to enjoy the compliment. How would he know what a well-run yacht interior looked like? "I'm going to polish the glassware that you just put in the cupboards, put away the laundry, and then I'm going to use the cordless vacuum on the sofas and wipe down the woodwork in the saloon."

"I'll do the glasses and laundry, if you do the saloon?" he suggested.

"Landon, you really don't have—"

"Let's put our energy into getting this yacht shipshape rather than argue over what I do and don't have to do."

I smiled—there was no way he was giving in and I liked that about him. A lot. "Thank you," I said. He was right that I wasn't someone who enjoyed accepting help. I was much more comfortable when I knew I was responsible for everything. That way, I only had myself to blame when something went wrong. But Landon made it impossible to say no. He charged in and just did it. Further, he didn't seem to resent staying up, and he wasn't making frat boy comments about making it up to him. "I'll do this then," I said, taking the wireless vacuum from its holder, still suspicious.

I worked quickly, vacuuming up pecan shells and polishing the wood free of fingermarks. It was tempting to leave it until morning—tell myself that August would have loads of time at the beginning of her shift before guests got up, but that kind of thinking didn't bring the big tips. These rich guys often got up at anti-social hours to make a business call or catch the headlines. We needed to be two steps ahead at all times.

I kept glancing toward the galley, wondering why Landon was so intent on helping me. There must be a reason. I couldn't imagine it was because he wanted to get into my panties. He'd done that already, and he'd seemed more than happy with my suggestion that we pretend it never happened, despite his charming reply. There had to be more to it. He was super handsome, good in bed, and seemed to have befriended everyone on deck. And now he was giving up precious sleep to help me. I had to figure out what his deal was.

"Okay, that's the saloon done," I said as I reentered the galley to find Landon holding a wine glass up to the light.

"I've just got a couple of these left to do. The laundry's folded and put away."

I liked that he'd taken his time over the glasses and not rushed it just to get the job done. "Okay, well, I'll set up for breakfast." I began to pull out everything August would need to set the breakfast table.

"Given you're chief stew, isn't it tempting to give these late shifts to your stewardesses?" Landon asked.

"Is that what Peter does to you guys?"

He shrugged. "I think so. Not that I'm complaining. That's how it goes. I'm bottom of the rank."

"Well, I don't operate like that." I'd never noticed Peter pull rank particularly. I couldn't imagine doing that to my stewardesses.

"I noticed," Landon said.

Was he watching me or was it just him being naturally observant? I'd done my best to avoid Landon, but there were certain things I'd noticed about the way he worked too. He seemed to listen very intently to anyone who spoke to him. And he noticed *everything* around him. I wasn't sure if it was some army thing or if he was just nosy, but it was almost like we were all being watched or something.

"How are you finding yachting? Is it like the army?" I asked, determined to figure him out a little more. To know him like he seemed to know me.

He laughed. "Not at all. But I'm enjoying it." His eyes glanced down my body and then he grinned when he realized I'd caught him. I could hardly chastise him. I couldn't look away from his hard abs that were revealed every time he reached to put a glass away.

"You think it will be a career for you?"

"I doubt it," he said as if his mind was completely made up.

"How come, if you're enjoying it?" Just as I thought—he was a drifter—couldn't commit to women or a job.

He pulled in a breath. "I just don't think it's the life for me."

I wanted to ask him what other options he had. But I held back, hoping he'd tell me without me asking him.

"You're very good at it," he said. "The people, the demands. Keeping cool under it all."

I tried to dampen down the sense of pride I felt at his compliment. "I've been doing it a while now."

"Do you find it hard to keep your smile up all the time?"

Was he accusing me of being a faker? "Not at all. The guests are demanding, true. The living conditions are cramped, and it's hard work. But this is not a bad life. I'm very grateful for what it's given me." Yachting saved me. It had given me a future. I'd had no qualifications, no references, no future, but this life took me and gave me a roof over my head, food in my stomach, and most of all, it gave me hope. Hope for a better life than the one I'd left behind. It also meant I had more savings than I could have ever dreamed of. "I have no reason not to smile."

I looked up when Landon didn't say anything and found him nodding.

"Speaking of grateful," I said. "Thanks for your help tonight. You've saved me from going to bed after the sun came up." I closed the cupboard door and scanned the galley for anything out of place, but everything looked good.

"No problem at all." Landon was still looking at me.

I glanced away and wiped my hands down my skirt. "Well, I owe you," I replied.

"I didn't do it to bank a favor," he said. I hadn't noticed the amber specks in his eyes before.

"Why did you do it?" I asked, still confused.

"I like you. I respect your work ethic and the way you serve the clients. And I want to support you."

This guy couldn't be for real. His comment might be one of the nicest things anyone had ever said to me. "Careful, I might start having expectations of you." I prodded him in the abs, trying to ignore the flip my stomach did when my finger connected to the hard muscle.

He grinned. "I'll do my best to live up to them."

For a fleeting moment, I wondered why this guy didn't have a serious girlfriend or a wife. "Maybe you would. I won't count on it."

He frowned but didn't say anything. "Let's get to bed," he replied, finally.

My heart began to thud through my chest and heat swept from my throat up my face. Did he mean . . . ?

Landon chuckled and rested his hand on my shoulder, guiding me out of the galley. "Not together. Wow, you really don't have very high expectations of people, do you? You thought I was polishing glasses to get a blow job?"

Thank God. For a moment there, I'd thought he was suggesting that we repeat our one-night stand. Because that would be a gigantic mistake, I had to keep reminding myself. "People have done a lot worse for a lot less." I took the stairs down to the crew quarters.

"How did you get so cynical, Skylar?" Landon asked as he followed me. "One of these days, I'll get you drunk and you can tell me what happened."

I swallowed. He just assumed I had a story. He somehow knew something had made me the way I was, and maybe at some point I *would* tell him. Landon had a way of making me feel I could trust him, that I could talk to him and that he'd listen and maybe even somehow make it better. I'd never felt that about any man. Even my girlfriends didn't know the whole story.

When we got to the bottom of the stairs, I turned. "Thanks again, Landon. I appreciate it."

He stepped toward me, so close that the fabric of his shirt pressed against mine. He looked at me silently before he said. "No thanks needed."

For a second, I thought he would cup my face and kiss me, and I decided in that moment to let him—perhaps it was his kindness or maybe it was just fatigue. Instead, he dipped his head and pressed his lips to the top of my head.

"Let me take your nightmares. Have only sweet dreams," he whispered before turning and disappearing into his cabin.

Landon couldn't take my nightmares away. I'd lived them. And I had no intention of going back. Keeping my expectations low and men off my agenda was the best way I knew of keeping my dreams as sweet as possible.

THIRTEEN

Landon

The squawk of the seagulls overhead was louder onshore than back on the yacht, and without the breeze the temperature had notched up a couple of degrees. Twenty-four-hour shore leave pulled me back to the beginning of my army career. We'd rock up at the local bar, drink until we were sick, and take home the nearest warm, female body. That was what had passed for fun back in those days. My nights out now were slightly more sophisticated, the booze more expensive, and the women . . .

My thoughts flashed back to Skylar as I made my way up the hill to make my call. It was clear that she was good at her job from the outset but the news about the additional guest had seen her switch into a different gear—organizing the interior, discussing options with Chef, and even directing Peter about what his team should expect without him realizing it. She was hard working, good at what she did, and charming with it. After helping her clear up the other night, I'd wanted to kiss her. I'd stopped myself—I knew better than that. But I found myself gravitating toward Skylar in a way that was unexpected.

I found a café, went inside, and found a table in the corner. Reynolds had been happy for me to send what info I had over the Wi-Fi on the yacht, but it wasn't my style. This might just be an information-gathering job but that was still no excuse to leave such an obvious trail of breadcrumbs. Walt might come across as a harmless, charming businessman but he was anything but, or I wouldn't be on the job. He hadn't gotten rich by being stupid. Who knew what kind of security and surveillance he had in place, so I was going to take precautions. I'd agreed to call Reynolds with time-critical information like the new guest who had arrived, but photographs and more detail would have to be transferred ashore.

I sat, ordered a plain black coffee, and pulled out the burner phone Reynolds had given me, took out the sim, and began downloading the photographs I'd taken. I'd gotten good images of everyone on board, including the business associate who'd arrived last night.

I swapped the sim in the phone. I'd brought a couple of dozen with me, storing them in the lining of my toiletry bag.

I typed out an email detailing the few comings and goings there had been, the snippets of conversation I'd overheard, and attached the photographs then quickly logged off and dialed Reynolds' number as my coffee arrived.

"Just got your email," he answered.

"How did you know it was me calling?"

"Because I didn't recognize the number, and you're a thorough, paranoid fucker, hence the change in number."

"Maybe I better change up my game," I said.

"How's life on the ocean waves?"

"Different to the army. These guys sure know how to spend some money."

"Where are you?"

"Some café."

"Itinerraire?"

I glanced at the menu that confirmed Reynolds' guess at my location. So the new guest I'd told him about must be interesting enough to take a trip from London. "I think you know the answer to that."

I glanced up and saw Reynolds on the other side of the glass door, scanning the tables, presumably looking for me. He spotted me and headed my way.

"So, when did you get in?" I asked.

"This morning."

"The new guy on board made a trip worthwhile?"

He nodded. "An intermediary, but still."

There was no way a member of any terrorist organization was going to rock up to a yacht in Cannes. A go-between would be as good as it got and potentially as dangerous for the crew. People terrorists trusted weren't the kind of people you wanted moving in next door to your parents.

Skylar was back on the yacht. And August. And the rest of the civilian crew.

"Is the additional guest still on board?"

"As far as I know. I heard the interior crew members talking about dinner for six tonight, so that suggests he's there for another night. No one's been told how long he's staying. The chef was complaining about it this morning."

Reynolds nodded.

"I have quite a lot of access on the boat. I could do a search of the target's room. Or even the new guest's room."

Reynolds winced. "Not at the moment. Things are too . . ."

"Don't you want to maximize your asset? You know I'm more than capable of getting this stuff."

"The stakes are too high, mate," Reynolds said. "Our client doesn't want to blow it at this stage. We're too close."

"I won't blow it."

"I know that, but my client doesn't know you. The new guest may well have his own security measures. He's used to being a target of surveillance."

"I know but this isn't my first rodeo, and—"

"I get it. But all I'm saying is . . . I have to tell you what the client wants. They are going to have their own people onshore, and they think they can get what they need that way. You and I both know you're in prime position, but my hands are tied. I can't sanction a search of any cabin."

Plausible deniability. Reynolds had to tell me not to search the cabins even if he knew that I was capable of doing so without getting caught. "I get it." If I uncovered something incriminating, I could inflict a serious wound on a terrorist organization responsible for the deaths of fellow soldiers. And civilians. I couldn't sit back and not do all I could. It just wasn't possible.

FOURTEEN

Landon

I wasn't sure how, but Harvey had found a curry house in the center of Cannes.

"You're not drinking?" Harvey asked, handing his menu back to the waitress after ordering.

"Not tonight," I replied. "Want to make sure I can get up bright and early tomorrow."

"Well that will please your bosun." Harvey tipped his beer bottle at me before taking a swig.

"It's what I live for," I replied.

"So how was your first ten days as a yachtie? Are you used to mindlessly doing what you're told yet?" Harvey asked.

"Hey, I was in the army, remember? Doing what I'm told comes naturally."

Harvey chuckled. We both knew better. Part of the selection process for the SAS was about establishing if recruits knew when to take orders and when to ignore them.

The SAS weren't just the elite, we were different—mavericks in our field.

"Regular time off is better though, right?"

"It's all fine. It's not like it's a career. How's your client? A decent human being?"

Harvey shrugged. "The money is like a disease, you know? It warps peoples' values. But this guy doesn't have any real enemies from what I can see and from what Reynolds has said. He's just a bit paranoid."

"Well, that's good, I suppose."

"But boring," Harvey replied. "How's your job? There must be more of a real threat or you wouldn't have taken the job. I've never known you to do anything for the money."

I shrugged. "Most of the challenge is making sure I have enough sunscreen on. That midday sun is a bastard." Harvey knew I couldn't discuss anything about the job I was on.

"Just take care of August," he said.

"Absolutely," I replied.

"If I'd known you two were on the same yacht, I may have suggested she get a job on another boat."

"Well, it's just as well you didn't know then," I said. "But seriously. She's not in any danger." Not with me around, anyway.

Harvey grinned and took another sip of his beer. "Speaking of women, how is the beautiful Skylar?"

"Still beautiful, but if I'd known we were going to be on the same yacht, I wouldn't have gone there."

"Maybe the gods wanted you to have regular sex while you were at sea."

I chuckled. "You know that's not my style. And anyway, I'm not Skylar's type." Every time I was close to Skylar, I felt a pull toward her. I found myself having to hold back. It wasn't a familiar feeling I had around women. But then again, in my line of work, I didn't spend much time with women. Skylar was a new experience for me in a lot of ways.

"Thanks, mate," Harvey said as the waiter put the last of what seemed like fifty dishes on the table. When the waiter left, Harvey glanced over my shoulder. "Speaking of."

I turned to find Skylar and August coming toward us. My stomach lurched as Skylar locked eyes with me and her smile faltered. Jesus, this girl did nothing for my ego.

"Hey guys." August bounded up to the table, ignoring me as she looped her arms around Harvey's neck and kissed him.

I should have looked at the rota—I hadn't realized that August and Skylar were off as well. Otherwise I wouldn't have suggested meeting up with Harvey.

"Hey," I said as Skylar took a seat beside me as Harvey and August continued to paw at each other.

"Hey. I wasn't expecting to see you," Skylar said.

"I imagine not. Otherwise you wouldn't be here."

"There was no fun to be had at the three bars we went to, and then we couldn't get into this yacht party, so we gave up," August said.

Skylar just shrugged and looked at my curry.

"It's vindaloo. Which means hot. But help yourself." I waved at the selection of food that we'd ordered.

"Awesome. I'm so hungry, and I love curry," Skylar said, her eyes going wide at the array of food.

"You like curry?"

"It's carb-tastic. The naan, chapatti, the rice—it's all so good."

I chuckled. "I thought girls hated carbs."

Her nose twitched as she helped herself to a plate. "Not me. We had a cook when I was about fifteen who always did curry on a Friday night." She frowned. "She didn't stay long."

Her family had a cook? I hadn't found out anything really personal about Skylar, but the way she was wired made me want to know more. I would never have guessed she came from money.

"Reminds me of home, too," I said.

"You eat it a lot in the UK, right?"

"Yeah. It's man-food," I said in a growly voice and grinned.

"Interesting. Which is why you and Harvey are here?"

I shrugged. "Absolutely."

"You feel the need to overcompensate because you're not secure in your masculinity?" Her face was blank of expression, and for a moment I thought she was serious until she broke out into a grin. "It's a shame, but I'm happy to vouch for you."

I chuckled. "So curry night in your family was home-made?" I asked. Did Skylar's family have serious money?

"Kinda. Did you have takeout?" she asked, not answering my question.

"If we were lucky." I wasn't going to be thrown off course. I wanted to know what Skylar would share with me. "Do you have brothers and sisters?" I asked.

Skylar shook her head and glanced down at her plate. "No. My mom . . . It was a lot for my mom, having me."

"A lot?"

Skylar shrugged. "Yeah, one kid was probably too much."

I didn't respond, wanting to hear more. What kid

thought they were a lot for their parents? It was kind of heartbreaking hearing her talk like that.

"What about you? Any siblings?" she asked. I wasn't getting anything from this girl.

"A brother." I cleared my throat and took a sip of water.

"Is he in the army, too?"

I laughed, glancing at Harvey to see if he'd heard the question. Anyone who'd ever met my luxury-loving brother would be amused at the question. Unsurprisingly, Harvey hadn't heard. He was lost in an alternate reality with August. Hayden would never have survived in the army. He was far too reliant on his home comforts. "Nope."

"You don't like to talk about yourself much, do you?"

"That's the pot calling the kettle black," I replied. There was a lot about me that Skylar didn't know, and I'd had plenty of opportunity to tell her. The fact that I was just killing time before I took up a new position. That I'd just sold my business for more money than I could have possibly imagined. That I knew more about Walt Williams than she did.

"Most men like to talk about themselves a lot." She sighed and bit into her naan as if she hadn't been fed for a week.

"Is that anything to do with the type of man you date?"

"I don't date," she replied. "Not really."

"Because not enough men fulfil your criteria?" I asked.

She shrugged. "Maybe."

The less she gave me, the more I wanted to know.

"You must have plenty of men who want to measure up," I said. Skylar turned heads. Although we had our backs to the rest of the restaurant, I was pretty sure that if I turned around, I'd find most of the men in this place sneaking glances at her.

But she wasn't the archetypal pretty—a rail-thin model, or the overly botoxed wanna-be actress—who hung around Cannes. She was old-school beautiful. Classic.

"You flirting with me?" she asked, grinning.

I was trying to get to know her, although it wasn't my typical style with a woman. I shifted my chair so I could look at her better. "Would it matter if I was?"

She shook her head. "Nope. Doesn't affect me. You're definitely *not* my type."

"Is that right?"

"You're an excellent kisser," she said as if she were remarking on my job performance.

"Erm, thank you."

"It's a good skill to have." She pinched her eyebrows together as if she wanted me to know she was being entirely serious.

"Well, you're excellent at a lot of things," I said. "Naked things. Dressed things. Eating curry."

"Careful, we might end up friends," she replied. "Especially given our two best friends don't notice us any time we come out."

"I guess we just have to make the best of a bad situation and agree to be friends. Friends who fancy each other a little bit," I said, wanting to see how she reacted to me admitting that I found her attractive.

"Fancy each other? Is that a British thing?" She strung out the word, elongating the "a" which sounded cute.

"Yeah—you know, find each other attractive. Like each other."

"Okay," she said. "I can admit that I fancy you a little bit. Not that it means that I want anything to happen between us."

I laughed. "Good to know. And I fancy you a little bit, too."

"What are you two giggling about?" August unwrapped an arm from Harvey and took a swig of his beer.

"We're not giggling. We're occupying ourselves rather than sit here and watch you two dry hump each other," Skylar said.

I chuckled and scooped up another bite of curry.

August sighed. "Well, if you're not going to bang, which, for the record, I think you totally should, you would have such beautiful babies together—"

"We're not going to bang. Say another word about it, August, and I'm going to stab you through the eye with this fork," Skylar said, waving a fork in the air, grinning.

"Okay, so as I was saying, if my best-case scenario isn't going to happen, then maybe you can be each other's wingman. Landon, you can find my friend a rich, hot, single, straight husband, right?"

"He can help her stay out of trouble until she finds one," Harvey interrupted.

"Sounds like I need to be more like a chaperone," I replied.

"And I don't need either," Skylar said. "Tonight, carbs are enough."

I chuckled. I didn't spend much time with women outside the bedroom, but the more time I spent with Skylar, the more I wanted.

FIFTEEN

Skylar

As soon as we'd left the curry house, August and Harvey disappeared, leaving Landon and me alone to go back to the yacht. Together. Landon's geography was increasingly a problem for me. If he wasn't around, I wouldn't be thinking about him. If he hadn't been at the curry house, we wouldn't have ended up talking and he wouldn't have asked me a thousand questions as if he wanted to know me from the inside out. And if I hadn't slept with him, I wouldn't be thinking about his hard thighs or rough beard that reappeared every evening despite the fact that he shaved every morning.

And that was a problem because I didn't want to be attracted to Landon or any man. I didn't want the complication. I liked to keep things clean and straightforward. I didn't date. I didn't *want* to date.

"You'll get your cabin to yourself tonight," Landon said as we boarded the *Sapphire*.

"Which will be nice because August has been known to snore."

Landon took my hand to help me onto the main deck and didn't let go as we headed inside. I should have shaken him off, but I liked the feel of him. He was so strong, so solid. I swore it wouldn't have surprised me if he was bullet proof. "Did you ever get shot in the army?" I asked, remembering the scar I saw the first night we were together.

He dropped my hand and guided me into the saloon with his palm in the small of my back. "A couple of times," he said, as if he was telling me he'd been to Amsterdam for the weekend.

"Wow, really? Was it serious?"

He shrugged.

All the rich men I was around in yachting had little to say but spent all their time talking. Landon seemed to have plenty to say but no inclination to share it with me, though I got the impression it wasn't personal. He wasn't the sort of person to share stuff. And that made me want to know him even more.

"You ever shoot anyone?" I wasn't sure what I wanted him to say. The idea of anyone shooting a gun . . . it was something I'd never come to terms with.

He smiled at me as I glanced up at him. "Skylar, I was in the army."

"I'm not sure how I feel about guns," I said almost to myself. If my mom had carried a gun, she might still be alive.

"You can't have an army without weapons. That's just how it is."

"I guess. But have you ever killed anyone?" I asked.

"Stop asking me questions I can't answer. I might have to kiss you to shut you up."

I bit down on my lip to stop the grin that threatened to take over my face. If he tried to kiss me, I might not stop him, which would be the beginning of a potential disaster.

"There will be no kissing," I said, narrowing my eyes at him. My resolve was weakening. I didn't want him to put it under any more strain. I needed some time away from him, time to remind myself of all the reasons why Landon kissing me would be a terrible idea. It wasn't kissing in isolation that was the issue; it was all the places it could lead. And those places were nowhere I wanted to go. I'd been to the place where peoples' hearts ruled their heads. Where passion overruled reason, and although in books and movies it seemed like utopia, I knew it to be the exact opposite.

"Can't answer or won't?" I asked, wanting to steer the conversation away from our lips.

"Does it matter?" His hand dropped from my back, and he nodded toward the crew mess.

"Friends share things. They talk. And you told me we were friends, so is there anything you'll tell me about yourself?"

He slid onto the banquette as I stood in front of the coffee maker, fiddling with the filter. "People's characters are more interesting to me than facts about their lives," he said.

"But doesn't one influence the other? What has happened to people forms who they are, and who they are influences things that happen to them."

When I didn't get a response, I glanced over my shoulder to see Landon staring at me. "You're a constant source of surprise to me," he said, getting up from the table and walking toward me. I stepped away from him, but my ass hit the counter and he closed the gap. "But I have to get to bed." He was leaving? He dipped his head and pressed a kiss on the top of my head like he had done before when he'd helped me clear up. It was a protective kiss. A kiss from someone who knew I didn't want to be kissed. That I couldn't be.

Couldn't, I reminded myself.

But he'd only just sat down. "You don't want coffee?"

"A little too much, I think," he replied. "But I'll make do with a cold shower." He held my gaze and then turned and headed to our sleeping quarters. "Goodnight, my sage, sexy friend."

I smiled.

Shit, I shouldn't be smiling.

I abandoned the misbehaving coffee machine and grabbed a glass of water. I needed to sober up. I had to deal with the reality of life rather than fall into some Landon-soaked fantasy. He'd done the right thing—for both of us—when he'd gone to bed. We'd already admitted to the attraction between us. That was bad enough. This time of night, with the warm breeze, the lights of the distant shore, and his increasingly rough beard, things between us were verging on dangerous.

I wouldn't end up like my mother. I didn't want her life or her death. And so I had to shake off the thoughts of Landon, the feel of him, the way I liked being with him. I wouldn't be a victim of love or passion—the things that had killed my mother. That wasn't my future.

SIXTEEN

Skylar

The sun was creeping up in the sky as if it were slowly stretching and opening its eyes, and the water was completely still, like ice on a lake. The hustle and bustle of the day on the Med hadn't yet begun. It felt as if I was the only person in the world who was awake, and it was a beautiful morning, which was precisely why I didn't mind the early shift.

Best of all, it was quiet. Apart from whoever was on the bridge, no one else was up. No clatter of pans from the galley, no laughing guests, no announcements over the radio. I glanced at my watch. The peace wouldn't last more than another ten minutes, but it would keep me going for the rest of the day.

I moved around the galley, setting up a tray of coffee cups and juice glasses. Walt would be awake soon enough, and I wanted to make sure I had everything ready for him.

Just a few minutes later, he plodded onto the main sundeck in his long white robe and sunglasses, took a seat at the dining table, and unfolded a copy of the *New York Times* I'd left out for him when I'd set his place just a few minutes earlier.

I'd call that perfect timing.

I filled a cafetiere with hot, black coffee and placed a plain croissant on a side plate. That was the way Walt liked to start every morning. He was a creature of habit, which worked for me. It made it easier to work out what he liked and what he didn't, which made it easier to please him. And that made it more likely that he'd tip well.

I lifted the tray and headed outside.

"Good morning, sir," I said.

Walt put his paper down and pushed his sunglasses over his head. "A beautiful morning made all the more lovely by seeing you," he replied.

I grinned. He was such a nice guy. The more I interacted with him, the more I liked him. "Your coffee, juice, and croissant." I set everything down in front of him, unfolded the napkin, and placed it on his lap.

"You do think of everything, Skylar."

"It's my complete pleasure."

"I was hoping you could arrange for a dinner off the boat this evening."

"Absolutely. A beach picnic or—"

"No, I want to go to Alain Ducasse at l'Hôtel de Paris."

My heart sank. It was the best restaurant in Monaco, perhaps in the South of France, and it booked up months in advance. Walt had money, but so did everyone dining there. I wasn't sure if I could get a big table at short notice.

"I'll see if I can arrange that right away. For six people? What time were you thinking?"

"Eight o'clock sounds about right, but I'll need a table of ten."

My shoulders dropped. He'd set me an almost-impossible task, but it was impossible tasks that created an opportunity for a big tip. "I'll tell Chef and arrange for you to leave the yacht around seven thirty, if that works?"

"I know it's short notice, but it's important, Skylar. A private room would be preferable," Walt said, taking a sip of his coffee. "It's a social event with important business contacts, so we'd like to be able to speak freely. And I'd like you to join us if you're free?"

My skin flashed cold. He'd dropped that last request in so seamlessly that I barely registered what he was saying. "You want me to come to dinner?"

"You shouldn't feel obliged, but it's a beautiful restaurant, and the wives and girlfriends of my associates will also be joining. Like I said, it's a social evening. Hopefully we can share some lovely food, great wine, and wonderful conversation."

Walt had been a little flirtatious, but not overly so, and I certainly hadn't expected a dinner invitation today. It was the last thing I wanted to do, but in yachting, no one said *no* to a guest.

I smiled widely. "I can't think of a better way to spend an evening." Frankly, I'd much rather give myself the pedicure I'd been promising myself. Would I have to fend off his unwanted advances? I was all about the tips, but there was a line in the sand. There were no sexual services available on board the *Sapphire*.

Voices in the saloon drew my attention, and all five of Walt's guests came through the sliding doors and out onto the deck.

"Good morning," I greeted everyone. "Can I get you all what you usually have or would anyone like something different?"

"Let's start with the usual and then see if your chef can surprise us," Walt said.

"Absolutely." Perhaps if I talked to the captain, he would step in and deem Walt taking me to dinner inappropriate. Even if it was a business dinner.

I headed back to the galley. I'd have to get coffee, juice, and pastries out immediately and think about Walt's request later.

"Morning, beautiful," Anton called out from where he was peering into the fridge.

"Did you even know it was me?" I asked.

"Of course. You have delicate footsteps. Unlike August."

I giggled. We all teased August about her Bigfoot impressions.

"All six of our guests are up. But it looks like you're off the hook for dinner."

Anton's head popped out of the fridge. "Why? What's happening?"

"He's asked me to book Alain Ducasse."

"In Monte Carlo?" Anton asked.

"Yeah. I'm not sure I'll be able to. I'll have to call in a few favors."

"Jesus, and then I'll have to cook for him the day after he's eaten at a three Michelin star restaurant. Shoot me now."

"Anton, your food is excellent—he's said over and over how pleased he is."

"Maybe, but I'm not Alain Ducasse."

"No, you're better," I replied.

"And you're a terrible liar."

We laughed and he prodded me in the shoulder.

"We should do a barbecue tomorrow. Maybe on the

beach. Instead of competing, let's do something different. I'll try to arrange some entertainment. It will be the opposite experience," I suggested.

"That's a great idea. Hopefully you can find some kind of fire-eating, singing acrobat and no one will notice the food."

"I'll do my best." I paused. "Can I ask you a question?"

"Shoot," Anton replied just as Landon wandered into the kitchen.

"Never mind," I said.

"Spit it out," Anton said.

I tried to ignore Landon, who leaned against the counter watching us both.

"Walt just asked me to join him for dinner," I said.

Anton's eyes widened, and he stopped cracking eggs into the bowl in front of him. "What? And that's allowed because this isn't a charter yacht and he's the owner?"

I sighed. "I guess. But I'm not interested in Walt."

"Good," Landon said, and my pulse tripped in my wrist at his reaction. I tried to ignore it. I shouldn't care what Landon thought about anything, least of all me being asked out on a date.

"Why not?" Anton asked. "You said you're looking for someone wealthy who was single."

I tried not to focus on Landon's gaze heating my cheeks as he stared. "Well, he's a client. I don't want him to think I'm for sale, but at the same time he's responsible for my employment this season."

Anton winced as if he understood the impossible situation I was in. "If you don't want to go, you shouldn't feel any pressure to agree."

The fact was, I *did* feel pressure. He was my employer, and the person responsible for the entire crew's tips. I should just suck it up and get on with it. "It's just dinner. And it's not like it's just going to be the two of us. It's a business dinner, but with wives and girlfriends. There would be ten of us."

"Anton's right," Landon said. "You shouldn't go. He shouldn't have asked—business dinner or no business dinner."

I'd never heard Landon voice an opinion about anything on the yacht. When we were out with Harvey and August, he was much more relaxed, and on board he seemed to keep his head down and fade into the seascape. I glanced at Anton, whose raised eyebrows told me he'd thought Landon was acting a little out of character too.

"I can't say no," I replied, finally decided. I'd wear something nun-like, no makeup, and make it clear there was no sex on offer.

Anton sighed. "It *is* the word that can't be used in yachting. But there's got to be a line, Skylar."

Landon stayed silent, but his jaw tensed and he fisted his hands. Was he possessive of me particularly, or would he react in the same way to any woman in my position?

Anton frowned. "He's a powerful man who's used to getting his own way. If you say yes to dinner, then you have to decide where to draw the line."

"You think he'll pressure me to have sex with him?"

Landon inhaled sharply. If I didn't know better, I'd think he was jealous. "It's a bad idea, Skylar. Anton's right. Even if he doesn't pressure you tonight, what if he asks you to dinner again? What happens if next time it is just the two of you? It's harder to say no a second time."

Landon was making sense.

"What if I mentioned a boyfriend? I could explain to him that I was dating someone."

"Then why would you say yes to dinner with Walt?" Anton asked.

"To be polite," I said.

"A boyfriend doesn't count if you're on a date with someone else," Landon said.

"I've already said yes. I can't back out now."

"Of course you can," Landon said.

"I don't have an excuse."

"You don't need one," Landon replied.

I glanced at Anton.

"I think Landon's right. It will be difficult to say no next time if you've said yes this time. Maybe the captain could step in and say something."

"And I've already said yes; I have to follow through. If he asks again, I'll cross that bridge when I come to it. Maybe I can say that my boyfriend proposed or something."

"I think it's a really bad idea," Landon said.

It didn't matter what Landon thought. I wasn't quite sure if he was being protective or an ass. Either way, it was none of his business. Another one of the benefits of not having a boyfriend or a husband was that I didn't have to ask anyone's permission to go to dinner. I could handle myself. It was one night, and Walt seemed like a great guy. How bad could it be?

SEVENTEEN

Landon

My legs were restless—I wanted to get out, run. I wasn't used to being as confined as I was on the boat. On deck was bad enough, but in the crew quarters with the low ceilings and cramped conditions, it was almost unbearable. If I could just find a way in to the dinner tonight. I'd already called Reynolds to let him know it was happening. No doubt he or his client would have someone cover it, but I was used to being in charge. At the center of things. I hated only getting half the picture.

And there was the added complication of Skylar being present tonight. She was a nice girl—a civilian. She didn't need to be dining with arms dealers and go-betweens for terrorist organizations. She'd mentioned she was trying to get a reservation for ten, which included the guests on the boat and her. But that left three unallocated seats at the table. God knew who the additional guests might be. More intermediaries or would it be someone more dangerous?

I hated feeling conflicted. I liked solutions to be clear.

The right result for Reynolds' operation was to have the most powerful and dangerous guests at the dinner tonight, but that wouldn't be the right thing for Skylar. If I could just go to the dinner tonight, I could observe who the other guests were, listen in to their conversation, *and* protect Skylar.

"All deck crew, meeting in the mess immediately," Peter called on our radios.

I checked my watch. Just hours until everyone left for dinner. I finished arranging the rope on the deck and headed down to the mess.

"You've hardly said two words today. You okay?" Peter asked as we waited for the others to arrive.

"Yeah, fine. Just concentrating, I guess. I was actually hoping to talk to you about taking on a bit more responsibility. I know I'm the junior deckhand, but I'd really like to take the opportunity to challenge myself." What I wanted was to take the tender ashore this evening. That way I could follow them to the restaurant and carry on my observations.

"It's early in the season. We have plenty of time."

That was the problem—I didn't have plenty of time.

"I guess I'm impatient," I said. "I'm best when I'm being challenged."

"I get it. But I need to be fair to everyone."

I wasn't talking about suddenly wanting to captain the fucking ship. I just wanted to take the tender out tonight.

The two other deckhands appeared, and I shifted so we could all sit around the mess table.

"As I said when I put up the schedule this week, everything's subject to change. The owner wants to go to dinner off the yacht tonight. Tom, I'm going to need you to take the tender out. You might have to stay over there until his dinner is over," Peter said.

Tom had been on shift since seven this morning, and who knew what time Walt and Skylar would head back to the boat. Monte Carlo was a twenty-four-hour town. It could be three in the morning before Tom got back to the boat.

"I'd be happy to take the tender out tonight," I said, seeing my opportunity.

Peter shook his head. "Too soon. You've only been on the yacht for days."

"He's good though, Peter. A natural. When we did the trip out to the caves yesterday, I let him take over for most of it, and going ashore is easier."

"But he's not been out at night before."

I could see that that would be a problem. I was sure I could handle it, but Peter wouldn't be doing his job if he let me.

Fuck.

"What's the weather doing tonight?" I asked. "It might make more sense to suggest going into the marina."

"What's with you?" Peter laughed. "That's the captain's call, not ours."

"But you could suggest it. It's much better and more impressive for the owner."

"I don't disagree with you, but a suggestion like that is way over our paygrade," Peter said.

"Who's suggesting things over their paygrade?" The captain's gravelly voice rang out as he headed in and over to the fridge. He rarely spent time in the mess. He had most of his meals in his room.

"Nobody, sir," Peter said. "We're just sorting out logistics for this evening. That's all."

Peter was going to kill me, but the trouble I was going to get into was exactly why I'd been successfully recruited into the SAS. I didn't like following orders and chains of command that didn't make sense to me. "Peter is covering for me. I suggested the *Sapphire* go into the marina tonight to allow the owner easier access on and off the boat. I thought it would be more convenient and look as if we'd gone the extra mile."

I tried to ignore Peter's eyes boring into the side of my cheek.

The captain pulled out a covered plate of food that Chef had clearly left for him. "Yes, I agree. I was about to tell you that's what we were going to do. I like that we're on the same page, Landon." He pulled open a drawer, took some cutlery, and headed out.

Shit, Peter wasn't going to kill me just once. To go over his head and then have the captain compliment me for doing it? Once wouldn't be enough. He'd resurrect me and do it all over again, but I couldn't regret speaking out. This way, I'd be able to follow the guests to the restaurant, find out who the additional diners were, and perhaps overhear some of the conversation. On top of that, I could keep an eye on Skylar.

I just had to do it without being caught—by the captain or any of the crew or Reynolds, Walt, or any of his dinner guests. If I was, best-case scenario I'd lose my job. Worst-case scenario, I'd end up dead.

EIGHTEEN

Skylar

"I don't understand why you're not more excited. Walt is wealthy, charming. Handsome. Isn't he your dream man?" August asked from where she was lying on her bed.

"I am excited," I replied as I did up the top button on the pussy-bow blouse.

"You could have fooled me. And what's with that blouse?"

"What do you mean? It's expensive." I didn't like to spend a lot of money on clothes. Or anything really. I tried to save as much as possible. But this blouse was an exception. It was a couple of years old, but it had cost me nearly a hundred dollars when I bought it. I figured it still owed me.

"Yeah, and it looks like something my mom would wear." August winced. "Sorry, I didn't mean . . ."

I shook my head. "Don't be sorry. Just because I don't have a mom doesn't mean you don't either. And anyway, you've said how your mom has a great sense of style."

"For her age, yes. But you're twenty-six. Not fifty-eight."

"I'm going for sophisticated. Alain Ducasse is a high-end restaurant." Frankly, I didn't want Walt getting the wrong idea. Sex was not part of the package. And if I made that clear, hopefully he wouldn't ask me out again.

"I thought you wanted Walt to find you attractive?"

"August!" I looked in the mirror. I liked this blouse. What was the matter with it?

"I'm sorry, I just—it's not a sexy blouse. But . . . maybe that's the point."

I was pretty sure August was about to launch into one of her theories. "What's the point?"

"Perhaps you don't really want Walt to find you sexy."

My heart began to thud. I didn't want her questioning my criteria. I didn't want to have to justify that decision—tell her what had happened to ensure I never wanted to fall in love or depend on any man. "Well it's difficult with him being the client. I don't know him, and I don't want to feel pressured into anything."

"I thought so. And you shouldn't feel pressured. But, if a marriage of convenience is what you want, then isn't Walt an option?"

Shit. How did I get her to drop this conversation? "I'm not saying he's not an option. I want to go to dinner without him assuming I'm going to drop my panties for him."

August narrowed her eyes and drew in a breath. "I have a theory."

I rolled my eyes. "I thought you might."

"Walt is the first man that I've known you accept a date from. You have this list of criteria that's almost impossible for any man to live up to . . . and even now, with Walt, you don't seem that into him despite him ticking a lot of your boxes."

Had August busted through my defenses and figured out I didn't want a man? "And your theory is what?"

"That you maybe should go off type. Perhaps there's a reason that you and Landon not only hooked up that first night but ended up on the same boat."

"Yes, there was a reason, and it's called coincidence. This isn't cupid bringing two destined lovers together, August. Get a grip."

August shrugged. "I'm just saying—I know chemistry. I've seen the little looks you give each other."

"There are no looks." Landon and I didn't flirt—we barely spoke to each other. There'd been how he'd helped me clear up after that big night. And he had talked about taking a cold shower after the curry. We had admitted a mutual attraction that night, but that hardly counted as flirtation. There had never been even a suggestion that we repeat the night we met. Neither of us wanted anything more.

"There are *plenty* of looks."

"You have the wrong end of the stick. Landon is a nice guy. A little . . ." I tried to think of a word to describe him. Dominant fit, but wasn't exactly right. Controlling sounded as if he abused his power and he definitely didn't. "I don't know, he's a little overfamiliar." Protective, maybe, and I wasn't used to it. Being independent was important to me. It wasn't that Landon challenged my independence. He couldn't. He had no claim over me. It was as if it was innate in him—like his need to solve problems, to fix and protect was in his DNA.

"Overprotective is nice. Harvey is like that."

"I'm not used to it." What had happened to my mother

had made me face the harsh realities of life, and it was better that way—I wasn't in denial about how awful this world could be.

August sighed. "Walt might be the kind of guy you're looking for, but not necessarily the kind of guy you need."

"I don't *need* anyone."

She shrugged. "True. You make plenty of money yourself. So why don't you find someone to love, rather than someone who can buy you a load of stuff?"

I'd much rather have things over love, but I didn't need either from a man.

"Is it because things were difficult when you were in the home?" August asked. "I'm guessing you didn't have many of your own things."

Discomfort prickled at my skin. I liked to look forward toward my future rather than back to my past.

"It's nothing like that. I just think love and passion are overrated and it's far better to be practical when it comes to who you're going to spend your life with. My list of criteria is no different to someone in a culture with an arranged marriage."

"You can't think that an arranged marriage is a good idea?"

"I think being practical about a life partner is a good thing." My mother had let her love and passion for my father rule her life—override her sense of survival—and she'd paid the ultimate price. I would never repeat her mistake.

Not for Walt.

Not for Landon.

Not for any man.

NINETEEN

Landon

Forgiveness rather than permission—it was a mantra that had almost always worked for me. I hoped it continued to work tonight.

After going over Peter's head, there was no way he was going to let me go ashore tonight, which meant I'd have to go without asking. If I got caught, I risked being fired and putting Reynolds' operation in danger. If I didn't go, I wouldn't be able to identify the additional guests at Walt's dinner and give Reynolds and his client the information they'd been looking for. I'd have to feign ignorance about the rule of not being allowed off the boat without permission. Peter would know I was full of shit, but hopefully I'd talk my way out of it. I'd managed to talk my way out of worse situations.

I watched from the aft deck while Walt and Skylar disappeared into a cab. When she'd emerged to meet him on the sundeck, it had taken every last bit of willpower I had not to run down, put her over my shoulder, and fucking disappear out of Monaco. Fuck the yacht, fuck Reynolds, fuck everything. She'd looked amazing—breath-stealing incredible. Like the kind of woman I'd dream up . . . and that pissed me off. I was on an operation. I didn't get distracted by a woman. I was laser focused and on mission. Always. What was happening to me?

I shook it off and surveyed my exits. I knew the crew well enough to know that with guests on shore, everyone would be focused on their free time rather than me. I hoped.

Laughter drifted down from the sundeck, so I headed in the opposite direction. I walked purposefully off the yacht as if I had every right to do so, and I didn't look back. Confidence in these situations was everything. The first rule of trying to be inconspicuous was not to look guilty. A simple rule but one so many forgot.

Within seconds I was out of sight, and I slowed my pace. At the end of the dock, I crossed the road onto the main street and glanced around, looking for a taxi. There were plenty of fast cars but no cabs. I guessed the rich didn't need taxis as they all had their own drivers. Unlike most of the rest of the ports in the South of France, there was a lack of people on the streets. There were no street entertainers or laughter. The only sound was the noise of the traffic, and the buildings looked like corporate offices and hotels. The place didn't have any soul.

As soon as I could, I dipped into one of the side streets and made my way northeast toward the hotel where Walt and Skylar and the eight other guests would be dining. I was determined to get photographs of everyone joining Walt.

I pulled out the burner phone I'd brought with me and dialed Reynolds.

"Another new number?" he asked.

"Old habits," I explained.

"Are you on your way?"

"Almost there," I said. "I'm going to get you these photographs, but you should know that there's at least one innocent party at the dinner who has absolutely no knowledge of anything that Walt is up to."

"We expected that to be the case, if this is an important meeting. He'll want to make it look like a social occasion."

"Exactly. Walt asked one of the stewardesses from the yacht to join him. I can assure you, she knows nothing of his business."

"Interesting. Do you know her well?"

"No." It wasn't exactly a lie. I didn't know Skylar *well*. Not compared to how August knew her.

"But you work with her, correct?" Reynolds asked. I could see where this was going, and I didn't like it. I'd called him to keep Skylar safe, but of course Skylar's safety wasn't Reynolds' priority.

"She's head of the interior. I'm bottom of the chain on the exterior. We have very little to do with each other."

"But the yacht's a small place. You could get to know her."

"I'm not going to get her reporting to me on what happened at dinner."

"Not reporting, exactly. But you could get her talking."

"Look, if you trust me, you trust me. I do things my way. What I'm not going to do is read her in and put her in even more danger."

"She might be in more danger if she doesn't help us. If our target has taken an interest in her then she could be a considerable asset."

My hand squeezed the mobile. "She can be an asset without being read in."

"Not if you two don't have much to do with each other."

"Like I said, you need to trust me." Perhaps I could create some kind of story that would ensure Skylar said no to a second date with Walt. There was no way I'd endanger her by telling her who Walt was, but I had to do something.

"Well, we'll see what tonight brings, but it's an option, Landon. We need to think about the operation."

I growled and took a left, the hotel coming into view. It wasn't an option. Skylar was innocent in all this, and I wasn't about to put her in danger.

"Where are you? I can hear car horns and traffic."

"I'm just coming up to the hotel."

"Make sure you get these photographs. We can talk about the crew member another day," Reynolds said.

We wouldn't be talking about Skylar. I wasn't going to put her in harm's way.

"I'll catch up with you later," I said and ended the call.

I glanced up at the hotel that, with its intricate, flowery architecture covered in turrets and cherubs, looked better suited to Paris than the edge of the Med. It didn't look real. Not the real I knew, anyway.

I stepped inside the lobby and took in my surroundings, trying not to be blinded by the expanse of white marble before me. Chandeliers hung from the huge, domed, stained-glass ceiling.

It would never occur to me to bring a date to a place like this. I might just be getting used to having millions in the bank, but I'd had a little money for a while now. I enjoyed good things in life, and London was a glamorous place, but this was a different level of living. I wasn't sure what kind of person would be comfortable here.

A man like Walt, I supposed, but it didn't seem like Skylar.

I crossed the lobby and saw the entrance to the restaurant.

"*Bonjour Monsieur.* Do you have a reservation?" the host asked in a thick French accent as I peered inside, trying to catch a glimpse of Skylar and Walt.

"No, I was just hoping to have a drink."

"Very good, sir. *Le Bar Americain* I think will suit you very well, if you just make your way . . ." He directed me across the lobby, but I didn't want a drink.

"There's no bar in the restaurant?" I interrupted him.

"I'm sorry, no. But if the Bar Americain doesn't suit you then maybe the lobby bar."

"Thank you." The lobby bar would have to do. At least there I'd have a view of the restaurant entrance. If I couldn't observe the dinner itself, I'd have to content myself with photographing everyone who entered and left the restaurant. Unfortunately, Walt wouldn't be so stupid as to leave with the three additional guests.

I took a seat at a small table where I'd be hidden from direct view, but where I could see people coming and going. I pulled out my phone. I'd have to be discreet as I took pictures of everyone who entered. Then I'd let Reynolds, or his client, sort through the patrons to find the people they were looking for.

I needed to do a thorough job or Reynolds would have another reason to get Skylar involved.

TWENTY

Landon

The fresh ocean air filled my lungs as I focused on the menial work of cleaning down all the chrome on the decks. It was almost like a meditation, neutralizing the adrenaline that had been pumped through my body last night.

Outside the restaurant, I'd captured image after image of everyone entering and leaving. Most of the shots would be useless, but I was sure I'd captured Walt's guests among the tourists and regulars, and I'd sent what I'd got to Reynolds. And I'd managed to get back on board without anyone noticing—the night had been a success. I just hoped it led to Walt's downfall.

Unexpectedly, Walt and his five guests had left the boat just after seven this morning. I'd brought up all the luggage from their rooms—it looked like they would be gone for a while. If only I'd been at the center of things. I would know whether or not Walt had really only been in town to have the meeting last night and now had left or whether something had drawn him away. At least it meant that he couldn't ask Skylar out again, which meant she was of less interest to Reynolds.

"All crew, all crew to the mess, immediately," the captain's voice rang out on the radio.

As I strode into the kitchen, Skylar walked in through the other door, gathering up her hair and fixing it into a ponytail. I couldn't remember ever seeing her with it up, and her long neck, which I knew tasted like honey, had me fisting my hands to ensure I didn't reach for her. So much for me ignoring Skylar and keeping focused on the operation. It wasn't working despite the fact I'd barely seen her since that first night. I kept telling myself I was good enough at my job not to let my pull toward Skylar compromise the mission. I hadn't made the money, celebrated the victories I had without being better than some guy who fucked up because he had his head turned. But could I enjoy Skylar *and* do my job? I was asking myself that question more and more often.

Reynolds suggesting I use Skylar had brought things to a head for me, and there was no use denying my ongoing attraction to her any longer. Skylar was physically my type —there was no doubt about that. But spending time around her, I found myself drawn to her. To the way she worked hard without it showing, the way she seemed to carry around a pain inside her in the same way soldiers who'd been in battle did, but she tried to hide it. It connected us by some invisible thread. I felt I knew her better than I did, cared about her welfare more than I should. I just couldn't explain it, and as much as I tried, I couldn't shake it. It was as if Skylar was really two people—the one she showed and the one she hid—and I wanted to uncover both.

"Hey," I said, patting the seat on the banquette next to me.

She tilted her head and a warm, inviting smile unfolded on her face. I couldn't help but grin back. "Hey," she replied.

"What have you been doing this morning?" I asked.

"Oh, you know, some time on the Jet Ski, a little yoga followed by a massage. You?" She grinned at me, but it struck me that was how she should have spent her morning, and for a second I wondered if I could make it happen.

She's not yours to fix and protect.

I nodded. "You're lucky. I've been polishing chrome. For hours. And tomorrow it will all need doing again."

She laughed. "That pesky salt water."

"It would be much easier if we weren't in the sea."

"Right?"

I didn't get to see this carefree side of Skylar very often. She usually had her defenses up. Or her affability was a mask she wore for the guests. I wanted more time with *this* girl—funny, playful, and fucking beautiful.

"You have a good time last night?" I asked.

"Better than I thought."

A mixture of unfamiliar emotions wrapped around my heart. I hated that she'd enjoyed herself with Walt. I wanted to be the one she enjoyed spending time with. I wanted to pull her close and keep her from harm's way.

What the fuck was happening to me?

I nodded, unsure if relief or anger would escape if I said anything.

"He was a perfect gentleman. You don't have to worry," she said.

"No less than you deserve," I replied.

"I don't remember you holding yourself back the first time we met." She grinned at me.

Her sweet honeysuckle smell, the whisper of hair

against my shoulder as she spoke, and then that bloody smile. This girl was a perfect storm of trouble. "Yeah, well, things were different then."

Different because then Skylar was just another hot blonde.

Different because then I'd not seen the glimpse of the woman beneath the mask.

Different because I didn't want her then like I wanted her now.

She turned to me, her eyebrows pulled together, confusion washing over her face, but before she could ask me what was different, the rest of the crew filed into the mess, silencing our exchange.

But this wasn't the end of it. It was only the beginning. Last night, seeing Skylar in harm's way, watching her go to dinner with another man—I realized that I wanted her. One night wasn't enough, and the myriad of reasons not to pursue anything more with her all seemed to dissolve into the sea air whenever she was around.

She might be a woman I was prepared to go all in for.

TWENTY-ONE

Skylar

"I'm exhausted," August said, collapsing onto the rattan chair next to mine with a cocktail. We'd found the cheapest bar in Monte Carlo that had a view over the ocean. It was still one of the most expensive bars in Europe, but it was worth it. The breeze from the water cooled the temperature to perfect, the twinkling lights of the marina provided the best lighting, and my drink had just the right amount of vodka in it.

"We all are," Peter replied from across the low wooden table. "It's been a long day. But it's done. No guests and a yacht where you could eat off any surface."

"Now we can party," August said.

After Walt and his guests had unexpectedly left, the captain had said that if the yacht was pristine by the end of the day, we could all have twenty-four hours leave. There was nothing more exciting than unexpected time off mid-season. We'd all worked frantically—nothing like freedom as a motivator.

"Who's getting a hotel?" August asked. "I'm pissed my boyfriend can't get leave. He's in freaking Italy."

"Hotels in Monaco are going to be pricey," I said. If we'd been in Saint Tropez or Nice or one of the smaller Italian ports, I would have definitely splurged to spend some time on dry land, but Monaco was a different world.

"Fuck it, I'm doing it," Anton said, pulling out his phone and tapping the screen. "I see it as an investment in my sanity."

"And your penis," August said. "Because no one on the boat is going to help end your dry spell, and you know the rule about bringing people back. Anyone else tempted?"

"I've booked something," Landon said, stretching his legs out in front of him, under the table, his shin sliding against mine. Had he meant to touch me?

"You've booked a hotel room?" I asked. "How come?" Was he planning to get laid? Why wouldn't he? He was single and hot. A wedge of frustration settled in my stomach. The idea of him with someone else . . . It seemed wrong. But I had no claim to him. I'd told myself over and over that Landon wasn't right for me. So why was I irritated at the thought of him kissing someone else?

"Oh, I don't know. I'm a thirty-two-year-old man who has an opportunity to have a room to myself tonight—I'm going to take it."

He looked at me as if he could read my thoughts and slid his leg against mine—this time it was definitely on purpose.

I didn't move. Didn't take my eyes from him. The rest of the table began to talk among themselves, leaving Landon and me to have a semi-private conversation.

"What happened to you this afternoon?" I asked. I wanted to know why he was booking a hotel room in

Monaco. Was it really so he didn't have to share a room for the night? Or had he had a call from an ex-girlfriend last night after his shift who was in town, or maybe he'd found someone on Tinder.

"What happened?" he asked, grinning at me.

"You went ashore this afternoon for no apparent reason." Maybe he'd met someone earlier today and that was why he'd been so keen to be off the yacht.

Landon chuckled. "There was a reason."

"So what was it?" I should have dropped it. It was none of my business, but I didn't like the idea that he was keeping something from me. I wanted to be the person he confided in. I wanted to be his friend.

"I went to get migraine meds," he replied. "And I picked up some tampons for August at the same time, if you must know."

August turned toward us at the sound of her name. "He saved my ass. Or my vagina, depending on how you look at it," she said.

"You went tampon shopping for August?"

Landon chuckled. "Yeah. There were so many choices." He shook his head. "Who knew?"

Conversation descended into discussing periods and whether it was an assault on masculinity to shop for tampons.

"If you're scared to buy tampons, you've probably never been to war," Landon said and took a swig from his beer bottle. "Stuff like that really doesn't matter."

That silenced the table, and my desire to question him. I'd never met a man like Landon—a man who'd fought for his country, who had done *important* things. He was right, most people concerned themselves with stuff that really didn't matter. I'd learned that yachting. I'd gone from living in a group foster home to a multimillion-pound yacht. The difference was stark.

That was the thing about Landon, he was just different. His time in the army, his quiet dominance, and the way he made me feel when he was near me.

"I'm ready to eat," Landon announced. "Anyone want to join me?"

A rumble of voices agreed, and we all drained our drinks and set off to find a place. He might be the junior deckhand on the *Sapphire*, but off the boat, Landon was completely in charge. It didn't seem conscious. He was just confident, knew what he wanted, and went for it without worrying about anyone else. Not that he was rude about it, just single-minded.

It was sexy as hell.

While rich men enjoyed flexing their power because it made them feel good, Landon seemed to have power despite his lack of money. He commanded attention from the rest of the crew, including me.

We all piled out onto the street, and Landon and I ended up at the back of our party.

As he was almost a foot taller than me, he had to lean over to whisper in my ear. "Did I tell you how beautiful you look tonight?"

For some reason, Landon's compliment didn't make me wince the way some men's comments did. Everything about him was different and it had thrown me off kilter. His warm breath on my neck shouldn't have made me shiver. He shouldn't ease the ever-present knot in my stomach or have me wanting to slide my hand into his as we walked. He shouldn't make me feel safe. "You didn't."

"Well, you do. Not that it's any surprise."

"Because you're a gentleman who prefers blondes," I

said, nudging him gently with my elbow, trying to lighten the mood.

He pulled in a breath and scraped his hand through his hair. "I'm beginning to think I'm a man who just prefers you."

I focused on the cobbled street in front of us. "Me?" Had I been mistaken about the ex-girlfriend in town or the girl on Tinder? I tried to hold my breath to ensure I heard his reply.

"Yeah, you. I like you. More and more."

My stomach swooped, and I tried to think of a response. My head was telling me to run. Far away. I didn't want to fall for anyone. I'd worked hard to stay single all these years —to keep away from temptation. But now, temptation right in front of me, I found myself rooted to the spot, wanting to know what was next. "Okay."

"Okay?" he asked.

I nodded, unsure of what to say. Unsure of how I felt.

I knew I found Landon attractive. I knew I liked him too. But I also knew that I'd been single all these years for a reason.

He wrapped his large hand around my upper arm to steady me when I stumbled over a loose cobblestone. We stopped, and I looked up at him as he swept his thumb across my cheekbone. "I'm only going to ask you this once, and you don't have to decide now, but stay with me tonight?"

"Landon . . ." Somehow, I couldn't say no to him, even though I knew I shouldn't say yes.

"Think about it."

He placed his hand in the small of my back, urging me forward to catch up with the rest of the party.

TWENTY-TWO

Landon

I could hardly tear my attention away from Skylar for more than a second, and if I wasn't careful, I was going to make a fool of myself. Despite the fact that I knew if things developed between Skylar and me, I could make the job I was doing for Reynolds more difficult, I'd decided Skylar was worth the risk.

"I gotta go dancing, burn off some of this sexual frustration," August said from the other end of the table. "Who's in?" Everybody began to gather their things, down their drinks, and get ready to follow August. I'd never been into nightclubs, and I wasn't about to change the habits of a lifetime.

I set some euros on the table, resisted the urge to pay for Skylar's meal, stood and pulled on my jacket.

"I'm not going," Skylar said, her voice hushed and her body turned to mine.

"You want me to walk you back to the yacht?" I asked.

She shook her head. "No. I want to stay with you."

My pulse tripped in my wrist and my heart hammered against my ribcage. "Good decision," I said.

She sighed through her smile. "Well, I'm not sure about that, but it's where I want to be."

Fuck, she was at her sexiest when she wore her feelings on the outside like this. I knew that a big part of her didn't want to go with me, but I liked the fact that a bigger part did. Maybe it was just the thought of the sex that had changed her mind. It had been so good between us, but deep down I hoped that whatever kept drawing us to each other was more than that.

"Let's try not to make it too obvious. I don't want the rest of them gossiping," she said.

"They're drunk—I'm not sure they'd notice if Beyoncé walked in on the captain's arm."

She giggled. "They are."

I'd been watching Skylar's alcohol intake this evening. I didn't want the cocktails to make her decision to stay with me. But she'd stopped at two drinks, switching to water when no one was watching. "Still. Where are you staying? I'll meet you there."

"No way. I'm not having you walk alone at this time of night. We'll put them in cabs and then we'll go to the hotel."

She gave me a reluctant grin and nodded.

In less than five minutes, the rest of the crew had piled into two taxis, leaving the two of us to catch a third.

Skylar and I stood and watched them turn left up the street, then I turned to Skylar and took her face in my hands. "Finally, I get you all to myself." I pressed my lips against her forehead, just enjoying touching her again. It was as if being this close to her gave me something nothing else did. I couldn't describe it—energy? Power? It was as if she added fuel to my soul. Her fingers drifted down my forearms, and I moved my mouth to hers, desperate to taste her.

She stumbled, and I pulled away to steady her. "You okay?"

She put her fingers over her mouth and nodded. "The kissing thing just kills me."

I frowned. "What?"

"Nothing, come on, let's go." She slid her hand into mine, and I led her down the street until we were staring up at the entrance of the *Hotel de Paris*.

"You didn't book here?"

"I heard it was nice," I said as I pulled her inside.

"Landon, you can't. It's crazy expensive."

"Tell me what made you say *yes* to spending tonight with me?" I asked as I pulled out the room key they'd given me when I'd checked in earlier.

"What? You can't be serious about staying here."

"I am," I said as I pressed the button for the lift. "Fourth floor."

"You mean fifth floor. It's crazy how you Brits don't call the first floor the first floor."

I chuckled. "We do. It's crazy you Americans don't call the ground floor the ground floor. Now tell me why you said *yes*."

She sighed. "I don't know. Maybe it was the kissing thing." She turned her face to my arm and placed a kiss on my shoulder. "I think I was always going to say yes."

"You thought you'd just keep me waiting before you told me?"

She grinned. "You always knew I'd say yes."

Had I? Skylar wasn't the sort of girl to be taken for granted, and I knew she thought we were badly suited. We were looking for different things, but right now, tonight, this summer, I didn't care about any of that. I just wanted her.

"I knew you had your reasons to say no. But I like that you said yes. Even if you won't tell me why."

"It's not that I won't. I'm just not sure I can explain it. I know you're not who I should want. I shouldn't want anyone, yet I think about you more and more. I want to know where you are, what you're thinking, and who you are underneath. You make me feel . . . safe. Like being with you is where I should be. And it doesn't make sense to me, but as long as I know this is just about tonight, I—"

I pressed her against the wall and kissed her. She'd said exactly what I'd wanted to hear. She liked me despite her logic and criteria. Her need for me was bigger than all of it. Somehow that made her decision more important. More valuable. For all she knew, I couldn't provide for her, but she was here anyway. Just because she wanted me.

The lift doors opened, and I took her hand and guided her into the suite I'd booked.

"Wow, Landon." Skylar walked toward the windows that overlooked the sea and the marina. "It's beautiful." She spun to face me. "This is just . . . Are you enjoying your tips before you get them? How can you afford this? Holy shit, is that a bathtub?"

"Come here," I said as I sat on the bench at the bottom of the bed and kicked off my shoes.

"You know you have a tub in the middle of the room." She wandered toward me, still focused on the bath with the best view in Monte Carlo.

I pulled her between my thighs and began to unbutton her dress, trying not to get distracted by her hands in my hair or the way she traced the outline of my face with her fingertips.

The red jersey material dropped to the floor, revealing black lace underwear. I fingered the edge of her bra—I wanted to play with and palm her breasts, but I also wanted more, and if I started something now, bath time would never happen. I turned her around so temptation faced the other direction, then groaned as I glanced down to take in her tight, high arse. Jesus, this woman's body. I snapped open her bra and pulled the straps from her shoulders before hooking my fingers into her knickers and peeling them off. I couldn't resist the cleft in her bottom and smoothed my hand down the center of her arse, my fingers gently pressing into the valley between her cheeks.

I sighed and circled her waist with my hands before turning her to face me again, then pulling her toward me and kissing her once between her breasts. I wanted to take my time tonight. Explore her inside and out.

I pulled one of the soft, white robes from the bed and held it up, encouraging her to slip her arms into the sleeves. "You're dressing me again?"

"Until the bath's ready."

She grinned and lifted herself up on her tiptoes. "We're having a bath?"

She couldn't be more surprised than I was. I'd never bathed with a woman before. Never had the urge to, but with Skylar, I wanted to care for her. I wanted her to relax and enjoy this evening. And I wanted to sit opposite her and talk in warm water surrounded by bubbles. "Sit here," I said as I guided her to take my place on the bench while I saw to the bath.

I never took baths. But Skylar had changed what I did and didn't do.

I eyed up some of the bottles on the inset shelf on the waist-high wall that separated the bath from the bed and emptied the entire contents of one into the fast-running water.

In just a few minutes, the bath was ready, and I looked up to find Skylar watching me, her eyes wide, her bottom lip between her teeth.

"Now it's your turn," she said as she joined me, then began to undo the buttons on my shirt. She pulled the sides apart and pressed her lips against my chest, mirroring my earlier gesture. "You smell so good. What is that?"

I shook my head. "Nothing. Just soap."

"Maybe it's the soldier in you. You smell so . . . masculine." She ran her hands up my chest, tracing the shapes of my muscles before pushing my shirt over my shoulders. I took over, unused to being undressed by a woman, and stripped off my trousers and pants.

"You want to test the water before you step in?" I asked.

She shook her head, glancing at my growing erection. "Something tells me you'll have it right," she said.

I pressed a kiss to her mouth before taking her hand and guiding her into the bath.

"The water's perfect." She sank into the bubble-filled bath. "You going to sit behind me?"

I shook my head. "If we start the bath with you between my legs, then we won't be in long enough to get clean."

She grinned as she leaned back and watched me as I stepped in and sat opposite her.

"Are you going to tell me how you afford a hotel room like this?" she asked.

It irritated me that we were back to this subject again. I guessed it didn't make sense since she'd made up her mind that I was some kind of drifter, but I didn't like to focus on money. "You could afford to book this room if you wanted. Everyone chooses to spend their money differently."

She sighed and tipped her head back, the water sloshing up to her neck. "That's true. I thought for a minute you were a secret heir to a fortune, and you just hadn't told me."

"Nope. My parents are teachers."

"They're still together?"

"Yeah, thirty-five years now."

"That's nice. Romantic. Do you know that's probably the first bit of personal information you've shared with me without prompting?"

I chuckled and grabbed one of her ankles, lifting it onto my thigh and smoothing my hand up her shin. "Don't exaggerate."

"I don't think that's what I'm doing. You're not a sharer, Landon."

"Old habits," I replied. "But tell me more about you. What do your parents do?"

"My mother's dead. My dad . . ." She shrugged. "I've no idea where he is."

She might accuse me of not being one to share, but I could tell by the way she wasn't meeting my eye that there was something she wasn't saying.

"What happened to him?"

She shrugged, pushing her thumb into my leg as if she was trying to make a fingerprint. "Prison somewhere. Haven't seen him since I was fourteen."

The light in her eyes dimmed, and I didn't like it. "I'm sorry," I replied.

She forced a smile. "Not my problem anymore," she replied.

But it had been. At some point. And the memory of him still cloaked her in sadness.

"Come here," I said. "Stand up and sit in front of me."

Her smile morphed into something more genuine, and

she stood, the water and bubbles skating down her body as she did.

"That's better. You were too far away over there," I said as she sat back against my chest, and I circled my arms around her waist, stroking my hand over her stomach, cupping her breasts then releasing them.

"Are my boobs particularly dirty?" she asked.

"Filthy," I said, my hands covering them.

She giggled and entwined her legs with mine. "Is this your thing? Baths with women?"

I slid my hands down her stomach, enjoying the feel of her so close. "I can't remember the last time I had a bath. As a kid, I guess."

She shifted and turned her head to look up at me as if to ensure I wasn't joking.

I dipped my head and kissed her, expecting it to be a quick peck, but when I tasted her, I couldn't pull away and instead plowed into her mouth with my tongue as I brought my hands up to cup her breasts. She moaned and leaned back, eventually shifting her entire body and straddling me.

Her water-covered skin felt like silk under my fingers as I ran my hands up her back, then down to her perfect arse as we continued to kiss, our tongues crashing together and desperately exploring. I slipped my fingers between her legs, and when she started to squirm, I grabbed her hip with my free hand, holding her in place.

Exploring her warm folds, I found her clitoris hard and needy, and she gasped into my mouth as I pressed and circled. I held her tight as her body strained against my touch. As I pushed my fingers inside her, she sighed—relief or pleasure or both? We broke our kiss as she tipped her head back and clutched at my neck.

"Landon," she whispered. "Landon."

I let her rock back and forth as she began to fuck my hand, and I took in her wet breasts and smooth, wet stomach. I'd never seen anyone sexier. Her fingers tightened against my skin.

"I'm going to come." Her eyes flew open in panic as her gaze fixed on me as if she was afraid I was going to stop her. As if she wasn't allowed. But it was exactly what I wanted— to see this beautiful, sexy, slightly damaged woman come because of me. Her mouth formed that perfect "O" and her body tensed as our eyes stayed locked. Looking into Skylar's face as she came at my touch had blood racing to my dick, and it pulsed beneath her.

She cried out, then slumped against my chest, her body soft and warm. Withdrawing my hand, I pulled her close and kissed the top of her head.

"This view," she said after the rise and fall of her belly calmed.

"It's pretty spectacular," I replied, glancing down at her.

She shivered as I trailed my fingers down her back.

"Are you cold?" I asked.

"I can't tell."

I chuckled. The temperature of the bath had cooled. It was time to move. "Let's get you dry," I said, shifting her so I could climb out. When out, I bent, scooped her up, and she squealed before I set her on her feet and wrapped her in a big, white towel. I picked her up again and carried her to the bed.

"Don't move." I set her down, lying on her back, and then found a towel to wrap around my waist and another to dry her off with. I didn't want her to be cold. Kneeling by the side of the bed, I dried her feet, making sure I'd pressed the towel between each toe. Exposing only one small area of her body at a time, I began to dry her off.

"This is nice," she said. "I've never had someone . . ."

I wasn't sure I wanted to hear the end of that sentence, but I could take a guess that she meant that no one else focused on her, cared whether she was wet or dry, pre-orgasm or post. Happy or sad.

I worked my way up her body, and when I got to her thighs, I opened them wide, capturing every droplet of water, and held myself back from dipping down for a quick taste of her. *We have time,* I told myself.

I kept making my way up her body, stopping to press a kiss against a mole just underneath her right breast. I'd not noticed it when we were together before. What else was she hiding? I worked the towel down her arm and just as I dried between her fingers, she grabbed my neck.

"I want you, Landon," she said, twisting and lifting her thigh over my hip.

"So impatient."

"You have enough self-control for both of us."

I chuckled. Self-discipline wasn't something I lacked, but I'd enjoyed these moments. I'd relished keeping Skylar warm, drying her off—caring for her.

She trailed her fingers down my chest as I abandoned the towel, and she gripped the base of my cock.

I hissed and clenched my jaw, grabbing her wrist so she didn't move her hand.

"So you *are* human," she said. "And you do want me."

How could she think otherwise?

I reached for my wallet and found a condom. "From the moment I first laid eyes on you."

"Yeah, but I was carrying a tray of tequila. It might have been the booze you were focused on."

I ripped open the condom and slid it on my flint-hard cock before pushing Skylar to her back. "Wrong," I said as I pressed against her slick entrance. "I saw you the moment I walked into the bar."

I pushed into her with a grunt, and she arched up from the bed. She was so fucking tight and perfect, and her skin was soft and smelled like honey—it would be so easy just to fuck and come and be desperate for her again.

"You saw me?" Her voice was breathless and ragged.

"And I wanted you right from that second."

She groaned, and I wasn't sure if it was as a result of my confession or the slide of my cock. She brought her legs up, her thighs either side of my hips as I began to rock in and out of her, pulling every sharp breath from her lungs. It was even more perfect than it had been the first night. It was as if our bodies molded together, knew each other, understood what was necessary.

I buried my head in her neck, biting and sucking as her movements alternated between smooth and sharp.

"Landon, I can't. I just can't."

I upped my rhythm. She was close, and I wanted her completely lost to me, unable to stop what she was feeling from crashing over her.

"Oh God," she cried.

I lifted up on my hands. I wanted to see her again. Wanted her to look at me as she came.

Her eyes flew open, and the orgasm that had been creeping up my spine suddenly took over. As she came, I did too, the tendons in my neck tensing, the muscles in my body contracting as I pushed in as deep as I could go.

"Fuck," I said, unable to pull my gaze from her. "You're beautiful. And your body? It's as if it was made for me."

She placed her palm over my chest. "Maybe your body was made for me."

I chuckled and collapsed next to her, then pulled her toward me. "Maybe."

She pressed a kiss over my nipple and then went limp in my arms. I grinned. This post-orgasm haze felt different from last time. More comfortable. Was it the heat of the bath? The snippets of information we'd shared? Skylar was right; I didn't offer up a lot of personal information about myself. It wasn't in my nature and it certainly wasn't in my training. But she was the first person in a long time I'd *wanted* to share stuff with. Partly because I wanted to know things about her, and the easiest way to get someone to open up was to do it first—it was a key way of building trust, and I'd learned it early in my army career. But it was more than that. For some reason, I wanted her to know stuff about me. Stuff that it wouldn't occur to me to tell anyone.

"I like you," I said. From anyone else that wouldn't mean much, but me telling someone, a woman, how I felt about them was a big deal because I'd never done it before.

And from the way her eyes softened and the corners of her mouth curled into a smile, she understood that.

She skirted her fingers down my chest, and I grabbed her hand, circling her wrist and linking our fingers before she got too low.

"I like you too," she replied.

I didn't quite know how to tell her, but tonight wasn't going to be enough for me. I was all in. "I don't want to not do this again." I was being unusually awkward. I wanted her to understand what I was thinking, but didn't want to come on too strong.

"You don't want to not do this again? Does that mean you *do* want to do this again?"

Of course she'd called me out.

I squeezed her hand. "I know you have rules and criteria, but . . ."

"And so do you. What about your quick bang and here's ten dollars for breakfast, babe, routine?"

"Erm, I'm not going to offer a girl ten dollars to buy her own breakfast. That's insane."

Her chuckle reverberated against my ribcage. "Oh, that's right. It's a no-breakfast deal."

"You," I said, rolling her to her back, "are beyond cheeky." Sliding her hands up over her head, I pressed a kiss against her neck.

"But I'm not wrong," she said.

I worked my way down her body, kissing, licking, biting. I found her nipple with my mouth, flicked my tongue, and enjoyed hearing her moan. "Careful. If you complain, you won't get breakfast money," I said.

"Oh, I'm not complaining." Her voice came out husky and needy, which was just how I liked it.

I trailed kisses from one hip bone to the other, her fingers pushing through my hair, urging me on before I stopped and hauled myself off the bed.

She pushed up on her elbows, her hair falling around her shoulders, her skin reddened from my lips. "What?"

"Stand up and turn around."

Without questioning me, she did as I asked, and gently, I pressed her over so she was standing over the bed, bent at the waist, her hands resting on the mattress.

"This is how I saw you the first time around. Your back to me. Your perfect arse swaying from side to side." She whimpered as I rolled another condom onto my straining dick then caught her hips, holding her in place.

"Are you ready?" I asked, sweeping my hand between her legs, thankful that I found her wet and ready.

She nodded, clutching the bedcovers and bowing her head.

I pushed in slowly this time and found her tight as a drum. I gritted my teeth, cursing her effect on me and wondering at the same time how I could make it last forever.

She collapsed onto her chest, her arms shooting behind her, reaching for my legs, urging me forward, deeper. *So impatient.* I grinned as she gasped when I settled deeper into her than I'd been before.

"Landon, it's so—oh my God."

"Can you handle it? Can you cope with how deep I am? How fucking good it feels?" I bit out.

She turned her face into the mattress, muffling her loud groans.

I pulled out slowly, the room spinning as I tried to maintain my self-control. "Tell me that you don't want to feel me again. Tell me you can live without my dick in you." I thrust back into her when she didn't respond.

"I can't," she cried out. "I want it. Please, Landon."

Her begging was the last thing I heard as blood rushed through my ears and my pulse tried to break out of my skin. I fucked her relentlessly, ignoring the sweat trickling down my spine and the way Skylar stumbled as her legs gave way to her orgasm. I just kept fucking, desperate for release, desperate to make sure she always remembered how good this was. Desperate to have her need me again.

I knew that whatever happened between us tonight, it wouldn't be enough. Not for me. It wasn't just proximity that had me wanting her. It was something deep in her soul, behind the practiced smile and her list of criteria. I heard it calling out to me.

She needed me, and I wasn't sure that I didn't need her.

TWENTY-THREE

Skylar

Tiptoeing wouldn't help—if someone was going to catch me it was because they'd see me—but I did it anyway. It was just before seven. If I was lucky, the rest of the crew would still be out partying. Even if they weren't, hopefully, they'd all still be asleep, and I'd be back on the yacht and tucked up in my bunk before people got going for the day. Our twenty-four-hour leave wasn't over until lunchtime.

I crept down the stairs into the crew quarters, happy to find it was like the Marie Celeste. All I needed now was to find my cabin empty, and no one would realize I'd been out all night.

I poked my head around the door to find August tucked up on the bottom bunk, her back to the door. Shit. I'd have to think of something fast—where I'd been, who I was with, and why I'd stayed out all night. I'd really hoped to avoid that.

"Don't think I don't hear your walk of shame," August said, her voice thick with sleep.

"Shhh, I've just been to the bathroom. I'm going back to bed."

August turned and pushed up on her elbow, suddenly the most awake person on the planet. "I'm going to have to call the firefighters, your pants are on fire."

I laughed and shook my head. "Shut up and go back to sleep."

"Not until you tell me where you've been."

I needed more time. My head was too fuzzy with last night to think up plausible excuses. I unzipped my dress and changed into my pajamas. "Just around. Seeing Monte Carlo."

"With Landon?" she asked.

I scowled. "Wasn't he with you?" I'd noticed Landon always answered a question with another question if he didn't want to answer someone.

"You know he wasn't with us."

I shrugged.

"Well if you won't answer me, I'll have to ask Landon myself. Perhaps in front of Chef. Or Peter."

"August! What's awoken your mean streak this morning? And why do you just assume I was with Landon?"

"Come on, Skylar, I'm your best friend. I know how you don't like being the subject of gossip, and I won't say a word to anyone. I just want to know you had a good time. I like the two of you together."

I bit back a grin. August was always rooting for love. "We couldn't figure out where you were, so we ended up getting a few drinks. That's all." It wasn't a complete lie. Landon had made me drink some water somewhere between my third and fourth orgasm. Or had it been between my second and third? He'd said that he didn't want me to get dehydrated. I grinned. He was always looking out for me. Caring for me. I never thought a man could be so focused on *me*.

"So how many orgasms did you have during your '*drinks*'?" she asked, complete with air quotes.

There was no way she was going to stop questioning me. And if the shoe was on the other foot, I'd have every detail whether or not I wanted it. "Four," I replied as I climbed up onto the top bunk. "You better not say anything to anyone. I don't want the crew finding out."

"Shit, Four? Really?"

I climbed under my duvet and pulled the covers up, wanting to sink into the memories of Landon's fingers on my hips, his breath on my skin.

"He looks like he'd be fantastic in bed. Bossy. Gritty. Controlling," August said with a sigh.

"Gross, August. I hope you're not imagining it."

"So that's confirmation, then?"

He *was* bossy, gritty, and controlling. But Landon was more than that, too. He was caring and thoughtful and focused on my pleasure. "A little," I said. "But that's got to be the end of it," I said as much to myself as to August.

Landon had said he wanted to have me again, and as delicious as that thought was, I had to put a stop to it. All my energy had to be focused on my job and my tip, not messing about with a junior deckhand.

"Wait, why? You two seem to have fun together."

I wasn't sure if fun was exactly what it was, but we were drawn to each other. "Yeah, well that's all well and good, but not what I'm looking for."

"Why on earth not? Four orgasms—you're going to say no to that?"

Landon being so close by was a problem. He was too close. Too tempting.

"And it's not like there's anyone else that you like better around," she said.

"I'm not saying no to Landon because I might meet someone else. I'm saying no to Landon because he's Landon." The things he did to me. The way he made me feel. It was too consuming. I liked him, I respected him, and it seemed to be mutual. The more I got to know him, the more of a threat he posed to my plan. My focus. My need to stay independent.

"And you don't want Landon because he doesn't tick all your boxes? No euphemism intended."

Of course, I wanted Landon. I wanted him right that second. I wanted him to pull me into the shower and soap down my body before laying me out and doing very wicked things to me. "Landon's not an option."

"Well, we know he's single. And he seems like a nice guy. What if he was rich? Would you want him then?"

"He's not."

"I don't get it, Skylar—surely you want to be happy? You've got your list and you think if you meet a guy that can provide a tick against each one, that will make you happy, but what if you meet that guy and you don't actually like him? There's a lot to be said for . . . chemistry. For passion —great sex."

I groaned. Chemistry and passion were what my parents shared. And that was exactly what I was trying to avoid. "Then I'll end up on my own. It doesn't scare me."

"You'll end up a lonely old cat lady."

At least I'd be alive. And I liked cats.

"I just want to see you happy," August continued. "Landon doesn't have to be a forever man. You know what yachting's like—everyone's kinda passing through—you can just have a holiday romance and then walk away."

The problem was, I didn't know if I would be able to walk away, and I didn't want to end up desperate for someone who ended up letting me down.

Last night had been last night.

"How did you leave things with him?" August asked after a few moments had passed.

I sucked in a breath. I'd run off in the middle of the night without telling Landon I was leaving. As much as I tried to tell myself that he'd be relieved that I wasn't there when he woke up, something niggled at the back of my brain that told me he'd be pissed.

"I'm not sure how we left things. I just—August, it's not as easy as you make it out."

Landon had told me he wasn't ready to walk away after last night. And instead, I'd run. But now, listening to August, who was convinced it was so easy, I wanted to believe her, go find Landon, and have him kiss me in that incredible way he did. Would it be possible to let my defenses down for just a few weeks? Could I tear up my list and just do what felt right rather than what my history was telling me I should do? For a summer?

TWENTY-FOUR

Landon

After a night like last night, I should have been in a better mood. I pushed my sunglasses to the top of my head as I kicked off my shoes before boarding the *Sapphire*. I'd woken up to an empty bed more disappointed than I had any right to be. I'd not changed my mind about wanting Skylar again, but she'd made it clear I wasn't the man for her on several occasions. I was fucked off that she'd run off before I woke up, but I should have seen it coming.

"Hey," Peter said. "You made it back right on time."

I'd made the most of the hotel this morning. I wanted my irritation at Skylar to have simmered down before I saw her again, so I'd completed a punishing workout in the gym, watched some sports, and had a quick shower.

"I'll change and then be ready for whatever," I said.

"Where did you get to last night? You should have been with us at the club; we had such a good time. Foreign girls are so much hotter."

I grinned, trying to pretend I was interested. "Did you get lucky?" I asked, ignoring his question to me.

"Of course I did. The choices were fucking phenomenal. You missed out, man."

I shook my head in feigned disappointment. "I'll be back when I'm changed." One thing was for sure, I hadn't missed out last night. Not for a second.

I headed inside and toward the galley.

"Hey, Anton," I said as I passed through the galley.

"Landon."

"Hey," Skylar said as she closed the fridge door that had hidden her from view.

My pulse tripped in my neck, despite my irritation at her. She hadn't lost her ability to leave me breathless. She had her hair up and was back in her uniform of navy skirt and light-blue polo. Somehow she managed to wear it better than the rest of us. "Hi," I replied and turned to head through to the stairs down to the crew quarters.

It wasn't that I was going to be an arsehole and ignore her, but I really had nothing to say. She'd made her position clear. So had I. I wasn't about to beg her for more.

As I descended the spiral staircase, I turned at the sound of footsteps behind me. It was Skylar. I shot her a smile, but continued toward my cabin.

"Hey, Landon, can I talk to you?" she asked as I turned the handle to my room.

I turned around and waited for her to say whatever was on her mind.

She got to the bottom of the stairs and looked around. All the crew cabin doors were shut, and I couldn't hear anything, so people were probably either asleep or out.

"Erm, can you come into my room for a second?" she asked.

"I have to get changed. I told Peter I'd be right up." No doubt she wanted to ask me not to tell anyone about last night, but there was no need. I didn't offer up information like that to anyone.

"Just for a second. Please?"

I wasn't sure I'd ever be able to resist her when she begged. "It will have to be quick."

She smiled at me, relief in her eyes, and I followed her into her empty cabin.

With the door firmly shut, she held my gaze for a few seconds, chewing on the inside of her lip before she spoke. "I'm sorry I ran off this morning." She wrinkled her nose, as if she was bracing herself for me to be angry. I was irritated, disappointed, but she was obviously expecting a more forceful reaction.

"Yeah, well, I'll live."

She let out a breath as if relieved.

"I freaked out," she said, peering at her toes. "I wasn't sure what to do."

"So rather than wake me and talk to me, you decided to run off before I'd given you money for breakfast?"

I was trying to make light of the situation, but it seemed she knew me better than that. She frowned then took a step forward, placing her palm on my chest. "Don't say that. You know that it wasn't like that."

I sighed, trying to ignore the heat of her skin against my tense muscles. "It felt a lot like that. You didn't need to run off, Skylar. I understand that whatever you want, it isn't me, but do me a favor? Don't regret last night. It was too good to be something you wish hadn't happened."

She shook her head and pushed her hand up my chest. "I'm sorry. I didn't mean to come across like I was regretting what happened. Not at all. It's just you said you weren't done and part of me feels the same, and that's what freaked me out."

I exhaled. So her problem was that she wanted more. Or at least part of her did. I'd struggled when I figured out that I wanted her again. That she was different to me than other women. This draw I had toward her wasn't exactly the center of my comfort zone either. "You're freaking out because you want something you think you shouldn't?"

She tilted her head up to me. "Exactly."

I brushed my thumb across her cheekbone. "If it makes you feel any better, when I said that to you, I didn't have a plan of what I wanted. I'm not saying we should swap promise rings or start picking out china patterns. I just like you. And I want to keep liking you."

She dropped her shoulders and pushed her face into my hand. "It makes me feel a lot better. So, you're not expecting—"

"Anything. From myself or you. It's just for the first time ever, I . . ." My feelings for her were difficult to explain. It wasn't as if cupid had shot me with his arrow, and I was in love with this woman. More that she intrigued me. I wanted to be in her orbit. "I like you. That's all I'm trying to say."

She grinned at me. "You said that already." Before I could reply, she circled her hands around my waist and pressed her head to my chest. I couldn't ever remember being held like that by anyone. It was comforting. I followed her lead and gently wrapped my arms around her. "I like you, too. And I feel awful for running off. Let me make it up to you."

Whatever she was thinking, she had it wrong. I didn't want her trading blow jobs for forgiveness or whatever else she had in mind.

"When we get our next day off, if we're still in the area, let me take you to one of my favorite spots," she said.

Again, she'd caught me off guard. "Where's that?" I wasn't a man who liked to shop.

She looked up, resting her chin on my chest. "Careful. I might surprise you."

She did that so often, I was almost getting used to it.

"So what are you suggesting? We're going to hang out? Spend time together?" I asked.

"We have the summer on the *Sapphire* and then we both walk away. Let's enjoy the time we have," she said.

I couldn't argue with that. I knew I liked her and wasn't ready to walk away, but I'd been serious when I said I hadn't thought further than that. It wasn't as if a relationship was a well-trodden path for me. I might be able to let her go after a couple more months together.

Although something told me it wouldn't be that easy.

"Agreed." I pressed a kiss on the top of her head. Right there in that moment, I'd give her whatever she asked of me.

TWENTY-FIVE

Skylar

Another twenty-four hour's leave for the entire crew? I headed back to my cabin after the news, a little giddy. I hadn't expected another day off so soon. The lack of guests mid-season meant that more time with Landon was coming sooner than I'd thought. But I was ready, wasn't I? There was no pressure. I could handle a summer fling, right?

"Wanna go shopping?" August asked as she burst into our room. "Another day off—can you believe it? I hope this doesn't mean our tips are going to be shitty." She collapsed dramatically on her bed. "We're in the South of France. It's like we're on holiday."

"Can I borrow your backpack?" I asked, pulling out my bikini and two small towels along with sunscreen, a comb, and toiletries.

"You hitting the beach?" August asked.

"I've promised Landon I would go with him today. Do you mind?" I asked.

August sat up and raised an eyebrow. "Not at all. Are you two . . .?"

"We're not anything. We're just going to the beach."

"Not anything?" she asked.

"It was your idea to have a summer fling."

"So, you're taking my advice?" August asked as a grin crept across her face.

I really was. After years of swearing to stay away from all men, I was going to allow myself one summer of fun. If we hadn't been yachting, if he hadn't been British, based thousands of miles from me and only a deckhand for a season, things might be different, but it was as if Landon was designed for me. There was no way this could turn into anything more. Geography and circumstances wouldn't allow it. I just had to relax and let it happen and then walk away at the end of the season.

"It's super casual," I replied.

"Well, help yourself to my bag for your *super casual* day out."

August bit back another smile, which I ignored, instead picking up my phone and typing out a message.

Bring sneakers and swimming trunks.

He could borrow my sunscreen, and I had a towel.

I grinned when his reply came through.

I have no idea what sneakers are but I'm wearing trainers. I'm just going ashore now. I'll meet you somewhere. Send me the details.

My stomach somersaulted. We were doing this. We were going to spend the day together.

I typed out a meeting place near a taxi rank and stuffed everything into August's bag.

"You seem excited," August said. "It suits you."

"It's just because we're going to one of my favorite spots around here. I'd be just as excited if I was going with you."

"So you don't mind if I join you then?" she asked.

I glanced at August and her face gave nothing away. "What do I need?" She got off her bed and rummaged around in her wardrobe. "Bikini, sunscreen?"

Shit. Was she serious? I could hardly turn up to spend the day with Landon with August in tow. Landon wouldn't be expecting anyone to join us, and however much I wanted to deny it, I'd been looking forward to spending the day with Landon. Alone.

"August?" I winced. I was going to have to bite the bullet and just tell her straight. "Would you mind if Landon and I went alone?"

She turned and grinned at me as if she'd just won the lottery. "I'm messing with you. I'm not going to interrupt your romantic date. I just wanted you to admit this was more than a day out."

"I suppose it is. I just don't want—" I didn't want to admit to August or myself how much I was looking forward to spending time with Landon. I just wanted to enjoy the time I was with him and forget about the consequences. For a summer. "I just don't want to get in too deep. You know?"

"Just go with it. It's a day off, not a honeymoon."

I nodded. "Exactly. Are you going to be okay? Am I abandoning you?"

"Nope. I'm going to hit up Camille, see if she'll go shopping with me. Then I'm going to call Harvey, nap, and enjoy my freedom. I want you to enjoy yourself."

"Thanks," I said, pulling on my favorite, white, off-the-shoulder t-shirt and cropped pants over my bikini.

"Hair up or down?"

"You're beautiful either way." August shrugged. "Wear it down and take a clip."

I nodded, pulling a clip from under my pillow. "Okay, I'm off."

"Have fun." August blew me a kiss and I flew out of the door.

I hadn't wanted to do the obvious thing and take food from the galley, so I'd ordered a lunch from one of the shops on shore. I'd drop by to pick up our food and drinks and then meet Landon at the taxi rank, ready for our day together.

I'd never spent the day with a man before, not one I found attractive. Not ever someone I'd slept with. Landon would be the first. And last.

This summer, I was having a time-out from running from my past.

———

WHEN I SAW Landon waiting on the sidewalk, his back to me, facing the row of cabs, I stifled a grin. Even his back was sexy.

"Hey." I tapped him on the shoulder.

"Hey," he replied. "You look very pretty," he said, trailing a finger from my neck to my shoulder before he bent and pressed a kiss against my lips.

"Thank you. You look . . . handsome." Somehow, Landon always seemed to look stylish. Maybe it was because he was older than other deckhands, but he even wore his uniform differently. He filled it out and made it look as if it had been custom made to stretch over his biceps and across his broad torso. Today he wore a similar uniform of shorts and a polo shirt, but without any of the ship's logos.

His dark hair and skin looked perfect against the navy and white—as if he was one of the billionaire playboys who made their home here in Monaco.

"So, you ready for our day out?" I asked.

"Can't wait," he replied, his smile wide and genuine.

"Okay, well it starts with a cab." I spoke to one of the drivers in my best French and we settled into the back of the taxi. "The views along the coast are spectacular. Do you like to travel?" I asked.

He took my hand and threaded his fingers through mine. "Sometimes. I think travel lost some of its appeal after the army."

"I can't imagine you end up in the most glamorous of places."

"That's for sure. But I got used to the heat, so while the guys on deck complain about working in the sun, I'm just glad I'm not carrying a fifty-kilogram pack through twenty miles of desert in full uniform."

Landon didn't talk much about himself, and I'd never heard him talk about his army days.

"You were in Afghanistan?"

He nodded. "Lots of places in the Middle East."

"Do you miss it?"

He stayed silent for a few seconds as if really thinking through my question. "I went into the army wanting one thing and came out appreciating many."

"What did you go in expecting?"

"I wanted to serve. To make the world better. To protect people who couldn't protect themselves."

"But surely you did all of that?"

He nodded. "At the heart of it, yes. But on a day-to-day basis, it's not just the big things that impact who you are. Things like the self-discipline you learn and the problem-solving and the self-reliance. It's those things that had more of an impact on me than I expected."

"Do you miss those aspects?" I asked.

"No. Those skills are with me every day. They became a part of me."

"And I guess you were working security, which had similar requirements."

He just shrugged, clearly not ready to embellish on his experiences.

"Look at that view." I pointed out the window. "You can really see the Rock of Monaco from here."

"The what?" he asked.

"That sticky-out bit of land. It's called the Rock of Monaco."

He chuckled. "The sticky-out bit? You training to be a tour guide?"

"You knew what I meant. That's all that matters."

"So where are we headed? I thought women liked to lunch and shop."

I groaned. "When's the last time you hung out with a woman?" Maybe Landon's commitment to one-night stands meant he was just as inexperienced at hanging out with a lover as I was. "I guess there are things the army doesn't teach you—girls like to do more than lunch and shop."

"I guess I'm still figuring you out."

"All women or just me?"

"You're the only one who counts at the moment."

My pulse tripped in my neck. "Landon, a sworn commitment-phobe can't go around saying things like that."

"I don't share a lot. But what I do say, I mean."

He cupped my face in his hands and placed a kiss on my lips. I sighed at his touch and he pulled back, clearly happy to make me wait.

If we weren't going to make out then I wanted to know more about him. "You said you had a brother; are you close?"

"More so now that I've left the army." He grinned. "He's a good guy. Settled down now. Never thought I'd see it." He frowned as if he were putting pieces of a puzzle together. There was always more going on under the surface with Landon. I wondered if anyone knew his every thought. Or even a fraction of what went on inside his head. "But he's happy. That's the most important thing."

"Maybe," I said, staring out of the window.

"You're not convinced? If happiness isn't what's important, then what is?"

"Surviving. Having food in your stomach, a roof over your head."

Silence ticked between us.

"Is not having those things something that worries you? Here in the South of France on board a luxury superyacht?"

"Only every day," I replied.

Before he could question me any further, I caught sight of the familiar restaurant through the front window and the cab pulled to a stop.

"So I was right about the fancy lunch," he said, pulling his wallet out of his shorts.

"Hey, I'm paying for the cab."

He frowned. "No, you're absolutely not."

I pulled open the front pocket of my bag. "I absolutely am."

He thrust fifty euro into the hand of the driver before I had my wallet open.

"Landon, no. This is my day."

Ignoring me, he got out of the cab. I followed, rounded the trunk, and held out a fifty-euro note.

"Put that away. It's a cab, Skylar. I didn't just buy you the car."

"This is my day to entertain you. I didn't offer to pay for the hotel room, did I?" I hated people doing things for me. I always worried I'd get used to it. It was much better to only rely on myself.

"I didn't book the room for us. I booked it for me."

"Yeah, which is weird. So don't get me started on that."

"Why is it weird?"

"It doesn't fit with the whole soldier thing—wanting that kind of luxury when you're used to . . . whatever you're used to in the army."

He smirked and pulled my bag from my hands.

"Hey, what are you doing?"

"This is heavy; what the hell's in here?" he asked.

"I thought you were used to carrying six-million kilograms through the desert."

"I'm not saying it's too heavy for me. Jesus, woman, do you just love to argue?" He hitched the bag over his shoulder and knocked his sunglasses from the top of his head onto his nose. "Where are we going?"

"We're not going anywhere until you give me my bag and accept this money."

"Skylar, I'm paying for the cab and carrying your bag. Get used to it. We can stay here all day. Doesn't worry me."

"But I don't need you to pay—"

"But *I* need to."

I fisted my hands, frustrated that I couldn't think of something appropriate to say—something to prove him wrong. "I don't need anything from . . ." *Anyone*, I thought to myself.

"Are we going into this restaurant or what?"

"Absolutely not." I stormed past him and toward the

path that ran in front of the restaurant and down through the hills.

I hadn't gone more than five steps when he caught my wrist and pulled me to a halt. "Skylar. Come on. I don't want to fight with you. I want to enjoy the day. Let's just go inside and have a good time."

"Will you take the money for the cab?" I asked.

"I can't do that. It's just not . . . how I'm built. And I've never had a day out with a woman before. Indulge me."

He was sneaky. How could I say no to that kind of response?

"Let's just go inside," he said.

My heart sank. I wanted it to be just the two of us, even if we were only eating sandwiches. "You want to eat in the restaurant? It's pretty fancy. I'm not sure they'll have a table for us."

"You didn't bring us here to eat in the restaurant?"

I shook my head. "Are you disappointed?"

"Not at all. I just assumed—"

"That I'd be dragging you around Louis Vuitton?"

"Well, you did say that you were taking me to your favorite place."

"Think about it, Landon, have you ever seen me wearing designer anything?" I rolled my eyes. "And if we ever stop bickering, we might actually get there."

He chuckled. "But you're not going to tell me?"

"If you're hoping for a big surprise then you need to readjust your expectations. It's *my* favorite place, but you might hate it."

"Lead the way," he said, gesturing me forward, "and we'll find out."

The restaurant was full and the bustle and chatter followed us down the hill as we walked in single file. There was only a slight breeze in the air and although the sun was high in the sky, it was a dry heat and perfect for walking. I always preferred the Med over the Caribbean season because of the lack of humidity.

We walked in silence down the track, though we didn't meet anyone going the opposite direction. Often people from the restaurant walked a hundred yards or so to take pictures, but today we had the place to ourselves.

The trail turned sharply right and continued.

"You okay?" I called over my shoulder.

"Worried I won't be able to keep up?"

"Maybe? I don't know. You've been out of the army seven years. And you're older now," I said on a giggle.

Landon growled from behind me, and the next thing I knew, he'd tossed me over his shoulder, and he was jogging down the trail.

I squirmed. "Landon, put me down. I was kidding."

He ignored me until I screeched. "Stop, stop, stop! This is one of the places I wanted to show you!"

He stopped, set me down, and held me up as I stumbled. "You can't just do that," I said, smoothing down my pants.

"I think I just proved I can," he replied and winked at me.

I pushed his sunglasses to the top of his head. "Look." I gazed out to the sea. "Isn't that the most beautiful view?"

Sometimes it was hard to imagine that anywhere in the South of France could be completely unspoiled, but from this particular spot, it was more difficult to imagine anyone had ever been here at all. "I love how that tree grows out from the mountainside as if it's trying to walk down to the ocean," I said, pointing to the mountain pine that I always took a picture of every time I was here. "I have to get a picture."

I snapped a photograph on my phone and turned to continue our journey.

"Let's take another one," Landon said. "Us and the view."

I bit back a smile.

Holding up the phone, he snapped a couple of shots and then nodded and slid his phone back into his pocket. "Now where?"

"We admire the view and keep walking."

Finally, we got to the bottom of the hill. We were the only ones at the small, secluded cove, just as I'd hoped. I'd never seen anyone else here, but it wasn't like I could organize the solitude.

"Wow, how did you find this place?" Landon surveyed the high rocks on three sides of us and the view of the water in front of us. "Is it a private beach?"

I shook my head. "I just stumbled across it one day, and I like to try to come back every year. There aren't many places this pretty that you can have to yourself around here." I pulled the backpack from his shoulder and set it down on the pebbly beach.

"It certainly is pretty."

"No fancy restaurant but the view makes up for it, I hope." I pulled out the picnic blanket that I'd brought along with the food I'd picked up from the deli, the drinks, silverware, and paper towels.

"I brought towels so we can swim. You brought your trunks, right?"

"I have them on. You've gone to some effort here, Skylar."

There was nothing that went unnoticed when Landon was around. "It's beautiful, right?"

"You come here with August?"

I sighed as I tucked the bottle of water I'd brought under the blanket. "Nope. I like to come alone. It's peaceful." It was my corner of the Med where I came to get away from the toil of the season, the demands of guests, and the pressure of running away from my past. Here I got to take a time out from it all and just relax. "I thought you'd like it."

Landon took a seat on the blanket and pulled me down onto his lap. "I do. It's wonderful and I feel . . . kinda special that you brought me here." He cupped my face in his hands and pressed a kiss against my lips. "Thank you."

"You're not disappointed that I didn't make reservations at the top of the hill?"

He chuckled. "Nope. This is much more my thing. I just didn't expect it to be yours."

I shifted so I sat between Landon's legs and we could both look over the water. "Yeah, I'm not sure many people know me that well."

"You're a riddle, Skylar."

"I don't think so. I'm just a girl from the Midwest— we're quite simple when you get to know us."

Landon brought his arms around me, cocooning me with his body. "So tell me something so I can get to know you. Explain why a full stomach and a roof over your head are things you worry about?"

Had he known that I'd meant it literally? "You can't take anything for granted. Don't they teach you that in the army?"

I tried to make it sound breezy so I might get away with just a generic answer, but when he didn't respond, I knew I'd failed. I was at a crossroads, one side of a line in the sand.

I could choose to keep my history to myself, avoid and obfuscate, or I could take a step forward across the sand and tell Landon the whole truth. I could choose to trust him. I could let him in.

"After my mother died," I continued. "I went to live in a group home. That period taught me a lot about life."

He pulled me closer. "I'm so sorry, Skylar. How did she die?"

I slid my hand over his as I considered his question. "That's a question most people don't ask. They . . ."

"Are uncomfortable talking about death. I know. But I've *seen* it too often to be scared of the words."

Was it because Landon was familiar with death that I wanted to tell him or was it because he made me want to open up? I'd never told anyone how she died. People close to me knew my mother had died and that I'd ended up in a home, but I never said how she'd died or who had killed her. But there was something about Landon, about the way he had about him, that made me think he'd stand between me and a drunken tourist or me and a bullet. It was the same way he was holding me now. And it felt safe to tell him anything.

"My father killed her," I admitted.

Landon froze behind me but he didn't loosen his grip. "Jesus," he said.

"He was drunk. And they fought. They used to argue a lot. I was used to that. But it would pass quickly and the next day the hallway would be full of flowers, and the house would echo with laughter. I just thought that's how things were—up and down. Looking back, of course, there were signs of violence that I didn't recognize. The bruises. The time my mother broke her collarbone. It never occurred to me that my father—the loving, gregarious man who would tickle me breathless and make me toast in the shape of stars on the weekend—was violent and abusive." I took a breath as I remembered back to those times. "I remember getting upset one time when I heard them fight. I was little, seven or eight, and my mom explained that it was just what married people did and that I shouldn't worry—that it was like a thunderstorm and it would pass quickly. She said without the rain, the trees and flowers would die and so the storm was nothing to be scared of." I paused. That's what I'd been working so hard to avoid—the storms. I'd learned that sometimes when they came, the devastation they brought changed the world, or my world, forever. I tried not to think about that time now. I liked to stay in the present. There was nothing I could do to change the past, so what was the point in thinking back to that time? But I'd lifted the lid and was staring right at those memories that I had boxed away now, and I couldn't look away. "The gunshot. It was so loud."

Landon just held me while I let the memory engulf me. The blood. The sirens. All the people.

"Maybe it would have been different if I'd gone down. Tried to make them stop arguing."

"You couldn't have done anything, Skylar. You were a kid. It wasn't your job to save your mother."

I closed my eyes and took a deep breath. "When I found out my father had pulled the trigger, I remember making the decision right then that I'd never get married."

"So your criteria for a man is . . ."

"It's impossible to meet," I said.

"That makes more sense to me. You don't care that it makes you sound high maintenance or picky. You *want* to put men off."

I shrugged. As usual, Landon saw more than I showed

him. "I don't trust many people. Because people aren't who they say they are. My dad was a charming, joke-telling, family man, but underneath it was a jealous, possessive killer. It takes me a long time to believe that someone is really who they appear to be. I know as a child, you don't always see the entire picture, but the same is true when you grow up too—people are good at hiding who they are."

"That's very true," he said, not letting go. "How long were you in the home?"

"Until I turned eighteen. I left on my birthday. I had nothing. No one. Yachting saved me. I'd seen a magazine article about yachting and spent the little money I had on a one-way bus ticket to Florida. I slept on a bench in the depot the night I arrived."

"You're very brave, Skylar."

"I'm not the person here who signed up to protect his country." I prodded his thigh.

"Bravery comes in many forms," he said. "To survive what you did and to come out the other side, that takes—"

"Ruthless practicality," I finished his sentence. "That's why I don't talk about it much. There's nothing to be gained. I just like to keep the storm at bay, keep my path slow and steady."

"Well, ruthlessly practical works for you. You're very good at your job. You must love it."

I laughed. "I've never thought about it. I've just always focused on having a place to live, food to eat, and money to save so I never had to worry about having it in the future." My savings account was my umbrella from any unexpected rainfall. "What about you? The army must require prac-ticality."

"Yes, but I *loved* being in the army. And then working

private security. I couldn't do my job if I didn't love it. Passion for what you do is important."

"Yeah, my parents had plenty of passion for each other, so I'm not concerned that I'm not passionate about my job— Bad things happen when you feel so strongly."

"No soldier would ever enlist if they didn't passionately believe in what they were doing, Skylar. No one would run a marathon, climb a mountain. Passion can be a good thing."

"Maybe," I replied. Perhaps Landon was right and passion was good for some people. But not me. I needed to stay practical, down-to-earth. "I'm happy with my life."

"You make it sound like you just bought a watermelon or finished ironing."

"I'm just realistic. There are many people in the world who can't say they're happy. I imagine most of the kids I was in the home with can't. I'm lucky—I might not be passionate about my job, but not everyone needs to be." I shrugged. "It's a small industry. There's always work if you have good references and people like you, so it's not as insecure as it seems at first. I'm hoping to get a two- or three-year contract on the *Sapphire* after this season. But it's not like the army."

"I understand that getting to a place where you were established and had some savings was important, but what about now?" he asked. "Those savings you talked about. They give you options, right?"

"I'm hungry. Let's eat," I said.

"And I thought I was good at swerving around difficult conversations."

He let me go as I wriggled out of his lap and began to set the food out. "I'm not swerving. I've just never thought about doing anything else. I've tried for a long time to avoid the peaks and the troughs. Slow and steady has been my goal.

Being passionate about anything feels . . . dangerous." I paused. In what way would I want my life to be different? I'd done what I'd set out to do when I left the home—I'd survived.

"What about back before your mother died? Did you know what you wanted to do then?"

I shrugged as I offered him a plate in an effort to distract him. All my hopes and dreams of my future died with my mother. Before she'd been killed, there were a thousand futures I fantasized about. When I got to the group home, the idea of being a lawyer—of bringing justice to the guilty —was the only thing I wanted to do. When I'd told one of the workers, she'd laughed at me, so I'd buried that last dream I'd had alongside my mother and every one of the futures I'd imagined for myself. But I tried not to focus on what I'd lost. "I do long for my own room for more than two months a year." I grinned at Landon, wanting us to change the topic.

He paused and then took the plate I was offering. "Yeah, I get that. I enjoyed having a place to call home when I left the army."

"You have your own place now?" I asked, before popping a grilled artichoke heart into my mouth.

"Yeah, in London."

"On your own?"

He grinned. "Yeah—I'm thirty-two."

"I know, but London's expensive, right?"

He didn't answer.

"Was I prying? I'm just trying to picture you there."

"No, I was just thinking. I guess I like my own company a lot."

"That doesn't surprise me. You and Harvey are good friends, but I noticed you don't really talk about much."

"Yeah, but we know each other because of what we've seen. What we've been through together."

I pressed my index finger against the scar on his right shoulder. He pulled my hand away and kissed my fingertip.

Maybe we both had stories we didn't share with everyone.

"Come on," I said, wanting to lift the mood. "We need to find the perfect shell." I glanced around at the pebbles interspersed with shells.

"We do?" he asked.

"Of course. To remember today. A souvenir, if you like. It can't be too big, or too small. I like white ones." I always ended each season with a couple of shells from my most-enjoyable days.

"Wow, you even have criteria for the shells you collect."

I grinned. "It's very strict." I picked up a broken, mottled shell peeking out from under the blanket. "This one would never do. It's broken, for a start, and the color is just a little sad. I want something to remind me of sunshine and laughter."

"What about this one?" Landon asked, stretching to pick up another. "No breaks in this one."

It wasn't a bad choice. But it wouldn't do for me. "It's a little gaudy. But if you like it, keep it. Shell collecting is very personal."

"Gaudy? How can a shell be gaudy?"

"You know, all the curly bits you have there. The pink color. I like something more like . . ." I looked around and found the perfect one. I held it up so he could see. "There are no breaks. It's perfectly symmetrical, so white it's almost blinding, and—"

"Tiny. It's smaller than the pad of my thumb."

"This is the only time a woman will tell you this and not

be lying—size doesn't matter."

In a flash, he launched himself at me, pressed me to my back, and covered my body with his. "You have a problem with my size?"

He knew the answer to that. I shook my head. "You know that I don't."

"Right. I do know that. And if we weren't in public, in broad daylight, I'd be reminding you that you don't."

I gazed up at him, so handsome and serious. So protective and fierce. Every minute I spent with him, I wanted more.

He pressed a kiss to my lips, gently at first, then deepening it until it turned passionate and wild. He hardened against my thigh, and I shifted so I could feel him between my legs.

"Skylar," he growled in the most delicious way. "Don't tease me like that. I won't have you here out in the open—we have no idea who's watching."

He rolled off me and onto his back, then scrubbed his hands over his face.

"Anyone ever tell you you're paranoid? There hasn't been a single sign of life since we got here."

"It's how I'm built."

"Not to express how you feel?" I asked.

"No, it isn't about me. It's about you. Goes to my need to protect what's important, I guess."

Did he just say I was important? That he wanted to protect me?

I guess there was no arguing with that, except I knew the only person who could protect me was me. Landon was only in my life for the summer. I just needed to make sure I didn't start to rely on his protection. The only person I could rely on was me.

TWENTY-SIX

Landon

"You've caught the sun," I said, pressing a kiss against her nose as we reached the top of the hill. "It's cute."

"Do I look like Rudolph?"

"Only if I look at you straight on."

She shrugged. "It was the look I was going for. That's what I'll tell people, anyway."

"Shall we call a cab?" I asked, shielding my eyes against the sun and looking out into the distance.

"I think this one looks like ours," she said as a car came into view.

"How did you manage that?"

She laughed. "It's not magic. I just texted the guy ten minutes ago."

"You think of everything, don't you?"

"It's my job."

"I think it's more than that—it's who you are." It seemed second nature to Skylar to look after people. To think ahead and anticipate the needs and desires of those around her.

And I didn't believe it was just because of her job. More like her nature made her good at her job rather than the other way around.

The car pulled up and I held open the passenger door for her.

"I've had a beautiful day. What do you say to grabbing a shower and some dinner?" I asked, taking her hand and pressing her wrist to my lips as we traveled back to Monte Carlo. The scent of sunshine on her warm skin was almost good enough to eat.

She withdrew her hand from mine and pulled out her phone. "We can, but I haven't made any reservations." She began to tap through the pages on her phone.

I placed my hand over her screen. "You took care of the day stuff. Let me take over on the relentlessly practical stuff for now."

She frowned at me. "But, I can—"

"Skylar, you're not my maid, my stewardess, or my assistant." I curled her hair around her ear. "I want to do this. Making people happy is a two-way street."

What did I know about making people happy? Skylar and I had been on two dates, but instinctively, I knew I wanted to make *her* happy, to see that smile of hers. And once I understood what my goal was, I always made it my mission to make it happen.

"I should have arranged something," she said. "I just didn't know how today would go."

"Today has been a thousand times more than I could have expected," I said.

The corners of her mouth twitched. "Really?"

"I might not be a man who says a lot or is big on sharing, but everything I do say is the truth."

She slid her hand back into mine and leaned her head

against my shoulder. "That's the thing I like about you best. You're exactly who you say you are."

Except I wasn't just a deckhand this summer. And I wasn't the drifter Skylar seemed to assume I was.

I made hotel reservations on my phone while enjoying the feeling of Skylar's body tucked close to mine.

For the rest of the journey, we silently watched the softening light against the water before the noise of Monte Carlo pulled us from our appreciation.

"Hotel de Paris?" she asked, gazing out of the cab window.

"I like the view and the baths, apparently."

I didn't argue too much about her paying for the cab, even though it was like nails on a chalkboard as I watched her hand over her money. As long as she was happy.

"A home away from home," she said as I switched on the lights of the room we'd been in just a week ago.

"Let's use the shower first this time," I said, pulling off my shirt and then unbuttoning my shorts. "I need to fuck you in there."

"You can fuck me anywhere," she said.

I growled and pulled out her hair clip, letting her blonde waves fall onto her shoulders.

I walked toward her, and she stepped back, pulling off her top and shrugging out of her trousers.

Yanking her bra down to expose her breasts, I bent, covering her hard nipple with my mouth as I circled my arms around her waist.

Her fingers pawed at my neck as she gasped and shuddered.

I pulled back, lifted her off her feet and into the bathroom. "How I kept my hands off you all day, I have no idea."

"Well, you didn't. Not really," she said, stripping off her underwear.

We'd "made out," as she called it, in the sea for what seemed like hours, but I wasn't about to fuck her outside. There was no way I would risk exposing her like that. Kissing was as far as it had gone.

"Compared to what I'm about to do to you, believe me, I've kept my hands off you all day." I reached into the shower, turned on the spray then pulled her inside. The warm water began to wash the sticky seawater from our skin.

"Well, I want you clean first." She picked out one of the bottles of shower gel and poured out a handful, dunking it on my chest.

"You're going to wash me?"

She nodded, making small circles all over my skin—up over my shoulder to my neck, up over my face, across my back—slowly working a lather all over my body.

"You're very thorough," I said as she kneeled in front of me, making me tip my head back as she worked her palms up my inner thigh and around my balls but avoided my erection raging against my stomach.

"I like to think so."

She lifted my foot and placed it on her thigh, working the wash between my toes.

I'd never had a woman tend to me before. Never spent this long in a shower, just enjoying the feeling of the water running down my body rather than focusing on getting clean. But then I'd never met a woman like Skylar—sweet and caring was at her very core. How she'd managed to keep that at her center given what she'd lived through was a miracle and made her all the more special.

She gazed up at me from her knees. "It's like your body

is so powerful that it decides where the water goes." She traced the rivulets of the spray with her fingertips as drops ran between my muscles before grasping the base of my cock.

I groaned and fell forward, my hands braced against the glass, as she swirled her tongue over my tip and then took me deep in her mouth. She grasped my thighs and continued to lick, suck, sweep down my cock, and back up again, pressing her fingertips into my skin, urging me forward. When I banged my fist against the glass, she glanced up at me, a sweet, innocent look in her eyes.

I just couldn't get enough.

In just minutes, I was ready to come in her mouth, down her throat, over her face, and on her breasts. I wanted to cover her in my come. Claim her. Make her mine. Shit. Before now, women had always just been women. Skylar was everything. Every fantasy, everything too good to even imagine and more.

I reached under her chin and she glanced up again. I had to look away for a second or I was going to— "I'm going to come, Skylar." I tried to pull away, but she took me deeper, sucked me harder. Fuck. Just as I thought it couldn't get any better, this beautiful, complicated, delicious woman wanted me in her mouth. "Skylar," I growled. "I can't hold back."

She swallowed, my crown at the back of her throat, and I was lost. The beautiful woman whose mouth was clamped around my cock, the warm spray, the amazing day we'd spent together—it all melted into one, and I let my orgasm take over every muscle. I cried out, my words incoherent, every sensation washing over me.

I stumbled back to the built-in bench under the spray

and managed to open my eyes long enough to see Skylar grinning at me.

"Thank you," she said. "I enjoyed that."

I chuckled and pulled her to her feet and onto my lap. "Not as much as me."

"Don't bet on it. You taste so good. And it made me feel powerful, you know? You're this big, tough guy and I can make you feel like that? Come like that? I kinda loved it."

My cock twitched as she spoke so openly and matter-of-factly about sucking me off. This girl was something else.

"You're full of unexpected surprises," I said, burying my head in her neck, sweeping my hand down her stomach, my fingers lingering between her folds before reaching for her breasts again. She twisted her hips to meet my fingers as I teased her.

She turned to face me, but there was no way she was going to call the shots here. Not this time.

I gave her a quick, sharp smack on the bottom. "Stand up."

She jumped to her feet like she'd get a prize if she moved fast enough. Maybe she would.

I stood and shooed her under the spray. "Turn around, hands flat on the marble, legs apart." I grabbed a condom from beside the sink and rolled it over my cock, admiring the way Skylar pushed out her arse, desperate for what was next.

"Are you going to frisk me?"

I chuckled. "Maybe." Standing behind her as close as I could, I swept my hands down her stomach to her pussy. Despite the water, the silky wetness between her legs gave away how ready she was.

Without any teasing or preamble, I pushed into her as far as I would go.

"Fuck," she cried out. "It's so deep."

"Always," I replied, sweeping my fingers across her pussy, finding her clitoris and circling before she grabbed my wrist.

"If you do that, I'm going to come right away. I want to feel you inside me."

I growled and released her, grabbing her shoulder instead as I began to fuck her.

"Jesus, yes," she whimpered.

I tried to concentrate on the shapes her wet hair made against her back, because if I focused on her breathy, desperate sounds, if I noticed the way her skin yielded under my fingers or the way her muscles tightened around my cock, I'd be gone.

As if I wasn't already.

"Landon." She turned her head toward me. "I want to see you. I want to see the way you look at me. Like I'm everything to you."

I pulled out and backed up against the wall, guiding her toward me.

"I want to see your eyes when you come," she said. "It's my favorite thing."

Jesus, this girl was my fucking kryptonite. So sweet and vulnerable underneath all the confident drive.

I lifted her up, and she wrapped her legs around me as I plunged back into her. She gasped, clinging to my shoulders as I drove into her, pressing her back against the wall. I slowed at the change in angle so I didn't go off like a bomb.

"You're so beautiful, Skylar." I choked out my confession. It wasn't what she looked like that made her attractive. It was everything I'd found out about her since I met her. All the effort she'd put into today. The fact that she'd shared such a special place with me. It was everything wrapped up in this perfect, blonde package that was pulling me closer and closer to the edge of something I'd never felt before.

She kissed me on the corner of my mouth and then trailed her tongue along the seam of my lips before kissing the other side. "Thank you," she whispered into my ear as she wrapped her arms around my neck. "Thank you so much."

Her back arched, and she pushed against me as I crashed into her, our rhythms perfectly matched.

We both wanted the same thing when we were together like this.

Pleasure.

Release.

Each other.

TWENTY-SEVEN

Skylar

I flicked through the pages of the contract that Captain Brookes had presented me with—three more years on the *Sapphire*. It was good money, the basic salary more than I'd ever made and a guaranteed tip, which never happened. It meant security and certainty, and I should be more excited, yet I was anything but. All I could think about was my conversation with Landon on the beach and whether he'd been correct. Could passion, in the right circumstances, be a good thing?

August crashed out of the bathroom.

"Do you love yachting?" I asked her, glancing around at the cupboard that we called a bedroom. "Is it your passion?"

She fiddled with the towel wrapped tightly around her. "I feel passionately about the money. Does that count?"

I shrugged. I felt the same, but I couldn't shake what Landon had said to me. I'd gone through my life avoiding passion. I associated passion with anger, rage, and violence —a lack of control. But I'd never heard Landon even raise his voice, and I bet he'd never lost control ever in his life. Yet he was passionate about the army. Even now I could see the devotion to his old career in his eyes when he spoke about it.

"If you could do anything, what would it be?" I asked. "I'm guessing, not a yacht stewardess."

She pulled out a pair of panties from the drawer. "I have no idea," she said. "What's with all the questions?"

"I've just been thinking. I chose yachting out of necessity. Not because I wanted to see the world or that I loved cleaning and organizing."

"You are good at it though."

I smiled as August did her own version of an Irish jig to try to get her underwear on without dropping her towel. "Should I be doing a job I love instead of yachting? I'm not sure. I'm not the kind of person who needs to feel strongly about their job, am I? I'm not passionate." I'd spent my entire adult life trying to avoid becoming my father. I'd never thought that maybe the pendulum had swung too far the other way.

"Of course you are," August said.

I slouched back against the wall. All these years avoiding anything that was remotely passionate, trying to be Miss Slow and Steady, the tortoise and not the hare, but maybe there was something more.

"If you really don't like yachting," August said. "Why don't you save this season's tips and go and do something you *do* feel passionate about."

I laughed. "As if." I eyed the contract beside me. If I signed, which of course I would, the next three years of my life were planned out. My money was guaranteed. I'd have food and a roof over my head. That was all I wanted, wasn't it? "What on earth would I do?" I wasn't the sort of person who got to choose. I'd never been pulled toward something I wanted. I'd been running from what I didn't.

"I think about it all the time," August said, abandoning her towel and pulling on the rest of her clothes. "I just can't come up with an answer. The day I figure it out is the day I hand in my notice." She flicked back her wet hair and grabbed a comb. "Until then, I can cope with the good money and the beautiful weather."

"You think you'd give it all up that easily?"

"If I found the thing I was meant to do. Or if I was to get pregnant—or even find a relationship that was worth it."

Pregnant? I'd never considered that as a possibility. If I had a choice, would I choose children? A family? I didn't think about any of this stuff. I reacted to things that happened around me. The only planning I did was to put away money. Every dollar that sat in my bank account was an insurance policy against the bad times. A salve. "Is Harvey worth it?"

August shrugged as she applied mascara. "I like him, but he lives in England and I'm between the Med and the Caribbean. It's not like the stars are aligned."

"He might get a permanent job as yacht security or something."

"I'm not holding my breath, but you never know. What about Landon? I'm glad you've found someone. He's a great guy—you are a great match."

Prickly warmth spread across my skin. Landon was a great guy. But I knew he was only in my life for the summer, and there was no point in thinking about a future together. "Landon's Mr. Right Now. I keep telling you, it's nothing serious. You know I'm focused on my job."

"The one you don't like." She pushed the comb through

her wet hair and then stared at me. "As a kid, what did you want to do?"

It was the same question Landon had asked me. "I'm not sure." Except that I did know, but I knew it was impossible to go backward.

But I wanted to know *how* impossible. I pulled my laptop out of my locker by my bed and lifted the screen. Cross-legged, I fired it up and began to investigate.

TWENTY-EIGHT

Landon

None of us were particularly busy without any guests still on board and finding a quiet corner to call Reynolds was more difficult when people didn't have jobs to do and places to be. I'd locked myself in my cabin bathroom and turned on the shower as I punched in Reynolds' number to my phone.

"Another number?" he asked.

"I have no update," I replied, ignoring his observation.

"The target will be back on board tomorrow."

I hadn't been expecting that. "Okay, anything I need to know?"

"Things are escalating. My client wants to interrupt any trade before it's made but needs the deal to be sufficiently advanced to bring prosecutions. So our job is to try to collate as much compelling evidence as possible."

"Understood. I can do a sweep of his room, if that's helpful?" I'd checked out Walt's room before but found nothing.

"Absolutely not. As things are progressing, the target is

getting more serious about security. We have information that he suspects he's being watched, and anyway, he'd be an idiot not to assume he is and act accordingly."

The first thing I'd do in his situation would be background check everyone on my payroll, including the crew of the *Sapphire*. I'd also hire some counter-surveillance specialists to check out my homes, offices—and my yacht. "Well, Landon James' background is clear."

"And if they discover it's an alias?"

"It looks like I had a drunk-driving arrest and changed it shortly after."

"Good. We know he's done background checks on his staff in his office, including fingerprinting. He's starting to act like he has something to hide."

"I'll be sure to let you know who comes aboard tomorrow," I said.

"The client was very impressed with the information you got from the restaurant. It's just a pity we didn't have confirmation from that stewardess of who was actually around the table."

"You didn't need it. You had the photographs, and I'm sure they could identify the people they suspected were going to attend the dinner. And confirmation from one of the restaurant staff would be easy to get if you told me which individuals your client thinks attended," I said. "There was no need to have gotten anyone else involved."

"That may be the case, but we're going to need the stewardess' help."

My heart began to thunder. That was never going to happen.

"It's unnecessary. I've got it covered."

"Why are you so reluctant to get the job done? Skylar could really help put this guy behind bars."

I froze. I'd never told Reynolds her name. He must have been looking into her. "I'm not reluctant. Bringing a civilian inside is always a cost-benefit analysis. I don't think she'd be sufficiently helpful to make it worth it." What did Reynolds want her to do? Wear a wire? At the very least, she'd end up a witness in the trial of a very dangerous man. Worst-case scenario? Well, it wasn't worth thinking about.

"The first thing we need is a listening device planted on the target."

"That's straightforward as long as you give me something small enough."

"You don't have to worry about the size, but it would be better if the stewardess did it. Less conspicuous."

"Bullshit. It's much less conspicuous if someone who's trained does it. I know how not to get caught."

"Landon, you're going to have to read her in and convince her to help or someone else will. Lives are at stake."

I stood up. There was no way I was going to involve Skylar in this mess. She was too . . . relentlessly practical? She'd probably be a great asset, but no, there was no way I was going to ask her. She might feel compelled to say yes because it was me who was asking. I couldn't live with that.

"The client has intelligence that the target will have his next meeting—at the Casino de Monte-Carlo. We also know that he's going to invite Skylar as his cover as he did for the last meeting."

"Great, the Casino is open to the public, and this time you have plenty of notice. You or your client can get other people to observe."

"Except that his meeting will take place during a private poker match."

"So plant someone as a member of staff, put a listening device in the room."

"Landon, seriously, you know it's not as easy as it looks in the movies. But we're on a deadline here. If we don't act now then it's going to be too late. We're working on various options, but if Skylar is willing to wear a wire—"

"Absolutely not," I interrupted, shutting off the shower. I wasn't prepared to discuss this any further. The conversation was over as far as I was concerned. If Skylar got found out, got searched on the way into the poker match, she wouldn't get out of that place alive.

"So you're going to jeopardize the entire operation, let weapons fall into the hands of terrorists, put thousands of lives at risk because you want to ensure the safety of one individual? What has happened to you?"

As soldiers, we knew that we put our lives on the line for the sake of the greater good. We even knew that when assessing situations, the threat to civilian life was considered in the long run, not on an individual basis. We didn't consider one life more or less expendable than another. We dealt in numbers. Reynolds was right; sacrificing Skylar would probably save hundreds of lives if she successfully delivered the intelligence they needed from her.

But Skylar wasn't just any civilian. Not to me. Not anymore.

But like Reynolds said, if I didn't read her in, she'd get an approach from someone else. "You're right," I said. "It's difficult because I know this crew." I needed to buy some time to find a different solution.

"I get it," Reynolds said. "But you need to focus on the end result. On the mission."

The entire purpose of me being here was to prevent weapons falling into the hands of terrorists. I was here to save lives. My training said that Skylar should be read in. But my heart?

I needed time to think. To decide if I was willing to sacrifice Skylar or the operation.

"Understood. How long do we have until the casino meeting?"

"Two weeks, but she's going to need a couple of days to adjust, so the sooner we get her up to speed the better."

"Leave it with me. I'll see what I can do." I was going to have to come up with a plan and fast. Perhaps she'd turn down Walt when he asked her to join him, especially given she and I were . . . whatever she and I were. If not, then I'd need to think of something else.

Yes, it was selfish; yes, it put the mission at risk; yes, it meant dangerous terrorists might get their hands on weapons they wouldn't otherwise. But despite my training, despite knowing it was wrong, it seemed to be worth all that. To keep Skylar safe.

TWENTY-NINE

Skylar

A calm focus descended on the crew as we filed back onto the yacht from the jetty, where we'd lined up to greet Walt. Since the announcement that Walt would be back in a matter of hours, the atmosphere on board had shifted. No doubt people would be disappointed at the loss of their free time and wondering where the boat would sail next.

I just couldn't help thinking about what was going to happen to Landon and me. Our time in the marina had acted like a pause on real life. It had stopped the music and sent the crew into some kind of holding pattern. Landon and I had spent all our free time together and I'd started wondering if I could have a different life from the one I'd always planned.

Now the music had started playing again, but everything felt a little different than how it had been a few weeks ago.

"I wonder why he's back alone, yet the other guests arrive tomorrow morning. Why not all come together?"

August said as she slid her tray of untouched, filled champagne glasses onto the countertop in the kitchen.

"He probably just got away sooner than his guests," I said. "Or they're coming from different places."

"We don't even know if it's going to be the same five as before. I have no idea what menus I'm going to prepare," Chef Anton said, pulling out a tray of eggs from the refrigerator.

"I'll take him his tequila and see if I can get any more information," I said, pulling a lowball glass from the cupboard.

"See if he wants anything to eat now, and then what time he wants dinner served."

"Will do," I said, setting out the tequila bottle and glass of ice on the tray and heading out of the kitchen.

As I passed through the saloon, I spotted Landon's back as he pulled up the fenders now that we'd moved off the dock. Walt seemed engrossed in the *Wall Street Journal*, ignoring the activity that went on around him.

"Skylar," he said as the sliding doors swished open. "How absolutely wonderful to see you. And you've brought my favorite tequila. Clever girl."

I glanced across at Landon, but he still had his back to us.

"Yes, I managed to track it down."

"Well, you must taste it at some point. Perhaps tonight. Would you keep me company at dinner, since my guests don't arrive until tomorrow?" he asked as I passed him his tequila.

Dinner?

"You want to have dinner off the yacht tonight?" I asked, wondering if Landon could hear us.

"No, we can have it just here." He patted the table he

was sitting at. "The chef the captain brought aboard is just superb. But then again, I'm sure you know that."

I didn't know what to say. I couldn't think of anything more awkward than eating on the yacht, my own team waiting on me. And could I have dinner with another man when Landon and I were . . . spending the summer together? I just didn't know how to say no to a guest.

My head was spinning, as if I'd forgotten how to be a good yacht stewardess, taking everything in my stride, refusing to let any request be too much. I was flustered and confused and needed to organize things in my brain.

"That's such a kind invitation." Was it my imagination or was Landon taking his time winding the rope up? Was he interested in my response? Would it matter to him if I went to dinner with Walt? "Obviously, I'll have to check with the captain." I needed to buy myself some time to figure out what to do. I didn't want to upset Walt. He was the client, after all.

"Of course, darlin'." His Texan accent seemed a little more pronounced since he'd been back aboard. "You follow protocol and come back to me."

"What time would you like to eat?" I asked, glancing up as Landon finished what he was doing and made his way up the starboard side of the boat.

"Eight is fine. Wear something pretty."

I smiled, flipped my tray under my arm, and headed back into the saloon.

Dinner was just dinner, right?

But then why did I have this dark feeling clawing at my insides? Instinctively, I wanted to run to Landon. He was logical and clear thinking. He would know what to do. But it scared me how more and more I'd begun to rely on him. I couldn't pretend that every moment I spent with Landon didn't make me yearn for more of him. But I knew I had to resist him. I understood that whatever it was we were in the middle of was temporary. We'd known it from the start, and nothing had changed.

It was just . . . I knew I'd miss him more than I should when the season was over.

The thought made my heart ache and my eyes sting.

As I reached the kitchen, I dropped the tray on the counter and made my way through the galley.

"You okay?" Anton asked.

I nodded, scared if I said anything, every mixed-up thought in my brain would tumble out. After plodding down the stairs, I knocked on Landon's cabin door.

No answer. But why would there be? We'd only just come on duty. But I wanted to feel close to him, feel him, smell him, so I opened the door, hoping to just lie on his bed for a few minutes.

I stepped back as I caught him coming out of the bathroom.

"I knocked," I said.

He pushed his hands through his hair. "Hey."

"Hey," I said, closing the door. "Did you hear Walt invite me to dinner? On the yacht." I rolled my eyes.

"Yeah. He likes you. And he *is* the client." He grinned and pulled me into his arms. He seemed to think it was a big joke. I liked the fact he was so confident that he didn't see Walt as competition, but I suppose I had hoped he'd step in and . . . What had I expected him to say?

I knew that Landon and I were only together for the summer, but that didn't stop me from wanting to hear something different from him.

I don't want you spending time with any other man but me.

Don't go to dinner with him.
I want you.
I want to be with you.
I'm falling for you.

But I knew better than to wish for things from men, and every comforting phrase that I longed to hear from Landon was entirely unrealistic. It wasn't who he was.

"You think I should go because he's the guest?" I looked up at him.

"I don't want to tell you what to do, Skylar. But if you're asking me my opinion, I think it's bullshit and he shouldn't have asked."

There was no good reason to turn down Walt's invitation to dinner. It was just a meal, after all, and it kept things easy for me. I wouldn't be disappointing a guest and the man who signed my paycheck.

THIRTY

Skylar

It should have been the most perfectly romantic night. The sky was about to burst it was so full of stars, and the air was warm without being muggy. One of the crew had arranged for music to be piped through to the deck.

The problem was I was spending the evening with the wrong gentleman. Being here with Walt had made me realize what I felt for Landon was more complicated than I'd thought.

Walt had talked about his ranch back in Texas, as well as his plans to replace one of his helicopters. He'd asked me again where I'd gone to college and what my parents did and seemed to have genuinely forgotten that I'd told him both things before.

"I thought I might take you shopping before my guests arrive tomorrow," Walt said.

"Shopping? Is there anything in particular you're looking for?"

"Well, I was hoping to take you to a poker match next

week. Do you like poker?"

Perhaps I should have said no to Walt the first time he asked me to dinner. He might have been upset, but at least he wouldn't have asked me again. And now to join him in a poker match? It was the last thing I wanted to do. "I've never played."

More time with Walt was the last thing I was craving. I hadn't seen Landon since he'd told me dinner with Walt was my decision. But still, it was his arms I wanted around me, his company I craved. I wanted him sitting in front of me, topping up my glass.

"Well, I will enjoy teaching you," Walt said.

Even though I would have preferred Landon to stake his claim to me and to have insisted I refuse Walt's dinner invitation, it hadn't watered down my feelings for him.

What I felt for Landon didn't compare to anything I'd ever felt for any man. Nobody had ever made me feel as safe, as protected, and as accepted as he did. I'd spent all these years resolutely single and I'd done it easily. I'd never craved any man's touch, never thought I'd be wandering around deck with an empty tray looking for empty glasses just to catch a glimpse of a man.

I wasn't sure if it was love, but it was something I'd never experienced before, and I knew there was no going back.

"That would be lovely . . ." I couldn't do this. I knew Landon accepted that me spending time with Walt was part of the job, but I felt like I was leading Walt on and at the same time being disloyal to Landon. It might get me fired. And I might end up with no tip, but I had to be straight with Walt. "But, I want to be completely clear with you, Walt. I enjoy your company *as a friend*."

Landon had shown me that I could trust a man to be

exactly who he said he was. He'd made me consider that I might have a future outside of yachting.

Landon had opened my eyes to a new world.

He deserved my respect, my loyalty, and for me to be completely transparent with Walt about my interest in him.

Walt patted me on the hand. "And I feel the same way, Skylar." He continued to chew on the pork tenderloin that Anton had made.

"So, no need to take me shopping," I said.

"Friends can go shopping together, can't they? And I'm sure as shit they can play poker together. Listen, I get that we will never be lovers—I have a twenty-two-year-old girl-friend back in Dallas, and she keeps me plenty busy. But I like the platonic company of pretty girls. Always have. Say you'll play poker with me? You never know, you might end up a little richer at the end of the night."

Walt's response hadn't been what I was expecting. Not only did he not fire me, he wanted to be my friend. It didn't make much sense. It was unusual that guests wanted to hang out with crew, but it did happen. It was usually toward the end of a boozy evening, when most of a party had gone to bed, that guests wanted the crew to start partying with them. But given I'd been upfront with Walt, I figured a night at the casino wasn't going to be the worst night of my life.

"Sure, that would be lovely, but no need for any shop-ping. I have a trusty black dress that will do just fine."

"A woman who doesn't want me to take her shopping? Well, you are a breath of fresh air." He chuckled as he set his knife and fork down. I was desperate to clear his plate and disappear downstairs. I couldn't wait to get back to Landon, sink into his arms, and tell him how I'd told Walt we were strictly in the friend zone.

THIRTY-ONE

Landon

"This bed wasn't made for two," Skylar said as we lay on our sides on my bottom bunk, her back to my front.

"This bed wasn't made for one," I replied, burrowing my face into her neck, and she giggled.

The sound wound around me, and I pulled her even closer, wanting to feel the vibrations of laughter deep in my belly. I'd never been with a woman like this—fully clothed, but touching, on a bed, knowing it was going to lead nowhere. We were both there to just enjoy each other's warmth and comfort.

I couldn't ever remember feeling this fucking content. It was like Skylar had pulled out my DNA, taken one of her polishing cloths to it, and had irrevocably altered my biological makeup. Would things shift back again at the end of the summer? Would I miss this . . . closeness?

"What are you thinking about?" she asked, smoothing her hands over mine, which I had clamped around her waist.

"Nothing." *You*, I didn't say.

"Tell me something I don't know about you," she said.

I exhaled. I wished I could tell her why I was on the yacht. "Christmas is my favorite time of year."

She jerked in my arms and turned her head toward me. "Really? How . . . sentimental of you. It's my least favorite holiday," she said.

I didn't ask why. Christmas without parents would be tough. Christmas in a children's home? I couldn't imagine. "I even like that Mariah Carey song and fake snow. Dry turkey, bad jumpers. The whole thing."

"Mariah Carey? Really? The Pogues one is much better suited to my mood around that time."

"I think I could change your mind. Christmas in London is pretty spectacular."

Shit. Had I implied that she should come to London at Christmas? Because that wasn't what I'd meant at all. I might be wondering if I'd miss her at the end of the summer, but that didn't mean I was inviting her back to London.

A beat of silence followed and then she said, "I've never been. The Caribbean season is in full swing then. Christmas is just like any other day—serving drinks and making beds."

Didn't she want a day off from all that? I *wanted* her to have the rest of her life off from it. I needed to snap out of it. It really was none of my business, but I wanted to make Skylar's life better. In the SAS, I was used to trying to improve things for strangers, for nations. As the owner of a private security firm, I was paid to get results. Now I was lying here, wanting to help Skylar—wanting her to have a happy life. A life where she didn't have to worry about food in her belly and a roof over her head. "Is that your plan next? Go to the Caribbean?"

She paused before she said anything, and I didn't know whether it was because she didn't know or whether she was considering what to tell me. "I guess."

"You guess?"

"I have my plane ticket, if that's what you mean?"

That wasn't what I'd meant. I'd hoped she'd thought about what we'd talked about at the beach and had been thinking about what else she could do with her life, but now wasn't the time. In ten minutes, our break would be over, and we'd be back at our stations. I didn't want to leave her unsettled. "So, you know my guilty pleasure is Christmas. What's yours?" I asked.

She relaxed in my arms, and I could almost hear her think. After a couple of minutes, she announced, "Celine Dion."

I chuckled. "You seemed to take a little while to come up with that. Are you messing with me? Is this some kind of special interrogation technique I don't know about?"

"Hey! I didn't judge you for liking Christmas and Mariah Carey," she said.

"Mariah wrote that Christmas song and it's a classic!" I said, flipping Skylar on her back and crawling over her.

"Celine, man. Her voice is the best in the business," she said as I dipped and kissed her neck.

"What else don't I know about you?" I asked. If I could stay here for the next week, just hearing what Skylar had to say about everything, I was pretty sure it would be the best week of my life.

"Hmm. Ice skating. I've always wanted to try it."

"You never have?"

She shook her head. "I'm sure I'd be terrible at it. But I'd like to know."

"Maybe if you listened to Celine Dion while you skated, it would help."

"You never know." She grinned up at me. "Have you been?"

"Yeah," I said. My parents took Hayden and me every Christmas in London, but Skylar didn't need to hear that. "Not for years, but at Christmas they have temporary rinks around London, so yes I've been a few times."

"You're trying to convince me Christmas is great again, aren't you?"

I chuckled. "I wouldn't dare."

"If anyone could, you could," she said, shifting back around so she was tucked into my chest.

The breath caught in my throat. For someone so cynical, so jaded, she sure did have a way of making a guy feel special.

THIRTY-TWO

Landon

It was unlike my brother to call, but it had come just at the right moment. I'd hoped that Skylar would somehow solve my dilemma and refuse Walt's invitation to dinner. But ever dutiful, she'd accepted, and ever loyal, she'd even told Walt that her feelings were strictly platonic.

If only she'd been a different girl. A less special person.

Of course, he hadn't given a shit that she wasn't interested, because he was just using her as a cover.

And it meant I was back at square one: sacrifice Skylar and put her in danger, or compromise the operation and live with the fact that if I didn't help bring Walt down, potentially thousands of needless deaths lay on my conscience. Either way, I was an arsehole. Perhaps Hayden could help.

"How's yacht life?" he asked as soon as I answered.

"Fine," I snapped.

"Everything okay?"

The last thing my brother and I did was talk about our feelings, but all I could think about was Skylar. "When you met Avery, did you know that she was different right from the beginning?" The first time I'd met Skylar, I thought she was hot. Perhaps the most attractive woman I'd ever laid eyes on. I'd flirted with her, made it my mission to fuck her, and enjoyed every second of her naked. I hadn't expected to see her again. And that had been just fine.

"I'm not sure if it was right away. She's clearly beautiful, which is hard to ignore. But I had a lot of shit going on at the time. I'm not sure I thought much about anything. Why do you ask?"

Somewhere along the line, Skylar had become important to me. Someone I liked to fuck, but it was more than that. I liked her. Thought she was funny and clever and sold herself short. "I think I might have gotten myself into a bit of a mess."

"Interesting, little brother. Over a girl?"

I growled. I wasn't in the mood to have the piss taken out of me. I should never have answered the phone.

"It was bound to happen sooner or later," he said. "It's not the reason you're on the yacht, is it?"

"No, I'm on a job for Reynolds, before I start with MI6 next month. I told you."

"There really is no rest for the wicked. Who's the girl?"

"Another crew member."

"Fucking typical. The only time you're forced to spend time with a woman and you fall in love with her."

"Hey, I never said anything about falling in love. And it's not just because we're cramped up on this boat." Maybe if I'd never seen Skylar again after that first night together, she would have disappeared from my thoughts like so many other women before her. But after that day on the beach, watching as she searched for sea shells and showed me the view, after understanding who she was, where she'd come from and what she'd survived—I didn't just like her. I respected her, wanted her to respect me. There was no going back for me after that. She was honest and loyal and hardworking. She cared about other people's happiness over her own. "I just don't know where my boundaries are at the moment. I don't know how to separate work and . . . not work." It wasn't love.

"Sounds like you need a change of pace, which is why I called. Avery and I are flying down to Nice tomorrow. I have a meeting, and there's no way Avery was going to let me come on my own when she could accompany me to her old stomping grounds and catch up with old friends. Let's have dinner."

The thought of seeing my brother was like a cool cloth over my forehead. I rarely got flustered, but when I did, my family brought me perspective. "We're just off the coast of Monaco at the moment."

"Which is perfect. Just a short helicopter trip for us," Hayden said. "Can you get the evening off?"

I'd need to hang around to see who turned up on the boat tomorrow, but if I asked Peter and told him my brother was in town, I might get the night off. "It would be good to see you."

"Might take your mind off your women troubles."

"I don't have fucking women troubles." I needed to hear from Hayden that the job came first. That duty and honor and the greater good were what had driven me for so long— he would remind me who I was. Because at the moment, Skylar had clouded my vision, and I couldn't see straight.

THIRTY-THREE

Skylar

Having a cup of coffee in a café in Monaco seemed indulgent, but it gave me a place to sit and brainstorm . . . and at least I was off the yacht for a few hours—a surprise from the captain for doing a twenty-hour day yesterday as he included dinner with Walt. I glanced up at the blue sky, then the boats in the marina. It all looked so beautiful. But just like every yacht crew worker, I knew the picture to be slightly less perfect.

Yachting wasn't my passion. And Landon had helped me see that it didn't need to be my future. But was I really going to turn down a three-year contract? Certainty? Guaranteed money, food, and lodging? For a girl like me, who'd been working toward all those things for so long, it seemed a lot to give up just because I thought I might want to do something else.

Despite not having a plan or even an idea of where I'd be in twelve months, I knew it couldn't be on board the *Sapphire*. Landon and I may well go our separate ways after this summer, but he'd changed me. Stopped me running. Encouraged me to look around and show me no one was still chasing me. And I'd be forever grateful.

For the first time since my mother died, I had realized that I had options. Choices.

I just didn't know which direction I should take.

I opened my notebook and glanced down at my list. At the top was the three-year contract on the *Sapphire* followed by a list of options that seemed entirely impossible.

My phone vibrated on the zinc table, and I grinned. No doubt it was Landon. I'd had at least five messages in the last two hours.

But it was Avery. Again. I hadn't answered my old friend's calls last night because I'd been on duty, having dinner with Walt.

"Hey," I said, as I accepted the call.

"Finally," she said. "Are you super busy? Can you talk?"

"Nope. I've got the day off because yesterday was so crazy."

"Sounds like your captain is a softie. Which is good because I need you to get the night off tonight. I'm at the airport. We're flying into Nice later today—that's why I was calling you like a maniac last night. I really want to see you and August."

"The yacht's in Monte Carlo, for tonight at least. And I'm free until tomorrow morning." Landon had the night off as his brother was in town, and we'd planned to spend the night together when he was done. The timing couldn't have been better. I could catch up with Avery while Landon had dinner with his brother, and then we could meet up and spend the night together off the boat.

"Fucking-fantastic. I can't wait."

Seeing Avery was exactly what I needed. She'd left

yachting and chosen a different path. Plus she knew me almost as well as August did. She'd be able to help me assess some of my choices. And I could tell her everything about Landon.

"I'll make it happen," I replied. "I need to talk to you about . . . a lot of stuff."

"This hasn't got anything to do with the guy you've been seeing, does it?"

I laughed. "Not really, well maybe a little. He has opened my eyes to new possibilities. In the future." Landon and I were . . . I didn't know what we were, but he'd always made it very clear he wasn't about commitment or long-term relationships. I'd been convenient to him over the past few weeks, but I was grateful for the time we'd spent together.

At the back of my brain, buried deep, there was a small hope that when we got done with the season, what had been a summer fling might develop into something more. Maybe things had changed for him like they had done for me.

"You didn't get the contract?" Avery asked.

"The opposite, actually."

Avery squealed. "I can't believe you didn't message me immediately. I'm so happy for you."

"Yeah," I said with a sigh.

"I'm not sure that I should be happier about it than you are. What's going on?"

"I've just been thinking about a lot of stuff. About what I really want. About what I wanted—the hopes and dreams I had before my mom died. I've been thinking that maybe the three-year contract isn't the way to go."

"Wow, this is huge, Skylar."

"Am I being an idiot if I turn this down?"

"To follow your dreams? It's what I've done, and I've never been happier."

I bit back a grin—partly because I was so happy my friend was happy, and partly because right off in the distance, I could see that maybe I could have that kind of happiness for myself. The kind that settled in your soul and kept you warm at night. The kind I hadn't known in a very long time.

"I'm not even sure if my dreams have stayed the same. Or if any of them are even realistic. I just think that maybe if I don't chase them now, I never will." If I took the three-year contract, whatever Landon had awoken in me would wither and die. I would be permanently on the path, running from something that had long since stopped chasing me.

I didn't always have to be the girl whose father shot and killed her mother.

I didn't always have to be the girl who was scared of being hungry and homeless.

I didn't always have to be the girl who didn't trust anyone but herself.

Landon had shown me that.

"Gah," Avery spluttered. "I think it's wonderful that you're thinking that there's more to life than a three-year contract. And I'm going to be able to hug you in the flesh to celebrate."

My phone started beeping. "Avery, I have a call coming through on the other line. I'll see you tonight."

I hung up and answered Landon. "Hey."

"I just spoke to my brother," he said. "I should be done with dinner by ten. That gives us an entire eight hours."

I grinned but didn't say anything, not wanting him to hear my smile in my voice. "I have dinner with a friend tonight, too. So, maybe I can meet you at a bar. I'm not sure where we'll go yet."

"I'm really looking forward to seeing you, Skylar," he said, his tone suddenly serious.

I couldn't imagine a time that I wouldn't look forward to seeing Landon. "I'm really looking forward to seeing you, too."

He sighed on the other end of the phone. "I should go. My break's over and the other guests are just about to arrive."

"Yes, go. And I'll see you tonight after ten."

I had plenty to do to keep me busy until then. I had my whole life to figure out. And a three-year contract to turn down.

THIRTY-FOUR

Skylar

If I couldn't spend the entire evening with Landon, dinner with Avery was the perfect alternative. I grinned at the hostess as I made my way through the door of the restaurant she'd texted me about. I got to spend tonight with my friend and later a man who, whether or not he knew it, had changed my life. I'd decided I was going to come clean with Landon later. Tell him how my feelings for him had grown, how I'd never felt this way about anyone, as well as how I intended to turn down the contract with the *Sapphire*.

I didn't want him to feel I had expectations of him beyond this summer. I just needed him to know he was a good, kind, honest man who had let me see men in a different way. We'd agreed to a summer fling, and if that was still all he wanted then I'd live with that. But it wasn't all I wanted. For the first time ever in my life, I wanted a man. But not any man. I wanted Landon James.

"Skylar?" a familiar, gravelly voice called from behind me.

I turned and came face-to-face with Landon. My smile took over my face. "What are you doing here?"

His eyes skimmed down my dress and back up, and a trail of heat followed his gaze. He slid his hand around my waist and kissed me. "I was about to ask you the same question. I thought you were having dinner with one of your girl-friends?"

"I am. Here." I pressed my palm against his chest, enjoying the reassuring firmness of his muscles. "What about you? Are you—"

"I'm meeting my brother."

"May I help you?" the hostess asked.

"Yes." I didn't want to be rude, but I wasn't ready to leave the circle of Landon's arms. "I'm joining some friends. The table will be under the name of Wolf."

"Mr. and Mrs. Wolf have already arrived. Let me show you both to your seats."

"Oh no," I said. "We're not together." I glanced up at Landon, who was frowning.

"Actually, I think we are," Landon replied.

Before I could answer, I spotted Avery waving from across the restaurant, and Landon gestured for me to follow the hostess. I glanced over my shoulder, and Landon was following me.

"Skylar, Landon!" Avery bounced out of her seat and pulled me into a hug. Out of the corner of my eye, I saw Landon getting a hug from Hayden. Were Hayden and Landon brothers?

"Hi," I said, trying to put all the pieces together. "Nice to see you." Hayden kissed me on the cheek and pulled out the chair across from Avery.

"So, did you just bump into Landon at the door?" Avery asked.

"You're brothers? But your last name is James."

Hayden snorted. "You and your aliases. Do you ever wonder how the rest of us cope with just one name?"

"So how do you know my brother?" Landon asked, his brow furrowed.

"Aliases?" I asked.

"You two are on the same boat together?" Avery said. "This is so great. Skylar was my second stew when I met Hayden."

"Why did you say your name was James?" I asked, searching through reasons why two brothers would have different surnames. "I would have put two and two together if you'd have said Wolf."

"Ahhh, that's the point," Hayden said. "My little brother doesn't like anyone putting two and two together when it comes to him."

I turned to Landon, and the way his eyes didn't meet mine sent a shiver up my spine. He wasn't Landon James?

"It's not like people are using my surname on board a lot. I'd pretty much forgotten I was James on board," he replied.

"But why would you use a different name in the first place?"

He took a deep breath. "Habit. I'm not good at being open about stuff."

"Let's get you some drinks." Hayden called over the waiter while all I could do was stare at Landon and wait for some kind of explanation.

"I need a whiskey," Landon said.

"What does Hayden mean about aliases?" I asked, not wanting to let this go. "Are you hiding something?"

Avery nudged Hayden in the ribs.

"What?" Hayden asked.

"You're not being very helpful." Avery turned to us. "Am I being dense—are you two . . . Is Landon the guy you've been . . . He's the guy at the beach, right?"

I was beginning to think the man beside me was anybody but the man I'd been at the beach with.

Landon shook his head. "It's nothing. You know that I do private security and military consultancy. It's just a habit. A safeguard."

What the hell was military consultancy? That didn't sound like the kind of job bodyguards did.

"Landon's underselling himself," Hayden said. "He's the best in the business, who just sold his very successful company. Which is why I'm expecting you to pay tonight, little brother. And I'm going to order some very nice wine."

"The best at what? Being a security guard?" What was Hayden talking about? "And what company did you just sell?" It was as if Hayden was introducing me to a stranger. I didn't seem to know anything about Landon.

"Private security is more than just being a security guard," Landon said.

"Which means what, exactly?" I felt as if I kept asking questions I wasn't getting answers to, and that made my stomach churn. I knew Landon, didn't I? I trusted him, and I didn't trust anyone.

"I had a business doing private-security work."

"Your own company?"

"My brother doesn't like to brag, but he had a very successful business," Hayden said.

I kept my gaze fixed on Landon, but his face was blank of any kind of expression.

"So you decided to retrain as a deckhand?"

"Sort of," he replied. "Can we talk about this later? And, Hayden, please can you shut the fuck up?"

"Landon," Avery said. "I don't know much, but I know Skylar, and whatever you are to each other, I know she deserves you to be transparent."

"The job I do doesn't always allow me that luxury," he said.

His words hit me, each one stealing my breath. He was admitting that he had been, and was being, less than truthful.

Our waitress arrived with our drinks, but the last thing I wanted was alcohol. My vision had been fuzzy for long enough.

"You're not on board to be a deckhand? I don't get it. Be straight with me, Landon."

Landon shot Hayden a look across the table.

"Don't be mad at your brother because he told me what you should have. He's not the one who's been lying."

"I've not been lying," Landon replied. "But I haven't told you the entire truth, either."

I waited for the explanation, desperate to stop the feelings of betrayal breaking free. But I got nothing. Only silence.

"Jesus, Landon. Who are you?"

He turned to face me and swept his hand over the back of my neck. "You know who I am."

I shrugged him off and moved my chair away. "No, I don't think I do."

"Hang on," Hayden said. "Is this the girl you were talking about last night? Are you two . . ."

I was vaguely aware of Avery shushing Hayden on the other side of the table, but all my focus was on Landon. I wanted him to explain what had happened since we'd stepped into this restaurant. I wanted to know who he was.

Was it possible that the man I'd opened up to, shared

things I'd never talked about, wasn't who he said he was? Had the man who had allowed me to trust again turned out to be the last person I should have trusted? His silence just multiplied my suspicion. I was giving him a chance to explain, but I was just getting semi-explanations and vague snippets of information.

How was it possible for me to have been so fooled by this guy? Looking back, his story about suddenly becoming a deckhand never made sense—he was too old and the way he described his decision made him sound like a loser, when he'd always been focused and diligent and instinctively good at work.

But I wasn't getting any more answers as I sat here.

"I need to leave," I said, pushing out my chair and standing. "I'm sorry, Avery, Hayden. It was great to see you both. But I need to go." I needed to get away from Landon James or Wolf or whatever he was calling himself.

I'd let myself ignore all my rules for this man. I'd let him in. I'd allowed myself to enjoy his touch, need his embrace. How could I have been so foolish?

He was a *liar*.

"Don't go," Avery said as she stood.

I couldn't even look at Landon. "I'm sorry. I'll call you, Avery. I just can't—"

Before I made a fool out of myself and let my sadness and frustration pour down my face, I needed to escape. I turned and fled from the table, desperately heading for the door as if I were underwater and wouldn't be able to breathe until I got out into the fresh air. I just wanted to go home, but I didn't have one. I'd spent *years* hopping from one yacht to another. I didn't belong anywhere. I'd thought Landon was someone I could have a future with, but he was *exactly* what I'd been running from for all these years.

THIRTY-FIVE

Landon

I wove between the cramped chairs and tables, following Skylar out of the restaurant. Reynolds would tell me this was the perfect opportunity to get Skylar up to speed on the operation. I could finally tell her everything and ask for her help, but I still couldn't find the words.

"Hey," I said as I caught up to her outside.

She shook her head and tried to walk around me.

"Skylar." I blocked her path and held her shoulders, dipping to try to meet her eye. "I'm sorry I didn't tell you more about my background—I just . . ."

She kept her eyes fixated on the ground.

"Skylar? Don't be pissed off at me because you didn't know something I *couldn't* tell you."

She tried to struggle out of my grasp, but I held her firm.

"Couldn't? Like you couldn't tell me your real name?"

"That would have just led to more questions that I couldn't answer." The easiest way to explain was to do what

Reynolds wanted—to enlist Skylar's help. I could tell her why I was on the yacht and who Walt was.

The hard line of her mouth told me she was far from placated with my non-answer.

"I need you to understand that I didn't lie about anything that mattered," I said. "Not between us."

"I *understand* that I'm not worth the truth."

I tipped my head back. "Of course you are." She was worth far more to me than she realized. She had me hesitating about getting her wired up and gathering evidence to stop a man who was going to sell weapons to terrorists. Jesus, the reason I couldn't find the words to do as Reynolds asked was precisely because she meant *so much*.

"You had your own business? Your last name isn't James, it's Wolf. Were you even in the army, or was that a lie, too?"

I didn't understand her anger but at the same time I cared that I'd upset her. I wasn't used to being bothered by anyone's feelings. I needed her to see it from my point of view. "Yes, I was in the army and then the SAS."

"The SAS?"

"Special Forces."

Skylar shook her head. "So not just some soldier. And you were probably just in it for the glory. All the stuff about passion that you talked about is probably bullshit too. Is anything you've told me even remotely true?"

"Special Forces operators don't talk about their work, even retired members. It makes them targets. Makes their *families* targets. These are just details. You know who I am. More than most people."

"These aren't just details. The things I've found out tonight are who you are. I feel like I've been with a stranger all these weeks. It's violating, Landon. Don't you see that?"

"I'm still the same guy. Just because you don't know—"

"No, you're not. That's the point. That guy knew how important honesty is to me. Apparently, you're happy for me to think you're some kind of drifter with no direction in life. You're prepared to deceive me and tell me half-truths and lies. I thought you were the first real guy I'd ever met; the first man I wanted to tell anything and everything to. The first one I trusted since my dad . . . I thought you were different."

She tried to twist away from me, but I wouldn't let her move. Her eyes filled with tears, and I began to realize how much of a betrayal my actions must look like to Skylar. She'd trusted no one since her father betrayed her in the worst way possible. To her, he'd pretended to be a loving husband and father and turned out to be a killer and a thief of childhoods. I'd betrayed Skylar's trust—something she clearly didn't give out easily.

"I'm sorry," I said.

"It's not good enough. You've . . . I just can't." She pushed out of my arms. "I was going to tell you tonight how I was planning to turn down the three-year contract because you'd inspired me to chase my dreams. I was about to confess how much you meant to me but—"

I reached for her and she pulled away.

"Skylar, I've been more open with you than I have with any woman."

She scoffed. "Doesn't mean a whole lot when you've never spent more than twenty-four hours with a woman."

She had a point.

"But I've never wanted to spend any longer with anyone. *That* should mean something," I replied.

She looked up at me, her ice-blue eyes filled with disappointment and sadness.

Now was my moment. I was at a crossroads with too many options, and all I wanted to do was turn around and go back to where I started. I wanted to confess everything to her, send her back to London with Hayden and Avery and keep her safe. But I knew it wouldn't be that simple. If I told her, there was a real risk she wouldn't leave. She'd want someone like Walt behind bars as much as I did. She'd stay. But it was too dangerous, and I couldn't risk her insisting that she put herself in harm's way.

Perhaps her hating me was a way out. Resignation trickled through my veins like summer rain—hot and suffocating. It was the perfect solution. If Skylar *quit*, she also left the clutches of Walt and the CIA or whoever Reynolds' client was. She was so professional, that a simple breakup might not get her to leave the *Sapphire*.

I had to rely on the fact that the only thing Skylar knew how to do better than maintain a yacht interior was to *run* from misery and pain.

The first chance she had, she'd run from Ohio—away from the memory of her dead mother and the group home she'd hated. Now I had to get her to run from the South of France. Away from the misery and pain that *I* would cause her.

"It doesn't matter," she muttered, her shoulders slumping.

"Exactly. It doesn't matter." I hardened my tone. Was I really going to do this? Could I drive her away to keep her safe?

"That's not what I mean," she said. "I thought you were different."

I rolled my eyes, hating myself every second, but I was going to have to do a lot worse.

"Jesus, Landon. I thought you'd changed my future, but

really, you're just a reminder of my past. And I don't know if I can live with that."

"Well, you're going to have to live with that because we're on the yacht together for weeks yet. You need to grow up, Skylar."

She blinked as if she couldn't focus properly or perhaps didn't recognize the man talking to her. "Grow up?"

Tears spilled down her face, and it was like an iron fist was wrapped around my heart. It hurt so much seeing her cry.

My heart raced as I held myself back from pulling her into my arms and confessing everything to her. But that would be selfish. I had to make it worse.

I took a deep breath. "Yeah. Grow up. You know my track record with women. It's not like I hid that from you. We were hardly going to grow old together. It was better-than-average sex. That's all. Nothing I'd write home about."

She pulled back. "Who are you?"

"I hope you're not going to make a fuss when we're back at work," I said, glancing around the square we were in as if I were barely interested in the conversation, as if I didn't know that accusing her of being unprofessional would cut her deep. I just hoped it was deep enough.

"Landon," she said. "This isn't you. What's the matter? Did something happen? You know you can tell me. You can trust me."

It was so typical of her to be caring and understanding in the face of me being so unpleasant. I was going to have to sharpen my knife. I knew how to cut her to the core. I just didn't want to. But I had no choice.

"Christ, Skylar, if your mother was this needy and desperate, no wonder your father couldn't put up with it," I said. "The apple clearly doesn't fall far from the tree."

She gasped and clutched her stomach as if I'd sliced her open. I shrugged, bracing myself for her anger, but it was only sadness I felt coming from her—disappointment in me —and it was like a bullet to my heart.

"I'm not listening to this," she said. "I have no idea who you are."

I'd done all I could, cut as deep as it was possible to do.

The fight had left her, and instead of saying anything more, she turned and ran. I hoped she didn't stop. She needed to *keep on* running. I followed her. I wasn't trying to catch her. I just wanted to make sure she was safe.

I needed her to be angry enough with me to give the captain her notice. I hoped the hatred she felt for me was enough to drive her to leave Europe and go somewhere far out of the reaches of Walt and the CIA.

I stuffed my hands into my pockets as I watched her get into a cab and drive away. I'd never see her again, but I wanted to burn the last memory of her into my soul.

She thought I'd been the one to change things for her, but she'd changed me completely. And she'd never know.

THIRTY-SIX

Skylar

As I poured the fourth top-up of coffee into the teenager's cup, I looked out of the window of the diner and sighed. Maybe I should have tried harder to get another yachting job to finish out the season—at least then I would be wait-ressing for better tips. I just couldn't handle the thought of being on the same continent as Landon, and if I knew nothing else, I knew now that I was capable of putting a roof over my own head and a meal in my stomach—I didn't have to stay somewhere if I was unhappy.

I still couldn't think about Landon without my heart growing heavy in my chest. My anger toward him was still there but quieter now, and disappointment rushed to fill the gap. How could I have been so completely wrong about him? The things he'd said to me had been so . . . The one man in all these years I'd opened up to and he'd turned out to be everything I'd spent my life avoiding.

I didn't really know why I'd come back to Ohio. I'd been upset and fled back home, after making up an excuse about a family member who'd been taken ill. But this wasn't home. It was just the town I'd grown up in. I didn't have a home.

The clock on the wall above the door said it was three minutes past the end of my shift. I turned just as Hetty emerged from the back.

"You get off now, my dear."

To do what? I didn't know anyone in this town. When I'd left, I'd never looked back.

I'd take some food back to my motel room and stare at the pile of textbooks I hadn't opened.

I'd rented a motel room the day I'd stepped off the bus, bought a secondhand car the day after. There was no getting about without it. This wasn't the South of France.

"Thanks, Hetty. I'll see you tomorrow." I pulled at the white apron strings at my back and headed out.

My car was parked in the back, and I slid onto the old pleather seat. I could afford better, but I was saving my money. I just didn't know what for.

I pulled out of the parking lot and took a breath as I headed across town. The only problem with where I was staying and where I was working was that I had to pass the group home I'd lived in after my mother died. I had no good memories of that place. No particularly good memories at all here.

So why had I come back? Florida was more home to me than Ohio. I hadn't been back here since I'd left on my eighteenth birthday. Since I'd escaped.

As I turned left onto Washington Drive, I couldn't even bring myself to look at the sign at the front of the building. I'd always hated the fact that the O in "home" was fashioned like a heart. It felt like more lies. There was no heart in the place. Just a bunch of people trying to get through their day. I exhaled as I passed the place and continued up the hill, then turned into the motel parking lot. This was home for me until I figured out what was next.

"Hey, Skylar," the maintenance man called from across the lot.

I waved and pulled my bag from the backseat. I'd bought a salad and a slice of cheesecake for dinner.

My cell began to ring from inside my uniform pocket. I knocked the door shut with my hip and pulled out my phone.

I winced as August's name popped up. I wasn't ignoring her, exactly. I'd just been avoiding her calls and replying with texts. That way I could more easily skip the questions that I didn't have answers to and reply *I'm fine* to her inquiries without worrying that she'd hear something else in my voice. But I couldn't avoid her forever.

"Hey, August," I answered as I locked my car and headed back to my room.

"Wow, you actually picked up."

"I just finished my shift."

"At your waitressing job? How is it?"

"It's fine. Pays the bills." I tucked the phone under my chin as I jiggled the key to the room in the lock.

"And how are you—don't you dare say you're *fine*, because we both know that's bullshit."

"I have a job, a car, and a roof over my head," I said as I glanced up at the stained ceiling of the motel room I'd been in for these past weeks. "How are things with you?" I asked to be polite, but I didn't want to hear about the life I'd left behind. I didn't want to hear about the *Sapphire*, the sun, or the cocktails. And I especially didn't want to hear about Landon.

"One week to go until the end of the season. I can't wait

for it to be over. It's been weird. And so much worse without you."

The end of the Med season had come around quickly. I never thought I'd be in Ohio when it did.

I dumped my bag, pulled out the food, and stuffed it into the tiny refrigerator that was noisier than it had a right to be given its size. "I'm sure you're coping just fine. And it's great that Captain gave you the chief stew position. You deserved it, and it means next season you'll have a track record, and you'll be leading your own team."

August groaned on the other end of the line. "Are you heading to Florida next week?"

"I'm not sure."

"I was going to suggest we find a place together."

I smiled. The chance to see a familiar face in a familiar place sounded tempting, but yachting didn't feel like the right fit anymore. "I'm not sure I'm going to do next season."

"Really? You enjoying being back home?"

I took a seat on the bed and glanced around. "It's not that." There was nothing about this place to make me stay— no friends, no family, no opportunities. But I didn't want to go somewhere else just to escape Ohio. I'd done that before. The next time I left it would be because I was heading toward something. "I think that yachting is over for me. It's been good. I've earned a lot of money—"

"But it's not where your future lies?"

"Exactly."

"Any thoughts about what you want to do?" she asked.

"A few. Except they all require a college degree. And that's a lot of money." There was only one thing I'd ever wanted to be—a lawyer.

"But you have savings, right? And you can work part-time."

I'd already figured out that with my savings and a job I could make it work, but there were a thousand other reasons why I hadn't applied anywhere. Landon had opened my eyes to the possibility, but his betrayal meant that I was questioning everything about our time together.

"But it's four years out of my life. And then grad school."

"Yeah, but college is fun. It's not like you're having to withstand four years of waterboarding. You can enjoy the journey not just the destination."

"Yeah, I wasn't expecting to get waterboarded. It's just a big time commitment."

"But not in the scheme of the next forty years."

"I guess. But then there's no guarantee of a job at the end of it."

"Might as well give up then," August said. "Come back to yachting, bury your dreams, and come clean toilets with me."

I laughed. August always had the most charming way of calling people out on their bullshit.

"There are no guarantees in life, Skylar. You, more than anyone, should know that. Go to college. Try it at least."

"Maybe I will," I said. August was right in a way. I didn't have a lot to lose. I could always go back to yachting if I changed my mind about college.

I took a deep breath. Landon had betrayed my trust, there was no doubt about that. He'd hidden what he did for a living from me, made me believe he was someone he wasn't, and I'd stupidly thought that what we had together was special. It was all lies. But being with him had made me realize that I was done running away. That I wanted something more than just a paycheck, and I couldn't shut those feelings down. I didn't want to.

I pulled out one of the study guides from the pile. I should really open one of these things. Just to see if I was even capable of passing an entrance exam.

"So now your future career is set, have you thought much about . . . you know . . . other *things*? And when I say other things, you get I mean Landon, right?"

"Nope," I replied. I'd thought of little else but Landon. The betrayal and disappointment he'd caused drifted into the misery of being back in Ohio, and it all hovered around me as if I were walking around in a big, dull cloud.

"These army guys aren't very emotionally evolved."

"How are you and Harvey doing?" I asked, taking the chance to distract August.

She sighed. "Things are fading out. We don't see each other much, and we're both so busy."

"I'm sorry. I thought it was all good between you."

"Don't worry about it. It wasn't as if we were some great love affair that ended in disaster."

"That's yachting for you," I said.

"But not for you," she replied.

"What do you mean?"

"I mean you and Landon were different. Worth fighting for."

"That's not true. We were—" I remembered him telling me how we were never going to grow old together. "Only for a summer."

"I don't believe that for a second. He's worn a gloomy expression since you left and never leaves his room unless he's on shift. And given that you fled the continent as soon as you split and haven't been answering your phone? It doesn't seem like it was just a summer fling."

Was Landon gloomy? Over me? Sounded unlikely. He

wanted me to quit, so I didn't make a fuss. He didn't try to talk me out of it.

"Have you heard from him at all?" she asked.

"Of course not. Why would I have?" I hadn't even hoped he'd call. I'd wanted to be as far away from him as possible. I'd invited lies back into my world when I thought I'd successfully banished them forever.

"I thought he'd apologized for whatever it was he did."

I hadn't told August what he'd said to me outside the restaurant—just that Landon had apologized for keeping things from me. I couldn't bear to think about how he'd taken the most awful things of my past and tortured me with them. I still didn't understand how the honorable, funny, protective man who I'd known for weeks had morphed into the cruel, cold stranger who'd watched from the upper deck as I left the *Sapphire* and hadn't said a word.

"An apology wouldn't change anything." Lying was a line in the sand for me, and Landon hadn't just skirted around the truth—everything about him, including his last name, had been made up.

But worse, when I'd been upset about the lies, he'd lashed out in the worst possible way—said things that would echo through me for the rest of my life. He wasn't the man I'd thought he was. I'd trusted him and he'd betrayed me. I'd thought he was one kind of man when he turned out to be the *worst* kind of man.

"So you just give up?" she asked. "Isn't it worth giving him a second chance? You two were so good together."

I rolled my eyes. August had clearly fallen for the good-guy act that Landon put on. "Landon's in my past. That's where he's going to stay." I kept telling myself that over and over again, but it didn't make the thoughts of him disappear. Those weeks with him had been so . . . real. At least for me.

The way he'd held me, looked at me. The way he'd kissed me. I'd let myself believe I could have a relationship with a man. Trust someone. But I should have known better. If I ignored lessons learned in my past, I would suffer the same loss and heartbreak time and time again. I had to look to my future. "I've moved on." I didn't have anything left to say. Landon and I had seen the last of each other, and that was all there was to it.

"Well, college seems exciting. I'm so proud of you—it's such a huge change."

"Nothing's set. And the admissions process is . . . There are no guarantees that I'll get in anywhere."

"You won't have a problem. When you want something, you find a way."

It was nice that she believed that, even if I didn't.

"Thanks, August. Listen, I have to go, but we'll talk soon."

"If you don't answer my next call, I'm on the next plane to Ohio."

I grinned. *That* I believed. "I promise I will."

I hung up, pulled myself off the bed, took a seat at the table, and opened the first page of the study guide. Staring at the books wasn't going to get me anywhere. It was time I started taking steps toward my future.

THIRTY-SEVEN

Landon

I glanced around Hayden and Avery's comfortable home. I'd been here a hundred times before, but this time I found myself wondering what it would be like to live this way. Out in the country. With a woman I loved.

"Can you put these spoons out?" my brother asked, handing me a bunch of cutlery.

"Who are you and what have you done with Hayden Wolf?" I asked.

"You think I'm not your brother anymore because I use spoons?"

"I guess I'm adjusting to the domesticity after having been on a yacht all summer." I was adjusting to a lot of things after this summer.

"I'm not sure I should be speaking to you," Avery said as she pulled out a tray of vegetables from the oven. "I don't want to take sides, but I'm on Skylar's. You have to know that."

Hayden rolled his eyes. "There are no sides to take. Breakups happen."

"Have you tried to reach her?" Avery asked.

I'd thought about it. Every day since I'd last seen her. But there was no point. She was understandably angry at me, and I'd encouraged her to leave. "No. I understand why she was pissed off." At least she'd not been brought into any real danger. That was the only thing that mattered.

"Because of all the lies," Avery said as if I were unaware of why Skylar was upset.

"Lies he had to tell," Hayden said. "It wasn't as if he'd lied about being single or having herpes."

"For the record, I don't have herpes," I said.

"Good to know," Avery said. "But Skylar's sensitive to people who don't tell the truth. She's had a difficult path."

"I know," I replied.

"You do?" Avery moved past me and put some plates out on the table.

"Yeah, she told me about her parents."

"She did?" Avery's face looked like I'd just told her I was about to go to the moon after dinner. "That's big, Landon. Skylar doesn't tell a lot of people her story."

I swallowed. From what Skylar had told me, not even Avery knew that it was her father who killed her mother. Compared to me, Skylar came across as open, light, and breezy, but there was a lot more to her than what was on the surface. It was part of the reason I was drawn to her. "The things I didn't tell her were to protect her. You know I hung around in Monaco after the owner of the yacht left for the summer?"

"Yes," Avery replied.

"Well, the owner, the one I'd been surveilling, was arrested in his hotel the day he walked off the *Sapphire*. For gunrunning. It's been in the press now. He was planning to sell weapons to a splinter group of the Islamic State."

"Jeez, Landon. Are you kidding?" Hayden asked. "You said it was a low-level thing."

"Well my involvement was," I replied.

"Are we talking about the owner of the yacht Skylar and August were on? Didn't Skylar go to dinner with that guy a couple of times?"

I nodded. "He wanted her as a cover—to join him at dinners with various people that he shouldn't have been meeting with."

"And you just let her go?" Avery asked.

"They only had dinner twice," I replied. The last thing I could be accused of was not worrying about Skylar's safety. "The second time was on the boat. The first time . . . Well, I was there outside the restaurant."

The corners of Avery's mouth twitched. "You followed them?"

"What? I was there taking pictures of suspected terrorists."

Hayden raised his eyebrows. "Sounds like there was a little more to it than that."

"At the time, it was all about the job, but believe me, I made sure that Skylar avoided being put in any real danger." They didn't need to know how close to danger Skylar had come, and how I'd put the operation on the line before putting her into the line of fire.

"Look, Landon, I know you're a bigger man-whore than your brother used to be—"

"Hey, less man-whore accusations, please," Hayden called from where he was collecting the food.

"Have you thought that maybe Skylar's the kind of woman who's changed things for you?"

230230230230 LOUISE BAY

Avery wasn't suggesting anything I hadn't spent the past month thinking about. "There's no doubt she was different."

I took a seat at the table and poured out the wine into three glasses.

"Isn't she worth fighting for?" Avery pressed.

"You just want your best friend and my brother to date so we can hang out more," Hayden said. "That's not a good reason for two people to be together."

"It's not just that," Avery replied. "I know Skylar. She doesn't talk about her past easily. Certainly not to a man. And I've never known her to be dating or even sleeping with someone."

Avery wasn't telling me anything I didn't already know. Skylar had trusted me with her story. With her body. With the real her.

"I know you were meant to be a summer fling or something," Avery continued. "But I've never even known her to do something like that. She's always so set on finding the perfect guy."

Avery clearly hadn't figured out that Skylar's criteria were a cover so she never had to date. She'd knowingly put barriers in place between her and a relationship. And I'd made it worse.

"From what I can make out, what the two of you had together was as real as it's ever gotten for her," Avery said.

"It was real." I'd spent the last month trying to pretend to myself that it had just been sex. Or circumstance. But being here with Hayden and Avery—with family—I was done bullshitting myself. There was no point. Hayden always saw straight through me. "But that doesn't mean it was meant to last. I had a reason to lie to her, and she had a reason to be pissed off about it. Sometimes you just reach an impasse."

"Yeah, with a colleague. Or a neighbor. Not someone you love," Hayden said.

My heart thumped. "No one's talking love. I said it was real. That's all." I might be done bullshitting but talking about love was a step too far.

"Real love," Avery said. "I saw it as soon as the two of you appeared at dinner. The way she looked at you? I've never seen her like that. And the way you touched her? Ran after her? Landon, you're lying to yourself if you're pretending you don't love her."

"Avery," I said, my tone like gathering thunderclouds.

"I care about you," she continued. "You're family. And I know that you don't open up to people."

I took a sip of my wine—I didn't want to listen to what she had to say. I wanted to be done with this conversation. Thinking about Skylar was futile. The damage had been done.

"I don't want you to lose something important just because you're too stubborn to see what's right in front of you."

"This isn't about me being stubborn. It's about who I am. It's about choices I made, and I'd make them again." I'd driven her away. I'd done it to keep her safe, and I couldn't take it back, and I couldn't regret it.

"Isn't it worth having a conversation and at least telling her how you feel?"

I had no right to think she'd forgive me for encouraging her to leave the *Sapphire*. For the things I'd said, for the lies I told. "She thinks I betrayed her. I can't be the man she wants."

"How do you know unless you explain?" Avery sighed. "You should also mention how you're a bit crap at communicating."

"Thanks, Avery. Helpful." I caught my brother's eye and he just shook his head. "I don't think she'd even listen." She'd looked so devastated as she'd climbed into the cab. I didn't want to be responsible for hurting her any further.

"You could try," Avery said. "It's not like you did it to be mean. And it wasn't anything personal. Was it?"

"She's better off without me," I said, pushing my food around on my plate. I might have *had* to lie to Skylar this time, but I wasn't good at sharing my feelings on my best day. I knew she deserved better than that. And the things I'd said to her? I hated myself, but knew it had been the right thing to do.

I might not be ready to accept that I loved her, but I did think about her. A lot. Hers was the first face I saw when I woke up, and the expression she'd worn when she climbed into her cab was the last thing I pictured before I went to sleep.

"I'm just going to say one thing, and then we can drop this," my brother said. "I thought I'd lost Avery at one point, and it would have been easy to give up, to walk away. But I knew if I did, I'd be losing someone I'd miss forever. Someone I could picture a future with, and I knew I'd be an idiot to walk away. And the idea that I hadn't done everything I could to keep her in my life was . . . Well, I couldn't live with that."

Silence echoed around the table.

Hayden and I rarely talked about our feelings, but I knew meeting Avery had changed him, and I couldn't shake the feeling that meeting Skylar was just as important to me as Avery was to him.

"Brother, I know that you're a man who likes to finish what he started—see things through—from an operation in the army to the arrest of an arms dealer," he said. "You're anything but a quitter. From where I sit, Skylar might be the mission of your life. Make sure you don't quit before the job is done."

Shit.

Hayden knew exactly what to say and it made me want to punch him. He and I both knew that for me, quitting when the stakes were high wasn't an option, and the stakes had never been this high.

THIRTY-EIGHT

Skylar

I bit down into my apple, shutting one eye and then the other as I stared at question number seventy-two in the book that promised to be a surefire way of acing any college entrance exam. I was sure I'd read somewhere that shifting *how* you looked at something sometimes shook an answer out of the brain. But no. I was stuck. Math just wasn't my strong suit.

I hadn't even changed out of my diner uniform. As soon as I'd gotten back to my motel room, I'd sat down and opened my books. I checked my phone. It had been an hour and a half. Time for a break, a shower, and a change of clothes. I could fit in another hour before bed. And then at least two before my shift tomorrow.

I groaned at the knock at the door. I was paid up for the next month—the date I'd set to sit the exam—so there was no reason for anyone to be interrupting my routine.

I dropped my apple into the trash, pulled open the door, and stumbled as I tried to figure out what was going on.

It was Landon.

In *Ohio*.

What the hell was in that apple? I glanced at the trash.

"Hey," he said.

"Hi," I replied, still unsure if I was imagining Landon on my doorstep.

"Can I come in?" he asked, his eyes narrowing in that sexy way he had.

What was he doing here?

I opened the door and straightened my dress, embarrassed that I hadn't changed when I'd got in. "I wasn't expecting you. Why are you here? How did you find me?" Avery and August were the only people who knew I was in Ohio, but I hadn't told them exactly where.

"I used to have my own private-security firm. When I was in the SAS, we did a lot of work that you'd normally associate with MI6 or the CIA. It wasn't difficult to find out where you were."

"Oh." I didn't know how to react.

"You weren't hiding, were you?" he asked as he took a step forward, and I backed into the room.

I'd wanted to escape. "Not hiding, exactly."

"But running," he said, reading my mind. "From me?" He closed the door to my room behind him and glanced around.

"Why are you here?" I asked again.

He drew in a deep breath. "To explain. To apologize. To see you."

I dropped down to sit on the bed, my limbs already heavy with resignation. "There's no need. It is what it is." I still replayed that final conversation we'd had over and over in my head. He'd been so . . . cold. So unfeeling.

"I didn't expect to be here. I've never felt the need to

talk . . . explain. I've always operated on the basis that I told people as little as possible about operations." He took a seat on the stool I'd been using to study. "It was always a strength of mine. In the army, I mean. And even when I started my own business."

I didn't need to ask him how he'd managed with women, because I knew he'd never had relationships that lasted more than a few hours. "And that's why you prefer one-night stands."

"I guess that's part of it. No one asks any difficult questions of a naked stranger. I've never had to navigate any other type of relationship."

"So, what are you here to say, Landon?"

He reached inside his jacket pocket and pulled out some paper. "I think this explains it better than I can."

He offered me the paper, and I took it, unfolding it to find a newspaper clipping. "It was in the *Times*. A British paper," he said.

Why was he giving me this? What did this have to do with anything?

I glanced up at him, and he jutted his chin toward the article.

I started to read.

It was about Walt Williams.

I glanced up at Landon when I got to the words *arms dealer* and *terrorist*. "This was why you were on the boat? To try to . . ."

"It was a job for a friend. I was there just to monitor who came on and off the yacht. And then he took you to dinner, to meet the wrong kind of people, and things began to escalate. No doubt he and some others at the table disappeared at some point during the meal."

I frowned, trying to remember. "Some of them went to smoke cigars."

"Right. That's what the dinner was all for. Walt was meeting with buyers. Or their intermediaries."

"Wait, I went to dinner with terrorists?" My heart began to pound. I'd thought Walt was some charming Texan oil tycoon.

"Friends of terrorists," Landon said. "Keep reading."

Walt had been arrested. Was awaiting trial. "Holy shit. He was selling arms to Islamic State?"

"A splinter group," Landon confirmed.

"He invited me to play poker with him and some friends. Was that . . .?"

Landon nodded. "That meet was a much bigger deal. For Walt and for the client I was working for. So much so that they got intelligence that Walt was going to ask you to accompany him and wanted you to help them build their case against him."

Landon went on to describe how he was supposed to recruit me to help him, and how he hadn't wanted to put me in the inevitable danger that getting involved might bring.

"I had no idea," I said, breathless with all this new information.

"When you found out at dinner, I still couldn't bring myself to tell you and recruit your help. It was the first time I'd ever compromised a mission. Put lives in danger because . . . because of personal feelings."

"But perhaps I should have helped. Maybe I could have—"

"No, Skylar. It was dangerous, and I knew we could get what we needed without involving you. I also understood because of the person you are, that you'd want to help, which was why I didn't tell you at the time. I would never have convinced you to leave."

He'd been looking out for me. Protecting me all along.

I would have been terrified if he'd asked me to help but I would have done it, and he was right, if he'd tried to convince me to leave and not help, he wouldn't have been able to. "I'm grateful that you didn't get me involved."

"And I couldn't tell you why I was on board the *Sapphire*. If I'd told you my background, that my name wasn't James, you would have had questions. Understandably. And then the entire thing would have unraveled."

"I get it. I understand this wasn't a game." I folded up the article. "But if you had . . . Those things you said after the dinner with Hayden and Avery. I quit because—"

"That was the point. I had to get you off the yacht and out of danger." He shoved his hands through his hair. "My mate said that if I didn't recruit you, his client would, and once you were involved you would have been a target on multiple fronts. You weren't safe on the yacht."

I exhaled. "So you didn't mean them?"

"Of course not," he said, frowning, as if he were in pain. "I knew how difficult it would be to get you to leave given how professional you are. I had to say the worst thing I could think up. I didn't believe any of it. My feelings for you are . . . almost the exact opposite to how I came across that evening. I could never mean anything . . . You're too important. I was trying to make you leave."

My heart began to pound. What Landon was saying changed everything. And it wasn't that I just had to rely on his word. I was holding the evidence. "Why didn't you tell me as soon as the arrest was made?" The article was dated two months ago. "All this time, I've been thinking . . ." I'd been thinking that he was a cold, heartless liar. But nothing had added up until now.

"I didn't think you'd want to see me. I assumed you'd forget about me soon enough."

If only I could have relegated him to the dungeons of my memory.

"I know what we had was . . . casual," he said. "You weren't what I was looking for—what I've always historically looked for, but . . . you were . . . you *are* important to me."

My stomach shouldn't have flipped like it did. I shouldn't be replaying the way he said *important* in my head.

"I regret not seeing that. I regret not understanding *how* important you were until . . . I won't say 'until it was too late,' Skylar. Because I can't accept that."

His stare was pleading and determined, and he reached for me then stopped himself.

"I don't know what to say," I replied. "All those weeks, I thought you were one person and you ended up being another. Even your name was a lie."

"But you said you understood?"

"I do. Honestly. But it's still difficult. Anyway, it just doesn't matter anymore. I'm here. You're back in England. We were going to end eventually anyway."

"I'm not sure about that," he said, holding my gaze. "If I'm honest with myself, and you—because that's what you deserve and what I'm really trying to be—I don't think I would have been ready to say goodbye at the end of the summer." He blew out a breath like he'd just made it to the top of a mountain, and I almost smiled. Something told me that talking about his feelings wasn't easy for Landon.

But he was trying.

And I had to appreciate that. He was trying *for me*.

"Our lives are so different, Landon. I'm just a waitress, at a diner, in the middle of the United States. You're in London doing God knows what."

"I'm going to be consulting for MI6. They want my skills and expertise, but I wouldn't be working for them full time. I've gotten used to being my own master."

He'd shared more about himself in the last twenty minutes than he had all summer, and I wanted to encourage him. "Are you allowed to tell me that?"

"I can't give you details, but yes, I can tell you that much."

I nodded, though I wasn't sure what to say.

"I live in a penthouse in the center of London," he continued. "My business has always done well, and I lived comfortably, but I didn't make big money until I sold it."

I swallowed. He was really, really trying. And it clearly took so much effort. He'd tracked me down and flown out here. He hadn't just called. My defenses began to look like a clumsy fort constructed by a seven-year-old to keep out an imaginary monster rather than the arguments of a grown woman.

"Tell me something else that's true," I said.

"I've wanted to join the SAS since I was fourteen. I meant what I said about Christmas and Mariah Carey. I'd have preferred to do my own ironing on the boat. And . . . I miss you."

I pressed my lips together and held back from launching myself into his arms. "Yeah, August's ironing wasn't great." I paused, trying to decide what to say next. "And I miss you, too."

He moved toward me, and I held out my hand. "But that doesn't mean that—"

"It means that you miss me," he said. "It's a start and I'll take it."

I closed my eyes in a long blink. "A start? Maybe it's better as an end."

"I can't believe that. Won't."

I pushed my fingers through my hair. "I don't know, Landon. I just can't see how—"

"Can I take you to dinner? You can ask me as many questions as you like, and I have nothing to hide."

"And then what? You go back to London and we become pen pals? You have a job waiting for you. A flat. A life."

He glanced over at my books. "My flat has a bigger table than this place."

"What?"

"You're studying. Avery told me she didn't think you'd be going back to yachting. And you don't belong in some shitty motel. It doesn't suit you, and I think you know that."

"Avery told you I want to go to college?"

"No. But you have a dozen books on your dressing table."

He always saw more than I showed him. "You were right the first time."

"So come study in London. See if you like it—it has some of the best universities in the world."

I couldn't hold back my smile. "You're crazy. I can't just come to London. We barely know each other. And I have a job and—" I was clutching at straws. There weren't many good reasons *not* to leave Ohio, but Landon wasn't a reason to say yes.

"I think we both know we're not ready for whatever we have to be over," he said.

There wasn't an hour in my waking day that I didn't think about him. "It's a lovely idea but . . ."

"Don't say 'but'. There doesn't need to be a 'but'."

There were a thousand reasons to say no to him. He'd hurt me—cut me to the bone when I'd opened myself up to him—but every fiber in my body wanted to say yes. "I need to think about it."

His face remained blank. Was that his training? There was so much I didn't know about the man in front of me, and everything was tumbling about between my head and my heart. I didn't know which way was up anymore.

"I need some time," I said.

"But you'll think about it? About us? About coming to London?"

"I'm still bruised, Landon. I get that you were trying to keep me safe. But my hard wiring tells me not to trust men who lie, whatever their reasons. You know I've spent my life trying to avoid repeating my mother's mistake. It's instinct now just to rely on myself."

"Skylar."

"I mean it, Landon. This is a lot to think about." It wasn't as if he was proposing or offering any kind of guarantee, which wasn't a bad thing. It was honest, at least.

"Okay. But I'm not going anywhere. Not far, at least. I'm checked in at the hotel next door. Can I take you to dinner?"

"It's been a long day and, really, I need to think."

"Tomorrow, then. Can we have breakfast?"

"I have to study, then I have work. And I really need some time to get my head around everything you've said."

"Promise me that you won't just skip out of town without telling me."

"You think I could do that?" He might have lied to me, but he knew me better than anyone, and I'd never do that.

"I just don't want this to be the last time I see you."

I hadn't noticed how tired he looked before now. I desperately wanted to go, sit on his lap, and take his face in my hands, and soothe him. But I had to hold back. Be sensible. I had to make sure I wasn't making a decision in the heat of the moment.

"I promise I won't leave town."

"Oh, I want you to leave town. I just want you to do it with me."

I smiled at his comment as he stood. "I think you're a little crazy," I said.

"I'm just a man who realized what he gave up a little late."

My stomach fluttered at his words. I believed him. It was me I didn't trust.

I didn't trust myself not to fall for this man completely. And that scared me. I wasn't sure I was ready to give in to that kind of passion in my life.

THIRTY-NINE

Landon

Three days. Three long fucking days since I'd last seen Skylar. I was trying to be patient, but resisting the urge to count every hour was becoming increasingly difficult. I turned right out of the hotel lift toward my bedroom, taking two long strides around the corner to see if anyone was waiting.

Nope. Just wishful thinking.

When I got to my room, I pulled the note that I'd left pinned on the door. I didn't want to risk Skylar turning up and me not being there and her thinking I'd given up. Because I hadn't. I wouldn't.

She'd said she needed time to think, and I got that. I just didn't like it. So I'd spent the last three days running to keep busy. I'd jogged past the diner where she worked. Past the home where she'd spent four years of her life after her parents had died. I'd run around the city she'd called home until she'd left it for a better life. I felt closer to her like this, but this town didn't represent Skylar. No more than yachting did. She was lost in both worlds and belonged to neither.

I wanted her to belong to me.

How long would it take for her to make contact? Or was she hoping I'd give up? I'd give her until tomorrow night and then go see her again.

My phone buzzed in my pocket. No doubt it was Avery checking up on me again. I'd been avoiding her calls. She was trying to help, but I didn't want to discuss tactics with Skylar's friend. I wanted to win her over because of who I was and what I offered, not because I'd maneuvered things to go in my direction.

Jesus. What had the girl done to me?

I didn't recognize the number, but it was local so I accepted the call.

"How was your run?" Skylar's familiar, sexy voice echoed down the line, and my heart clanged against my ribcage.

"Good. I'm just back. Did you guess or—"

"I saw you jog past the diner. Yesterday, too. I'm guessing you know where I waitress."

"I do. Seems I have to work at being less conspicuous."

"Yeah, it's a good thing you gave up the field work."

Silence filled the space between us. I didn't want to push, but I knew if I spoke, whatever I said would come out as a plea.

"Are you busy?" she asked.

"No. Never. Not for you."

"Okay. Good." Her smile curled around her words, and I couldn't help but picture a pink tinge to her cheeks. "Can I come over?"

"Yes, or . . ." I glanced down at my sweaty body. I needed a shower. "Or I can come to you?"

Movement at the other end of the corridor caught my attention, and I looked up to find Skylar, her phone to her ear, coming around the corner.

The pulse in my neck froze as she glanced up to find me standing there. She grinned and then stopped herself. "Hi," she said into the phone, pausing at the other end of the corridor.

I hoped she wasn't here to say goodbye. To say that she couldn't live with the uncertainty of being with a man who had broken her trust, no matter the reason. "You look beautiful," I said, almost stuttering. Her blonde hair was down, her jeans clung to her hips, and there wasn't a trace of makeup on her face.

As she walked toward me, her beauty was almost overwhelming. Breathtaking. And it shone from the inside. I knew how kind and sweet she was. How the smile covered up the pain she carried. I'd hate myself forever if today was the last time I saw her.

"I changed when I got back from work," she said and then hung up. She was so close I could almost touch her.

"I should shower," I said.

"I can wait."

"But I'm not sure I can." I pulled out the plastic key card from my shorts, opened the door then held it for her, gesturing for her to go inside. Did I want to shower before I heard what she had to say? I didn't want her to change her mind and leave while I was in the bathroom. I didn't want her to leave at all.

I couldn't take my eyes off her as she wandered into the room.

"Are you always this tidy?" she asked.

"Even before I joined the military." There were few signs that anyone had checked into the room. My toothbrush was in the bathroom but everything else was put away out of sight. "But you're a neat guest, too, I seem to remember." That first night in her hotel room had told me a lot about Skylar, but I could never have predicted I'd end up here, needing her like oxygen. "Take a seat. Can I get you a drink?"

She shook her head and took a seat on one of the two beds. "I'm good." She drew in a breath. "Thank you for giving me these few days."

My gut churned. That sounded ominous. She didn't look like a woman who was about to tell me she was ready to take a chance on a guy like me. "Skylar, I want to give you everything you need."

Her smile was reticent and unsure.

"I know it's difficult to believe," I continued. "And I'm not suggesting I'm perfect; I'm just saying give us, give me a—"

She held up her palm, and I stopped talking. Last-minute speeches were over.

"I've lived the last ten years determined not to repeat my mother's mistakes," she said. "I didn't want to waste my life on a man who promised me things that he couldn't give me or told me he loved me but showed me something different."

I winced, hating myself for not being able to take away the pain she so clearly felt.

I wanted to tell her how it would be different with me. How I would never treat her like that, but I held back. She came here to talk, and I wanted to hear it.

"The last few days, I've realized something. A few things, actually. I'll never get over what happened to my mother. Never get over finding her and then being told that it was my father who had killed her. It will stay with me my whole life." She paused. "But I realized that I'm not supposed to get over something like that. So there's no point in running anymore." Her voice wobbled, and I wanted so badly to reach out, touch her, comfort her, make it better, but I resisted.

"My need to survive, a desperate drive to put a roof over my head and food in my stomach was really the only thing that mattered to me for a long time. Until you."

I searched her face. What was she saying?

"I'll never be my mother. I've already had a different life. I've learned the lessons of my past. I'm a better judge of character. I'm not as weak. And despite the fact that you hurt me, I think I'm in love with you."

I tried to steady my breathing. It was no good. My self-control was shot. I stood. "What did you say?"

"For the first time in my life, I'm in love. With you."

It was as if I couldn't get oxygen into my lungs quick enough. I cupped her face, then pulled her up to stand. "I know that feeling. I love you so much that the thought of being away from you is terrifying. I'd rather take a bullet."

She slid her hand over my shoulder, hooking her thumb underneath my t-shirt and stroking it over my scar. "No more bullets."

"Does that mean you'll come to London with me?"

Her eyes welled with tears, and for a second I thought she was going to say no, but she nodded. "I've never been."

I wrapped my arms around her waist and lifted her, desperate to get my fill of Skylar. She was coming to London. I hadn't lost her. "I thought you might tell me no," I said, setting her back on her feet.

"This is early days, Landon. There are no guarantees. Neither of us are good at following our feelings. I just know that you coming here . . . It means a lot that you're prepared to fight for me."

"I can guarantee you that I'm going to do my best to be the man you need." I wanted to be everything for Skylar.

She bit down on her bottom lip. "I just want you to be you."

I nodded. "I know. And I'm going to do that. And if I get it wrong then you can bollock me, but it won't be because I don't want to get it right or because I haven't tried."

She grinned at me. "This," she said. "This I believe. And it's why I'm here."

"Because you can bollock me?"

"No. Because of your lack of bullshit. Because even when you're not telling the truth, you're still a good man. You're *you*."

I pressed my lips against hers, overcome with the need to be closer to her. I shivered as she ran her fingers through my hair then clasped them around my neck.

Relief turned to lust as I became acutely aware of her body pressed against mine. God, how I'd missed this. Just being near her, her honeysuckle scent filling the air and her skin against my fingertips. I never wanted to let her go.

"I've missed you," she said, pulling away from my kiss, her fingers trickling around my neck and down to my chest.

"I'm sweaty." I should never have gone running. I should have stayed in to wait—perfectly clean and groomed and ready for her.

"I like it."

I grinned. "You do, hey?"

"I think maybe you need to get me a little sweaty so we're even."

"I can manage that." I pulled her shirt over her head,

holding back a gasp at the sight of her breasts pushing over the top of her white bra. I threaded my fingers into the lace, desperate to feel her, then pulled her nipple between my finger and thumb.

She blinked, lazily fumbling at the hem of my t-shirt. I pulled it off and discarded my shorts before undoing her jeans and pulling them down her legs. I looked up at her from my knees. Jesus, she was beautiful. She rested her hands on my shoulders and stepped out of the denim, and I knew this was where I belonged. With her, ready to give her everything.

She had me on my knees in every possible way.

She slipped off her bra as I peeled off her knickers and pressed a kiss to her stomach.

"I need to shower," I said, ignoring my throbbing cock.

"I like you like this. I like you every way."

I ran my hands from her ankles up the back of her shins, thighs, and then over her bottom, reminding myself of how utterly perfect she was. "Sit down and lie back." I needed to taste her.

She sat on the edge of the bed, her thighs to either side of my chest, and lay back, her arms over her head. The sight of her sweet pussy tugged at my cock, and I leaned forward and breathed her in.

My Skylar.

She groaned before I'd even touched her. Just the heat of my breath inches away from her had turned her on—that was a real victory.

I grinned. The physical stuff between us had always been fantastic. I didn't expect it to have changed.

"I'm warning you," she said. "As much as I want your tongue on me, I'm going to need your dick."

I growled and pressed my mouth against her heat,

unable to hold back any longer. She was wet and slick, and I licked and sucked as if she were my last meal. I wanted to make up for all those weeks I hadn't seen her, all those things I'd said to her outside the restaurant. But most of all, I wanted to be buried in her—my fingers, my tongue, my dick. I wanted my body to be as lost to her as my heart was. Within seconds, she was writhing on the bed, begging me to stop, for more, for release. She pulsed underneath me, her clitoris engorged and hard. She was so close. If I were a cruel man, I'd have pulled back, made her wait. But that wasn't what she needed. She needed to come. She needed me to *make* her come, and I'd vowed I'd do my best to give her *everything* she needed.

I slid two fingers deep inside her, and she began to orgasm immediately. Her stomach contracted and her back arched as she cried out. Fuck, she was beautiful like this. She belonged to me. As much as I wanted to get her back to London as soon as possible, I wasn't sure I was ready to let her leave this room any time in the next year. I needed to own her like this. Needed to show her that she'd been mine since the moment I'd seen her in the bar and would be mine for the rest of time.

I grabbed my wallet and pulled out a condom, covering my cock as quickly as possible. I had to get inside her. Make her come again. That was my mission now. I wanted to make sure she understood that we'd never be apart again.

I nudged her legs apart and coated the crown of my cock with her wetness as she lay, dazed, in front of me.

"You ready?" I asked. "I'm going to make you come over and over and over."

She sighed, and I took that as a yes as I pushed into her as far as I could go.

She cried out and her nails dug into my arms.

Shit. The pressure was almost too much, and I had to clench my jaw and shut my eyes to hold myself back. How had I thought I could ever let this woman walk away from me? I'd never known anything like her. Never felt someone settle in my core like she had. Never wanted to care for someone, to protect someone, as fiercely as I wanted to shelter Skylar from the entire world.

I exhaled, opened my eyes, and caught her watching me. She traced a bead of sweat from my forehead down my temple. I began to rock in and out of her as we stared at each other. Her blonde hair fanned out behind her, and her limbs were loose and warm. "You're perfect," I whispered.

She shook her head. "No one is."

"Then you're perfect for me," I replied.

I folded over her, my chest against hers, our skin slick and sticky, and our mouths met. I couldn't get close enough. Couldn't possibly show her how special she was. I'd make it my mission to make sure I tried every day of my life.

She wrapped her legs around my waist, and I rolled to my back, ready to watch her above me. She pushed up on my chest and took my cock deep into her, as I pressed my thumbs below her hip bones. "Promise me you won't stop fucking me when we get to London," she said as she lowered herself onto my dick.

I could barely get my words out. "I promise. I'll never stop." As if she'd have to convince me.

She tipped her head back, giving me a view of her throat, then down to her perfect, ripe breasts, her dusky pink nipples, straining and desperate under my glare. How could she think I'd be able to stop? I'd never stop wanting her. But it was more than that. She'd created a need in me that I'd never experienced before. It was more than physical. I needed the way her caring for people was second nature, her relentless practicality, her love of Celine Dion. Her hard armor and her soft center—I wanted it all.

Her breathing became more and more strained as she tightened her thighs and tilted her pelvis back. I slid my palm up her stomach, relishing the feel of her hot, smooth skin.

Jesus. I'd do anything for this woman. Couldn't she see that? I gripped her waist and tipped her onto her back. "But I can't cope with the teasing. Not if you want me to last."

"I wasn't teasing," she said, her eyes wide and honest. "I just love the way you feel inside me. The way I'm so full of you."

She always knew exactly what to say. I groaned and rammed into her. "Like that?" I asked, unable to hold back any longer. All my muscles engaged as if I'd been trekking under the Afghan sun for days. I was spent, but knew I had to keep my focus on the goal.

"Yes!" she cried. "Just like that."

"I can't stop. With you, I just lose control," I said. That summed up my reaction to Skylar in every sense. She was the only woman who tore through half of my defenses and made me want to surrender the rest. She was the only woman I'd ever considered adapting for, the only one who made it impossible not to. She changed everything. I'd move to Ohio if she asked me to. I'd give up my job, my life in London. I'd do anything if it meant being with her.

My orgasm rumbled in the distance, setting a warning spark across my skin. My muscles continued to ache as I kept pressing into her. I drew up her knee, desperate to get deeper, to push her further. I wanted us to reach the same place. To exist in the same sense of bliss at the same time.

She whimpered and began to chant my name.

She arched her back, pressing her breasts against my

chest as her orgasm caught her breath in her mouth and made her eyes water as she looked at me: hope, happiness and understanding in her gaze. Her expression pushed through my body's last defense, and my orgasm tunneled up my spine, meeting hers with a vengeance.

"I love you, Skylar," I choked out as my orgasm continued to course through my body, setting my blood on fire and muscles into spasm.

I kept my gaze fixed on hers as we both floated back down to earth. She smoothed her palm across my face. "I love you, too."

I collapsed over her, still not ready for a single part of her not to touch me. I couldn't imagine a time when I wouldn't feel the same way. It was as if she were a part of me, and without her, there would be some element missing. I wanted to stay connected with her—physically, mentally, emotionally—forever.

She lifted her head and pressed her lips to my shoulder. I rolled to my back and tucked her into my side.

I'd love this woman forever. I was as sure of that as I'd ever been of anything in my life.

EPILOGUE

Skylar

I released the swinging door and stepped out into the fresh autumnal breeze of Holborn, London, and glanced down at the paper I was clutching and tried yet again to make sense of the scores.

"Skylar!"

I turned to see Landon trying to wave from across the street but juggling coffee cups.

My cheeks heated. He was so freaking hot. How had I gotten so lucky?

I beamed and waved my test results in the air.

"Did you pass?" he shouted from across the street, checking for a gap in traffic. Eventually he gave up and despite the blare of horns, pushed through the slow-moving cars and cyclists weaving in and out of the vehicles.

"There's no pressure. You can always take it again," he said as he reached me. "See this as a dry run."

"But I don't need to take it again. I passed," I said.

He searched my face, then tossed both cups of coffee

into the nearby trashcan and traced my cheekbones with his fingertips. "I knew it," he said before kissing me.

My knees buckled and I pulled at his shirt, trying to keep upright.

When he finally pulled back, he slipped his hand around my waist and guided me in the direction of the restaurant where we were meeting Hayden and Avery for lunch.

"So this means you can get into any university?" he asked.

I stared at the piece of paper that I hadn't dared put back into my bag in case when I took it out again, the score had changed. "I wasn't expecting to get this kind of result."

"You always underestimate yourself. You should know better by now."

"I'm getting there," I said. "Slowly." Being with a man who believed in me so completely was helping.

"Next stop law. In the US or here?" he asked, pulling me toward him and out of the way as a buggy plowed toward us.

"I guess the US makes sense."

Landon stayed silent.

"What do you think?" I asked.

"Oh, you finally want to talk about this?" He grinned and placed a kiss on the top of my forehead.

Every time he'd tried to bring up the topic, I'd shut him down. I didn't want to get ahead of myself. I'd been focused on passing the exam. If I couldn't do that, I wouldn't need to choose a place to study.

I prodded him in the stomach. "Yes, I want to talk about this now that I have this." I waved the paper at him.

"I want you to be happy," he said.

I sighed. "That's a cop-out. Tell me what you think."

"I want to hear your thoughts first. This is a big deal for you. A pivotal moment. It should be your decision."

"And then you'll tell me what you think? Even if I blurt out a lot of incoherent thoughts that I haven't let myself analyze in any detail?"

He chuckled. "I promise."

I sucked in a breath. "I guess the US makes sense. I know the system and the schools better. But then, nowhere in the US feels like home. Even though I've spent a lot of time in Florida, that was just because of yachting. And Ohio?" I shook my head. "I'm not sure that ever felt like home."

"Does anywhere feel like home?" he asked.

I wanted to say that being with Landon felt like home. When he held me, I felt warm, safe, and protected. Wasn't that what home was supposed to feel like? "I'm not sure," I replied.

"What about London?" he asked.

"London is complicated." For the last three months, I'd been blissfully happy. Landon had insisted I stay in his apartment, and I'd gotten a job in a little café in Covent Garden while I studied. Landon had started his new role and loved it, and our time together consisted of grinning at each other like lunatics—as Avery liked to tell me—cooking, Landon showing me his favorite parts of the city, and sex. Lots of sex.

It had been three months of pure perfection.

"Why's that?" he asked.

"Because the last three months have been . . . amazing."

He tightened his grip around my waist. "Agreed."

"But a degree here would be three or four years." If Landon and I split up, then I'd be faced with being in a country that did nothing but hold reminders of what I'd lost.

"I think the timing seems perfect."

"You do?" What was he thinking?

He stayed silent.

I tapped him on his temple. "Tell me what *you're* thinking."

He turned us sideways up an alley between two stores. If I lived here a hundred years, I wouldn't learn my way around.

"I want to be with you, Skylar. We can make that happen wherever you are, but I like London, and I think you've enjoyed your time here. If you haven't got your mind set on anywhere in particular, I was kind of hoping you'd choose my town."

How did someone so handsome, so completely capable, and so utterly charming get so adorable?

"You were hoping I'd choose London?"

"More than that. I was hoping you'd choose *me*. I was hoping you might marry me."

I stopped walking. Had I just heard that correctly?

"You don't have to decide anything straightaway." He turned to face me as pedestrians passed us from each direction. "But I want it out there on the table. The way I see it, we get married while you're studying. By the time you finish, we might be ready to start a family. Of course, I wouldn't expect you to stay at home or anything. I could, or we could get help, or . . ."

"That's what you see for us?" I asked. Married to a man I loved and who loved me. To a man who'd never let me down or disappoint me? To a man I could trust and count on? I'd never let myself dare imagine such a scenario.

"I know you only agreed to three months over here, but yes, I want us to be together. Forever. I love you."

I stared up at him. "I love you."

"I know I'm not the most romantic," he said. "And I still have to work really hard at sharing what I'm thinking and feeling, but I also know I couldn't love you more."

I bit down on my bottom lip. "Oh, I think you're romantic. In the way that I need. I can trust you. You want to make me happy. You're everything I could have ever wished for but hadn't dared hope for. I want to marry a man like you."

"So you'd say yes if I asked?" he asked as he snaked his arms around my waist.

I laughed. "Didn't you just ask?"

"That was me telling you what I was feeling. I figure you deserve a better, bigger proposal." He draped his arm around my neck, and we continued to the restaurant.

I gazed up at him. "I don't need bigger and better. I just need you."

Landon Wolf was the last man I'd ever expected to end up with, but he was the only man I would ever love. The only man who'd showed me he could be trusted. I knew as long as I was with him, I'd be safe, loved, and protected, and that's all I'd ever wanted in life.

Landon

Even though it was only five o'clock, it was already dark, and the December air created smoky ribbons trailing from the passing pedestrians' lips. I glanced at my watch. They wouldn't be deliberately late, but August's train might have been delayed.

"I never saw you as part of a couple," Hayden said as he pulled at his tie. Why had he worn a suit to go ice skating?

"No, I never saw that in my future—or yours."

"What is it with these women who burst into our worlds and knock us off our feet?"

"Not sure, but I'm happy to have been knocked," I replied.

Hayden chuckled. "It's a good job considering we're about to mount that ice on blades. What are we doing?"

"We're keeping our women happy?" I shrugged, trying not to grin. I wasn't going to tell Hayden, but I was quite looking forward to ice skating with my girl.

"Yeah, there's pretty much nothing I wouldn't do for that woman." Hayden nodded toward the three girls coming toward us, their arms around each other as they chatted, smiled, and laughed.

"Me neither," I said.

Skylar scanned the crowds for me, and I watched her face light up when she caught my eye. I was a lucky fucker, being able to make a woman smile like that. She released her friends and bounded toward us.

"Hey," she said, wrapping her arms around my neck and pulling me close.

"Hey," I replied, pressing my lips to hers.

"We're really going to ice skate?" she asked.

"Anything to make you happy."

She wriggled her cold hands under my coat and pressed her head against my chest.

"Hi, August. Avery," I said, kissing one and then the other on the cheek while Skylar clung to me. "You all ready?"

"What time is our booking for?" Skylar asked, finally releasing me.

"Urm, now?" I said, glancing over her head so I didn't catch her eye. It was as if Skylar's presence removed some kind of chip in me that allowed me to keep a secret from her.

"'Urm, now?'" she asked.

I guided her under the white-stone arch and toward the neoclassical courtyard of Somerset House where the temporary ice rink had been set up for Christmas. I wasn't going to be able to avoid her questions for long.

Two security guards opened a gap in the metal gates, and we stepped into the courtyard.

"Where is everyone?" Skylar asked as she craned her neck to look around. Usually, the courtyard would be packed with people queuing for their skating slot, or food or one of the exhibitions.

"It's just us."

She frowned as she turned to check if Hayden, August, and Avery were following. "It is?"

I shrugged. "I thought it would be good to have the place to ourselves," I said, still trying to avoid meeting her eye. It had taken some arranging. But it had been worth it to see the look of wonder on Skylar's face. She spun, taking in the Georgian buildings that surrounded us on all four sides.

"Wow, really? This is so totally cool. No lines. No waiting around. You're beyond wonderful." She pulled at my collar, and I dipped my head long enough to receive a kiss on my jaw. Skylar calling me wonderful was more than I could have ever wished for. I just wanted to live up to the compliment.

The five of us collected our skates and made our way onto the rink, hand in hand. Hayden's ability to ice skate had clearly left him some time ago, though he did his best to keep the two women to either side of him upright.

I couldn't help but grin at Skylar's pink cheeks and warm smile as we began to make our way around the ice to the familiar Christmas tunes from Sinatra, the Pogues, and Paul McCartney.

And then the Christmas music faded and the track I'd picked started.

Celine Dion started to play out from the speakers. I'd tried to pick the right song and this one, that was about how I was a better person because she loved me, seemed right. As I turned to Skylar, she shook her head and grinned.

"You finally admit that she's the best in the business?" she asked as we came to a stop in the middle of the rink.

"You've set me straight on that," I said, chuckling as I snaked my arms around her waist.

"Finally!" she replied. "Your surrender is the best Christmas present you could have ever given me."

"Really?" I asked. I hoped that wasn't the case.

She followed my gaze as the light display started. The stone walls that surrounded us on all four sides became screens as lasers projected the question "Marry me?" on one wall in large, red writing and then on the opposite wall, and then on the south wall and then on the north. The words began to slide across the walls, disappearing and then reappearing, dancing across the stone.

Openmouthed, Skylar watched the show.

I couldn't take my eyes off her. "I thought you deserved a proposal that was a little more romantic. In front of your family." I glanced over at Hayden, Avery, and August, who were huddled in a corner of the rink, watching.

She sucked in a breath, her eyes glistening with tears.

"Skylar, look at me." She glanced down at my chest and then up into my eyes. "Will you let me love you for the rest of our lives? Ice skating or yachting, rain or shine, in London or Monaco. Say you'll marry me?"

She seemed to take forever to respond, as if the ice we

were standing on had frozen her still. "Of course I'll marry you." A grin curled around her words.

I nodded. "Good," I replied, trying to hold myself back from screaming out loud about how fucking lucky I was.

"Good," she replied, mocking my timbre and accent. "My very-British fiancé."

I grinned and pressed my lips to hers as I lifted her off the ice then put her back down again.

"I might just change my mind about this holiday," she said.

"I want to turn every bad memory you ever had into a good one," I replied. That was my only mission now.

"I just want to create new ones with you," she replied.

I bent down and pressed my lips to hers, kissing her like it was my job, ignoring the jeers and whistles from my brother and the girls.

Nothing but Skylar mattered and, despite the cold, I'd always be warm with her by my side.

OTHER BOOKS BY LOUISE BAY

Sign up to the Louise Bay mailing list to see more on all my books.
www.louisebay.com/newsletter

International Player

Being labelled a player never stopped me from being successful with women. Until I met Truly Harbury.

Truly was the first girl who ever turned me down.

The first female friend I ever had.

And she might just be the first woman I ever fall in love with.

When an emergency means she needs my help running her family's charity, I'm happy to introduce her to the glitz and glamour of the London business world—taking her to dinners, coaching her through speeches, zipping up the sexy evening gown I helped her pick out.

The more time we spend together, the more I want to convince her I'm not a man to avoid, that we're not as unsuited as she believes.

She sees herself as the book-reading, science-loving introvert while I'm the dangerous, outgoing, charmer.

She thinks I love parties and people whereas she prefers pajamas and a takeaway.

What she doesn't realize is that I like everything about her–the way her smile lights up a room, how her curves light up my imagination, and especially the way her lips taste when coated with tequila.

She's the first woman I ever fell in love with. I just need to know if she could ever love me too.

The Wrong Gentleman

I'm an all-or-nothing man—100 percent focused on whatever has my attention.

First it was serving my country in the Special Forces. Then it was building my business. Right now it's the hot blonde at the bar who's about to become another notch on my bedpost.

But women never keep my attention for more than a night.

Until I peel off Skylar Anderson's clothes and her mask starts to crumble, showing me glimpses of the girl she's hiding. She's funny, sexy and vulnerable and throws me out of bed before I can catch my breath and suggest breakfast.

When I start my last undercover job on a yacht, turns out, she's one of the crew. I try, but I can't look away.

Her high ponytail shows off her kissable neck that tastes like summer.

Her short uniform reveals the killer legs that were wrapped around me last night.

And her provocative smile? I know what that mouth is capable of.

I want to explore her body, discover her secrets and sail off into the sunset with her.

I might want to go all in for Skylar, but she should stay away from me. I've got secrets of my own and they can only bring her trouble.

A stand-alone novel.

The Earl of London

Love left me off its to-do list.

I date. I'm all for giving guys a chance. I've just never met *the one*.

Until on a spring morning in the English countryside, a tall, dark stranger emerges from the mist. Logan Steele is all tousled hair, hard chest and lips so perfect I want to reach out and touch them just to check they're real. I'm sure that's a thunderclap of chemistry I feel between us.

Did I mention he's an Earl with a self-made fortune?

A billionaire who works tirelessly for charity?

And he's so hot, watching him is like staring at the sun.

But like I said, love isn't rooting for me.

When I find out Logan Steele is out to destroy everything I've dedicated my life to protect, the chemistry disappears and the hope that had blossomed my chest turns to rage.

It no longer matters that he quickens my pulse just saying my name, weakens my knees with a single touch and that he might just be the greatest kisser that ever lived.

I might believe in love but Logan Steele is definitely not *the one*.

A stand-alone novel.

The Ruthless Gentleman

As a chief stewardess on luxury superyachts, I massage egos, pamper the spoiled and cater to the most outlandish desires of the rich and famous.

I've never had a guest want something I can't give them. Until British businessman Hayden Wolf comes aboard—all sexy swagger and mysterious requests.

He wants me.

And Hayden Wolf's a man who's used to getting exactly what he demands.

Despite being serious and focused. Demanding and ruthless. He's also charming when I least expect it as well as being devastatingly handsome with an almost irresistible smile.

But guests are strictly off limits and I've never broken a rule. Not even bent one. My family are depending on me and I can't lose my job.

Only problem is Hayden Wolf is looking at me like I just changed his life. And he's touching me like he's about to change mine.

A stand-alone novel.

Duke of Manhattan

I was born into British aristocracy, but I've made my fortune in Manhattan. New York is now my kingdom.

Back in Britain my family are fighting over who's the next Duke of Fairfax. The rules say it's me--if I'm married. It's not a trade-off worth making. I could never limit myself to just one woman.

Or so I thought until my world is turned upside down.

Now, the only way I can save the empire I built is to inherit the title I've never wanted-- so I need a wife.

To take my mind off business I need a night that's all pleasure. I need to bury myself in a stranger.

The skim of Scarlett King's hair over my body as she bends over . . .

The scrape of her nails across my chest as she screams my name . . .

The bite of her teeth on my shoulder just as we both reach the edge . . .

It all helps me forget.

I just didn't bargain on finding my one night stand across the boardroom table the next day.

She might be my latest conquest but I have a feeling Scarlett King might just conquer me.

A stand-alone novel.

Park Avenue Prince

THE PRINCE OF PARK AVENUE FINALLY MEETS HIS MATCH IN A FEISTY MANHATTAN PRINCESS.

I've made every one of my billions of dollars myself— I'm calculating, astute and the best at what I do. It takes drive and dedication to build what I have. And it leaves no time for love or girlfriends or relationships.

But don't get me wrong, I'm not a monk.

I understand the attention and focus it takes to seduce a beautiful woman. They're the same skills I use to close business deals. But one night is where it begins and ends. I'm not the guy who sends flowers. I'm not the guy who calls the next day.

Or so I thought before an impatient, smart-talking, beyond beautiful heiress bursts into my world.

When Grace Astor rolls her eyes at me—I want to hold her against me and show her what she's been missing.

When she makes a joke at my expense—I want to silence her sassy mouth with my tongue.

And when she leaves straight after we f*ck with barely a goodbye—it makes me want to pin her down and remind her of the three orgasms she just had.

She might be a princess but I'm going to show her who rules in this Park Avenue bedroom.

A stand-alone novel.

King of Wall Street

THE KING OF WALL STREET IS BROUGHT TO HIS KNEES BY AN AMBITIOUS BOMBSHELL.

I keep my two worlds separate.

At work, I'm King of Wall Street. The heaviest hitters in Manhattan come to me to make money. They do whatever I say because I'm always right. I'm shrewd. Exacting. Some say ruthless.

At home, I'm a single dad trying to keep his fourteen year old daughter a kid for as long as possible. If my daughter does what I say, somewhere there's a snowball surviving in hell. And nothing I say is ever right.

When Harper Jayne starts as a junior researcher at my firm, the barriers between my worlds begin to dissolve. She's the most infuriating woman I've ever worked with.

I don't like the way she bends over the photocopier—it makes my mouth water.

I hate the way she's so eager to do a good job—it makes my dick twitch.

And I can't stand the way she wears her hair up exposing her long neck. It makes me want to strip her naked, bend her over my desk and trail my tongue all over her body.

If my two worlds are going to collide, Harper Jayne will have to learn that I don't just rule the boardroom. I'm in charge of the bedroom, too.

A stand-alone novel.

Hollywood Scandal

HE'S A HOLLYWOOD SUPERSTAR. SHE'S LITERALLY THE GIRL NEXT DOOR.

One of Hollywood's A-listers, I have the movie industry in the palm of my hand. But if I'm going to stay at the top, my playboy image needs an overhaul. No more tabloid headlines. No more parties. And absolutely no more one night stands.

Filming for my latest blockbuster takes place on the coast of Maine and I'm determined to stay out of trouble. But trouble finds me when I run into Lana Kelly.

She doesn't recognize me, she's never heard of Matt Easton and my million dollar smile doesn't work on her.

Ego shredded, I know I should keep my distance, but when I realize she's my neighbor I know I'm toast. There's no way I can resist temptation when it's ten yards away.

She has a mouth designed for pleasure and legs that will wrap perfectly around my waist.

She's movie star beautiful and her body is made to be mine.

Getting Lana Kelly into my bed is harder than I'm used to. She's not interested in the glitz and glamour of Hollywood, but I'm determined to convince her the best place in the world is on the red carpet, holding my hand.

I could have any woman in the world, but all I want is the girl next door.

A standalone romance.

Parisian Nights

The moment I laid eyes on the new photographer at work, I had his number. Cocky, arrogant and super wealthy— women were eating out of his hand as soon as his tight ass crossed the threshold of our office.

When we were forced to go to Paris together for an assignment, I wasn't interested in his seductive smile, his sexy accent or his dirty laugh. I wasn't falling for his charms.

Until I did.

Until Paris.

Until he was kissing me and I was wondering how it happened. Until he was dragging his lips across my skin and I was hoping for more. Paris does funny things to a girl and he might have gotten me naked.

But Paris couldn't last forever.

Previously called What the Lightning Sees

A stand-alone novel.

Promised Nights

I've been in love with Luke Daniels since, well, forever. As his sister's best friend, I've spent over a decade living in the friend zone, watching from the sidelines hoping he would notice me, pick me, love me.

I want the fairy tale and Luke is my Prince Charming.

He's tall, with shoulders so broad he blocks out the sun. He's kind with a smile so dazzling he makes me forget everything that's wrong in the world. And he's the only man that can make me laugh until my cheeks hurt and my stomach cramps.

But he'll never be mine.

So I've decided to get on with my life and find the next best thing.

Until a Wonder Woman costume, a bottle of tequila and a game of truth or dare happened.

Then Luke's licking salt from my wrist and telling me I'm beautiful.

Then he's peeling off my clothes and pressing his lips against mine.

Then what? Is this the start of my happily ever after or the beginning of a tragedy?

Previously called Calling Me

A stand-alone novel.

Indigo Nights

I don't do romance. I don't do love. I certainly don't do relationships. Women are attracted to my power and money and I like a nice ass and a pretty smile. It's a fair exchange—a business deal for pleasure.

Meeting Beth Harrison in the first class cabin of my flight from Chicago to London throws me for a loop and everything I know about myself and women goes out the window.

I'm usually good at reading people, situations, the markets. I know instantly if I can trust someone or if they're lying. But Beth is so contradictory and confounding I don't know which way is up.

She's sweet but so sexy she makes my knees weak and mouth dry.

She's confident but so vulnerable I want to wrap her up and protect her from the world.

And then she fucks me like a train and just disappears, leaving me with my pants around my ankles, wondering which day of the week it is.

If I ever see her again I don't know if I'll scream at her, strip her naked or fall in love. Thank goodness I live in Chicago and she lives in London and we'll never see each other again, right?A stand-alone novel.

The Empire State Series

Anna Kirby is sick of dating. She's tired of heartbreak. Despite being smart, sexy, and funny, she's a magnet for men who don't deserve her.

A week's vacation in New York is the ultimate distraction from her most recent break-up, as well as a great place to meet a stranger and have some summer fun. But to protect her still-bruised heart, fun comes with rules. There will be no sharing stories, no swapping numbers, and no real names. Just one night of uncomplicated fun.

Super-successful serial seducer Ethan Scott has some rules of his own. He doesn't date, he doesn't stay the night, and he doesn't make any promises.

It should be a match made in heaven. But rules are made to be broken.

The Empire State Series is a series of three novellas.

Love Unexpected

When the fierce redhead with the beautiful ass walks into the local bar, I can tell she's passing through. And I'm looking for distraction while I'm in town—a hot hook-up and nothing more before I head back to the city.

If she has secrets, I don't want to know them.

If she feels good underneath me, I don't want to think about it too hard.

If she's my future, I don't want to see it.

I'm Blake McKenna and I'm about to teach this Boston socialite how to forget every man who came before me.

When the future I had always imagined crumbles before my very eyes. I grab my two best friends and take a much needed vacation to the country.

My plan of swearing off men gets railroaded when on my first night of my vacation, I meet the hottest guy on the planet.

I'm not going to consider that he could be a gorgeous distraction.

I'm certainly not going to reveal my deepest secrets to him as we steal away each night hoping no one will notice.

And the last thing I'm going to do is fall in love for the first time in my life.

My name is Mackenzie Locke and I haven't got a handle on men. Not even a little bit.

Not until Blake.

A stand-alone novel.

Hopeful

How long does it take to get over your first love?

Eight years should be long enough. My mind knows that, but there's no convincing my heart.

Guys like Joel weren't supposed to fall for girls like me. He had his pick of women at University, but somehow the laws of nature were defied and we fell crazy in love.

After graduation, Joel left to pursue his career in New York. He wanted me to go with him but my life was in London.

We broke up and my heart split in two.

I haven't seen or spoken to him since he left.

If only I'd known that I'd love him this long, this painfully, this desperately. I might have said yes all those years ago. He might have been mine all this time in between.

Now, he's moving back to London and I need to get over him before he gets over here.

But how do I forget someone who gave me so much to remember?

A long time ago, Joel Wentworth told me he'd love me for infinity . . . and I can't give up hope that it might have been true.

A stand-alone novel.

Faithful

Leah Thompson's life in London is everything she's supposed to want: a successful career, the best girlfriends a bottle of sauvignon blanc can buy, and a wealthy boyfriend who has just proposed. But something doesn't feel right. Is it simply a case of 'be careful what you wish for'?

Uncertain about her future, Leah looks to her past, where she finds her high school crush, Daniel Armitage, online. Daniel is one of London's most eligible bachelors.

He knows what and who he wants, and he wants Leah. Leah resists Daniel's advances as she concentrates on being the perfect fiancé.

She soon finds that she should have trusted her instincts when she realises she's been betrayed by the men and women in her life.

Leah's heart has been crushed. Will ever be able to trust again? And will Daniel be there when she is?

A stand-alone novel.

KEEP IN TOUCH!

Sign up for my mailing list to get the latest news and gossip
www.louisebay.com/newsletter

Or find me on

www.twitter.com/louiseSbay
www.facebook.com/authorlouisebay
www.instagram.com/louiseSbay
www.pinterest.com/louisebay
www.goodreads.com/author/show/8056592.Louise_Bay

ACKNOWLEDGMENTS

Thank you readers for being patient with me while I worked on International Player and The Wrong Gentleman plus I was cooking a human being which made my brain ache and the desire to sleep overwhelming!

To Elizabeth - Next time you won't have to deal with my pre/post partum brain. I hope you notice a difference. Thank you, thank you.

Thank you to Sophie. I couldn't do this without you. Lenora says thank you for letting me spend time with her!

Candi-I love your brand of crazy and your voice notes. Thank you for your help.

To Najla - You are the best. You really are.

Thank you to all the bloggers and reviews and people who spread the word about my books. You're the coolest.

Thank you, Lenora. You are an angel baby and have let me finish this book. You put up with an awful lot having me as a mother and I'm forever grateful you stick by me and don't go find someone who would do it better. If in doubt, use Luther Vandross as inspiration—you're so amazing and you've changed my whole world.

Made in the USA
Monee, IL
12 May 2020